S'

Pilot

Best wishes John
for 2023.
— DT.

Stray
Pilot

DOUGLAS THOMPSON

Elsewhen Press

Stray Pilot
First published in Great Britain by Elsewhen Press, 2022
An imprint of Alnpete Limited

Elsewhen Press, PO Box 757, Dartford, Kent DA2 7TQ
elsewhen.press

British Library Cataloguing in Publication Data.
A catalogue record for this book is available from the British Library.

ISBN 978-1-915304-03-2 Print edition
ISBN 978-1-915304-13-1 eBook edition

Designed and formatted by Elsewhen Press

This book is a work of fiction. All names, characters, places, agencies, organisations, news media, governments, are either a product of the author's fertile imagination or are used fictitiously. Any resemblance to actual states, newspapers, broadcasters, companies, agencies (fascist or otherwise), places or people (living, dead, alien, or future) is purely coincidental.

Irn Bru is a trademark of A.G. Barr p.l.c.; Scottish International Airshow is a trademark of The Airshow (Scotland) Ltd. Use of trademarks has not been authorised, sponsored, or otherwise approved by the trademark owners.

For Ally (1955-2016), in whatever dimension.

The souls that throng the flood
Are those to whom, by fate, are other bodies ow'd:
In Lethe's lake they long oblivion taste,
Of future life secure, forgetful of the past.

Virgil, *The Aeneid*. (Trans. John Dryden)

01

A late summer evening in July. The landscape is uncharacteristically flat for Scotland. Good farming land on a flat east-coast plain with Pictish stones dotted here and there, testament to generations of culture reaching back into time beyond known history. The twentieth century brought an airfield, then a military base, to this stretch of coastline. Between the chain-link fencing of that and a large forest of densely-planted fir trees, sits a house on its own a mile and half from the nearest village. Within its kitchen sits Doctor James McCaffrey, resting for a moment at the last of his house-calls. Horizontal bars of yellow-orange light and shade from the lowered kitchen blinds fall across his hands and face, and the table at which he sits and writes into his personal notebook:-

Mrs Mary Tellman is eighty-seven years old and her memory is shredded. Human memory, indeed human consciousness as far as scientists have so far been able to tell, is not unitary but vested in many different layers and compartments of the brain that generate them like a cinema projector. For most of our lives, more or less in the flush of youth, we all enjoy the wonderful illusion that we are one entirely unified and integrated thing, a person, character. It's such an appealing and useful notion, that most of us go quite far to suppress any clues to the contrary. But the clues are many, mostly in very young children and in the very old, the latter of which seem even now scarcely to be studied for this purpose. The progressive failing of differing aspects of memory and consciousness that can be observed in the very old and dying, is like a slice through the mind of the human organism, in which an invaluable insight is briefly afforded, of how 'we' are made, how the magic-lantern illusion of 'I' is generated...

The unusually loud cooing of a wood pigeon causes Doctor McCaffrey to look up, to see it sitting outside on the window sill behind him, throwing its enlarged shadow across the kitchen floor and wall like some monstrous mother hen. He resumes writing:

...There are thought to be at least five different kinds of memory the human brain is capable of. Thus is it possible that Mary Tellman can remember the automatic and habitual such as locking her doors, or which kitchen cupboard her dinner plates are kept in, but cannot recall something said to her repeatedly only five minutes beforehand – never mind last week – while also being able to remember in detail events of sixty years ago. Thus is it possible that every time she wakes up from an afternoon nap she finds herself in a house that is completely unfamiliar to her, even though she has lived in it for the last eighty years. At that point, it must seem to her exactly as if she has travelled forward in time. Just a moment ago, as far as she is concerned, she was five years old and living with her parents in Ayrshire in the house she grew up in. When she wakes up she sincerely asks where her parents are, and is visibly devastated when someone such as myself has to tell her that they are both dead. Who else have I got left? she then asks, meaning aunts and uncles, apparently having at that moment no conception that she is a mother and grandmother herself with children of her own, that she had a husband once, whose picture still sits on her mantelpiece. Even when I direct her to look down at her own old and wrinkled hands, the idea that she has lived through the last eighty years, rather than been cruelly transported through them by some magical technology, still seems impossible for her to accept.

Movement in Doctor McCaffrey's peripheral vision catches his attention. He looks down to see a large spider working its way across the kitchen floor. Having disciplined himself since childhood to eschew revulsion in favour of fascination for all living things, he even tolerates it climbing over his shoe. He resumes writing:

This is not fiction, let alone science-fiction, but real. The genuine experience *of how this old person's life and world feel to her every day. And her case is not by any means unusual or uncommon. It is almost as if our capitalist society of endless consumption, and therefore fantasy of endless life, appears to have an elective blind-spot for death and anything related to it. Hence the relative silence surrounding senescence. Is it up to me to study it? I don't have the means or time, a simple G.P. in a rural practice, whose own youth is passed. But imagine the irony. If through telescopes and microscopes, out there on the edges of space and amid the interstices of the tiniest things in biological labs or the quantum racetracks of physicists: humankind searches and searches in vain for the meaning of life. While all the time here it is, hidden in plain sight, available for anyone to see, in the decaying mind of an old lady...*

As Doctor McCaffrey stops writing, a small sound from the next room catches his attention and he stands up and goes through to check on his patient before he will exit the house and drive back to his own home for the night. Standing at the door to the bedroom he sees that the sound was only a moth battering itself against the blinds, and that Mrs Tellman seems sound asleep now after taking her medication. Turning around and walking down the hallway past the living room, he notices three things: the sound of the radio constantly playing classical music at low volume to relieve the old lady's sense of loneliness, how old-fashioned the floral wallpaper is, and the black-and-white photograph on the sideboard of her as a little girl with her father standing behind her – a handsome smiling man in a pilot's uniform, his strong broad hands resting on his daughter's laughing shoulders.

02

The sun rolls down below the hills, slowly taking the entire landscape into darkness. At the light's last gasp, the shadows thrown across the house from the pine forest nearby are impossibly long. At this time of year the sun will roll on its back, hidden below the northern horizon for only a few hours before emerging again, triumphant. Its orange glow will weaken, but never truly leave the edge of the sky. A chill night breeze begins from the ocean a quarter of a mile from Mrs Tellman's house. The sea's wave-textured surface, like frosted glass, is progressively illuminated by the stars coming out and moon rising above. The sea sighs and sobs into the sand of the shore, an ancient sound that Mary finds soothing on nights when her ears can catch it through an open bedroom window. Around her house and in the woods, numerous nocturnal creatures stir, emerge, and quietly carry out their usual patrols around her property. Foxes in search of snails and voles, visiting deer in search of the luscious leaves of unusual bushes, their rough tongues allowing them to tug at thorned roses and gorse. A pine marten climbs onto her roof. A late brood of swifts shiver together in their nest in a hole in the eaves of her disused garage.

The sun yawns and rises out of the sea again around four o'clock, its circumradiant glow of orange and yellow building into intense rays of red light that cut a path across the swaying fields of wheat between the shore and the woods, to penetrate the blinds of Mary's window, leaving a brief flickering apparition of fire on the wall opposite her bed, amid which the shadows thrown from her overgrown pampas grass outside dance wistfully. She sleeps on, aware of nothing. Her hands and feet twitch occasionally. She is dreaming of 1948, the last time she saw her father, of her joy and excitement when he lifted her up in his arms.

03

Mrs Tellman's local authority carers always operate in teams of two, in their characteristic dark blue loose-fitting uniforms that render everyone safely hygienic and almost sexless. Today's shift is Magdalena and Christine; Magda picks Chrissy up outside her home first thing in the morning and they drive through the outskirts of Kinburgh and out towards Mary Tellman's house, chatting over the sound of the car stereo playing popular evergreen songs, the local radio station. *How was your holiday, Chrissy? Tenerife was it?*

No bad, ta. Kenny got terrible sunburn and drank too much Sangria, the dafty. Flight delayed for two hours on the way back, the usual shite. How did you get on with my stand-in while I was away then? My stunt double? Young Becky, was it?

Beyond the RAF airfield out of town, they turn off the main road and wind along the poorly maintained drive to the Tellman house. The car crunches over the gravel and weeds of the last hundred yards before coming to a halt outside the back door, into whose night-box Magda punches the memorised number and retrieves the key. The girls call out upon entry as usual: *Good Morning, Mary!*

After a moment, some vague moans of confusion come from the bedroom. By the time the nurses reach the room, Mary is starting to pull herself up, her white hair standing up in wild disarray like an artistic mime of inner confusion. *Who's that? Are you ma daughter? Where am I? Ah'm ah supposed to be here? Who's paying for this place? De ye ken whaur ma parents are? Ma mither? Ma aunty and uncle? Who huv ah left then?*

The nurses move around, preparing to change the bedding and to give Mary a wash, while supplying their stock answers to these questions to which they have long become accustomed. *Look at your hands, Mary. See how wrinkled they are? Now what age do you think you might be? Can you imagine your mother still being alive if you're this age? Don't worry. Ah said Dinnae fret Missus Tellman! It's all paid for. The whole house and everything. Paid for by your savings and your pension and your two children.*

Children? Weans, ye say? Whaur ur they? The old woman looks around startled as usual, as if the room and its walls might hold answers, as if these unfolding surprises are like some kind of inverted Christmas morning in which she gets to unwrap her own life.

A boy and a girl, a man and a woman, both married. Called…. Magda what did you say they were called again? Andy and Louise, that's it. I said Andrew and Louise, Mrs Tellman. They live far away from here. One in Australia and the other one in London. But Louise comes to visit you every month or two. Would you like me to bring you the phone and you could call one of them? You've just been asleep, Mary, your memory has gone and blanked itself again, emptied oot like a big jug o' watter, but it will soon fill up again, don't you worry yourself.

Frustrated at Mrs Tellman's particularly slow mental reboot this morning, Chrissy resorts to her final ace card to distract the old lady: the framed black and white photograph of Mary as a little girl with her airman father. Like a child with a particularly awesome toy, this always evokes silence and wonder in Mary, like a key with which to find her way back into her own identity.

Ten minutes later, with Mary changed into dry fresh bedding, Magda comes back into the room with a tray of tea and biscuits, to find that Mary is doing the full routine now, calling out, almost talking to herself, about the memory of her father: *If only they had foond a body, some trace o' ma faither, then we could hae grieved, tried to move oan. But ah still wait for him hen, e'en efter a' these years, still haud oot the hope, vain though it micht well be, that he'll come hame some day. Am ah a silly auld footer?*

Not at all, Mary. Chrissy answers. *It was before my*

time of course, but I remember my mother talking about it. All over the newspapers back in the forties and fifties, wasn't it? So you're not the only one that wanted to find him, that wanted an answer. You're not daft at all. Apparently they still get weirdos, UFO-hunters turning up occasionally, sniffing around the town, looking for mementos or wee green men or something. You're certainly no dafter than any of them, Mary...

*

Funny how you call her Mrs Tellman and I call her Mary, isn't it, Magda? Chrissy asks as they drive away ten minutes later.

Magda frowns in the passenger seat, looking down at her phone, checking her messages distractedly. *I never really think about it. I suppose you're right. Being respectful I suppose, but maybe it's too formal. Maybe it's a Polish thing. Which do you think she prefers? Maybe we should ask her?*

Chrissy shrugs and sighs as she looks left and right, turning onto the main road and rapidly accelerating so as not to slow down a logging lorry bearing down on them on the road behind. She winds the window down and takes a draw on her vaporizer, blowing out clouds of strawberry-flavoured smoke. *Have you ever wondered, Magda, what would happen if one of these times we told her something totally different?*

Like what? What do you mean?

I mean, if instead of telling her the usual stuff about where she was born, how old she is and where she grew up, what the headline news on today's newspaper is, what if we told her something far-fetched, like she used to be an aid worker in Africa or something, rather than working in the local post office. Or if we told her that astronauts have just found blue gooseberry bushes growing on Mars...

Magda laughs. *You're a sicko, Chrissy. Honestly.*

But she'd forget, wouldn't she? Completely forget an

hour or two later, or as soon as she nodded off to sleep. So why would it matter?

Why would we do it? And what if she didn't forget? Just for once, just our luck? What if she remembered for once and told someone else? Repeated our crazy nonsense to someone?

But nobody would believe her, would they? Anyone would just assume she was havering as usual, a mad old lady spouting nonsense.

But we would get found out, reprimand, disciplinary hearing, struck off and all that.

No we wouldn't. No one would find out, or care. No one could be sure. And anyway, only doctors get struck off. The likes of us minions, we just get suspended pending disciplinary hearing panels or some such bullshit.

Dishonourably discharged, like in the army? If you were going to risk your job, you'd be better to do it for something more surreal and daring.

Daring? Chrissy asks as they turn into the cul-de-sac of the Kinburgh council house estate where their next client, a blind old widower with emphysema, is waiting for them.

Yeah. Like telling her that aliens had landed in George Square in Glasgow or something.

Glasgow? Be serious, hen. Chrissy laughs aloud, throwing her head back as she parks and switches the engine off. *Even ah wouldnae believe that! Trafalgar Square in London more like. What self-respecting aliens would ever land in Scotland?*

04

Later rumours will become confused. Some will say that unusual lights had been seen over Kinburgh earlier that night. That a white-blue light hovered over the woods and briefly produced a single beam downwards like a stage spotlight, like a helicopter searching for an escaped convict, an hour before the pilot was seen marching out of there. Except that there was no noise. Others will say that his propeller aeroplane, a Hawker Sea Fury, was dimly seen and heard landing on the disused airstrip far out amid the sand dunes of the military testing range, whose tall barbed wire borders every Kinburgh citizen is taught to avoid since childhood. Still others will say that the pilot was seen walking calmly out of the sea itself in twilight, as if he could breathe water as easily as air. His airman's cap appearing first above the waves like a bobbing seal before the rest of him gradually emerged, walking, just walking on and on, staring straight ahead. His first footsteps in the grey sand, showing the imprint of the gripped soles of his military boots, the water running off his uniform, but his body heat and the mild July night progressively drying him as he walks through the pine woods, until he emerges at Mrs Tellman's house.

The old lady is not yet entirely bed-bound, and grateful for this and all other mercies that destiny still grants to her. She has always loved the dawn, and knowing she has earned the right at her age to sleep for the rest of the day if she so wishes, she sometimes gets up and treats herself to a sunrise vigil on her porch, rocking in her armchair, listening to the bird song rising up in a symphony of exultant joy, as if the birds are giving thanks to their god. The same god as everybody else's, surely.

Tonight – this morning, of course – is ostensibly not dissimilar to a hundred others over the last few decades, her children having grown up and left her here alone. But on this occasion something quite extraordinary happens. It happens like a moon rise, like an eagle swooping across a road to land on a rabbit. It happens like a car crash, both too fast and too slow to be anything other than itself, too inevitable somehow to be averted or refuted. It just happens. Like love happens. Or high tide happens. A non-returnable gift that immediately feels as if it has always existed and been part of the world, is pre-ordained, and can only be accepted. She sees and hears something stirring in the distance within the pine forest, coming closer. Thinks perhaps it is some wild animal, a large one, but notes that the footsteps sound oddly regular and rhythmic. Then it comes suddenly: the revelation is upon her. She see her father, still wearing his airman's outfit, stroll out of the woods and turn, walk smiling towards her. She recalls that walk, its military gait, straight back, gasps at its suddenly renewed familiarity.

Tears quickly come to her eyes, cloud them, even as she needs them more than ever now, to fully comprehend every detail of what and who is approaching. He appears un-aged, exactly as she remembers him on the day of his disappearance. All this is quite impossible of course. She is totally willing to accept she may be dreaming, just grateful for an illusion of such astonishing power and comfort. Except that it is not one. He is concrete, entirely real, flesh and blood and breath and eyes brimming over with a living spirit. He is kneeling down now, next to her on the porch and speaking then embracing her. The shock should perhaps be even greater for him, the change in her almost unimaginable, too much for him to take in. How can he even be sure it is her, that he recognises her? His own seven-year-old daughter transformed into an eighty-seven year old woman, face lined and shrivelled, wrinkles and creases now running with tears. The years in between, of all her womanhood and beauty, been and gone without him to witness them. *Daddy, Daddy... Faither! It cannae be! Can it? Whaur hae ye been?*

His American accent, the beloved tones of his soft southern drawl, his sun-dark face and white teeth, the smell of his sweat, come back to her. How she has missed him. More than can be said. Too painful to think of, to dwell too long upon. Places in her young mind she and her mother and brother had to abandon back then, board up and walk away from, to keep the pain and fear from hurting them, huddling together in the dark, sharing a wounded bed. They had to grow strong despite this, grow strong without this man who was their god to them, find other ways to light their broken world and strike new paths through it. But here he is back again, speaking and laughing and crying. *Mary... Mary, baby, baby... it's me. I'm back. I'm sorry, so sorry... I got lost, lost my way, something happened. Some strange people took me away for the longest time. I had no way to tell you, no way to send a message, no way to come back. Yeah, sure, it really is me. Here, pinch my cheek, pinch yourself, honey. They took me so far away, I saw so many things, things I don't know if I can ever even explain. But it's so good, so goddam good and mighty strange to be back. Your mother.... Eleanor.... I know, I know... when I saw you there at a distance a moment ago I almost thought you were her. But I know for sure that ain't possible. What year is it exactly, Mary? How many years have gone by?*

Tae think that every nicht ah prayed ye wid come hame. Ah never loast faith. Eighty, Ah reckon, Faither. Eighty year exactly. Ah won the Maths prize in Secondary School ye ken, ye wid hae been sae proud.

What about Sonny? Is your little brother here?

Oh Jesus, Faither, he deed o' a hert attack a few years back.

Oh no, no... Thomas buries his face in the old lady's shoulder, and shakes with shock and grief, wonders at her calm stoicism.

But dinnae ask me mair. Dinnae trust onny detail ah tell ye. Ma memory is nae sae guid these days, ye ken. The doactor says ah hae dementia... an nae buddy's goan tae believe this, that yuv came back. They'll aw sae ah imagined ye.

Why, Mary? You ain't demented as far as I can tell.

Dementia, noat demented. When you go awa', ah mean, when ye disappear.

But I ain't gonna disappear, Mary. I'm back. Here to stay. I got nowhere else to go. I'm home now. I need a place to stay. My old bed, if you still have it.

Help me up, Daddy. Lift me up in your airms like ye used tae, and ah'll show ye whaur yir room is and the bedding, mair or less whaur ye left it. But hoo can it be, noo? Hoo can ye nae be aged a single day, faither? How's yon possible?

Mary, I don't suppose Albert Einstein is still alive, is he? He can't be, I reckon, if you're this age. He would explain it better than I can.

Albert who? Wiz he the jeweller, the watch repairer in toon or something?

The pilot, Thomas Tellman, laughs and smiles a smile of irony and sadness fused, tears in his eyes. He looks up at the last stars still visible overhead as dawn fades into morning, and he carries his daughter, grown to resemble his mother, into the house. Einstein the watch repairer indeed. Time is broken, and even old Albert were he still in life, would have no answers, no way to fix this.

05

When Chrissy and Magda next return they are in for a fright. Mary's father's room has been preserved more or less untouched for the last eight decades. The door is kept closed, except on very hot summer days, and nothing has been added or taken from it, although occasionally the carers pile the odd towel or duvet there, using it as casual storage while they think the old lady isn't looking. Today the door unexpectedly opens, *opens itself* is how it must appear to Magda, as she walks past it in the hallway, and she screams with fright, dropping her tray of tea and biscuits onto the floor, where the porcelain smashes and the hot tea stains the wooden planks. *Holy Mary, Mother of God!* she exclaims in Polish. *Najświętsza Maryja, Matka Boża!*

The man standing in the doorway and looking back at her, dressed in antiquated pyjamas, smiles broadly, his eyes full of warmth and kindness, then to her amazement speaks back to her in her mother's tongue: *Dzień dobry. Nie martw się o to. Przepraszam, jeśli cię przestraszyłem.*

You speak Polish?! Who are you? Oh forgive me, that sounds so rude...

Not at all, Ma'am. I understand. You sure wouldn't have been expecting me to be here. My name is Thomas Tellman. I'm Mary's father.

Her... her... what?

Chrissy has arrived now with a mop and bucket for the tea spill, and her and Thomas face off for a moment, his dark brown eyes widening as if catching everything in some kind of net of calm attention that arrests them both. *My name is Thomas, Mary's father, I got home last night, Ma'am. I've been away for a long, long time. You are both nurses I see. You help my daughter? That sure is kind.* He holds out his hand to shake Chrissy's first, then Magda's, as if able to sense already their slight difference in rank, the more guarded and sceptical nature of the more senior of them.

Pleased to meet you. I'm Christine, and this is Magdalena. Mrs Tellman hasn't mentioned you before, Thomas. A grandson... then you must be one of Andy's children, Andrew Tellman, her son, hence that accent of yours. Did you grow up in Australia?

Magda, completing the mopping-up, backs past Chrissy, embarrassed, whispering under her breath: *American.*

I'm from Kentucky actually, the Bluegrass State... he begins to answer but is interrupted by Mary shouting from her room: *Faither, is that you ah can hear oot there?* Thomas and Chrissy enter Mary Tellman's bedroom together to see her sitting up in bed. Magda joins them a moment later with a fresh pot of tea, and all three pause to witness Mary begin her habitual lament of confusion after waking up after a long sleep, but with a surprising new variant this morning: *Where am I? Faither! Thank guidness yoor here. Ah dinnae recognise this place. Am ah kipping ower at some relative's place? Who are these girls, ma cousins?*

Mary, these ladies are your nurses I think, to help you about the house now that you're so old.

Really? But hoo kin ah affoart tae pay them?

Chrissy laughs and shakes her head. *You paid your taxes, Mrs Tellman. We don't cost you a thing, silly.*

Do the Air Force pay for you? The RAF? Thomas asks.

Ha! Now don't you start! I can only cope with one comedian at a time, thank you very much. Chrissy guffaws nervously. *Taxes I said. We work for the council, the local authority.*

Home Care. Magda chips in proudly, pointing to the logo on the left lapel of her uniform jacket.

Ahh... the British Health Service. Thomas nods. *So they went ahead with all that. That's just swell.*

Swell? Chrissy laughs. *You speak like out of a film, a movie.*

Sir... Magda adds wittily.

And I've not been called Ma'am since many a long year. You're a very polite young man. Now Mary, would you like a wee sandwich and a yoghurt after your tea? We could sit you up by the bay window while Magda and I change the bedding over? Your grandson here can help you through and sit with you.

Grandson? Whit!? Whit ur they oan aboot, Faither? Ah dinnae see onny kiddies.

Now Mrs Tellman, Magda intones, leaning in to help with the bedding. *You've just woken up, just a little bit confused. Just give it time and everything will all come back to you. We're here every day, us or the other girls, looking after you. You're forgetting how old you are. Not nearly young enough to be the daughter of this young man.*

Mary looks down at her wrinkled hands, and her brow clouds with doubt for a moment, dimly starting to grasp Chrissy's technical objections.

06

Rain patters against the window as Thomas sits on the edge of Mary's bed, having brought her a bowl of soup and bread on a tray. Mary's spoon clinks against the porcelain like the sound of distant church bells. Thomas stares into space, past the partially drawn white net curtains, into the overgrown garden outside. *I remember a story your mother used to tell me...* he says slowly as if deep in thought, almost in conversation with himself, *about a village that used to exist on one of the sandy peninsulas near here, centuries ago. Something happened, I can't remember what, and it all went under the sand then under the sea. Then for generations later, at real low tide or in storms, people used to say the top of the church steeple would become visible, or fishermen would hear or feel the reverberation of the bells, still ringing from the church of the drowned village. Local legend or fragment of truth, or some allegory, metaphor for something else? You Scots have such great fables. In the States, only the Indians had stuff that good, the Cherokee, the Chickasaws, the Shawnee. I look back and wonder at how they must have viewed the white man. Growing up, there was so much I never questioned, about belonging, and ownership.*

Whit happened to you, Faither? Mary looks up from her bowl. *Folks said you were chasing a big muckle silver light in the sky and got tae close tae it. They said your aeroplane blew up or something, but they never foond ony wreckage. Hoo can it be? Whit happened?*

Thomas runs his fingers through his short black crew-cut hair, rubs his face and eyes. *I blacked out, Mary, lost consciousness. I don't know how long for. When I woke up I was in a silver room, like some kind of hospital, white light everywhere, and silhouetted figures moving about, like surgeons.*

Whaur wur ye, Daddy? Mary stops eating, her gaze fraught with attention.

Inside the silver light I'd been following I guess. It was like a ship, but one that sails through the sky and space rather than water or waves.

Whaur did they tak ye tae? She resumes eating her soup, riveted by the unfolding story.

I didn't realise we were moving at first, it was so smooth. But we must have been travelling at incredible speed. They showed me other worlds around other stars, all so different from each other. Green skies, yellow oceans of ice, forests like turquoise seaweed swaying in crimson winds.

Whit ur they like, Faither? Ur they different from us? Whit is their world like?

They have no world, no home left. It died tens of thousands of years ago, became a desert, devoid of life. They are like nomads, wandering, travelling between many other stars, always looking for other life. They are monitors. That is what I came to understand I was to call them. The monitors.

Were they kind to you? They must o' fed ye, and kept ye' warm.

Thomas laughs. *They took good care of me, Mary, as you can see. I am in very fine health. But they are beyond kindness and cruelty, laughter or sadness, all of our concepts of good and bad. Those are all so relative anyway. They have their interests and motivations, as do we. But ours are unimaginably primitive in comparison. We are like dogs, Mary, or rabbits maybe. Imagine thinking you were a human being all your life, a thinking sophisticated being, then one day finding out you were actually a puppy, a hamster, who'd had a strange dream of being more complicated than it really was. That is the knowledge that I've come back with, that I live with every moment now.*

A guinea pig, Daddy?

Thomas laughs again now, but more darkly. Reaches out and runs his hands through his aged daughter's cruelly greyed hair. *Yeah, that's it. An experiment, Mary. And it's not over yet.*

Whit did they look like? Are they like us? Muckle or toatey? Grey or green?

I'll show you. Thomas smiles, and goes across the corridor to the bathroom and returns with something behind his back. He sits back down on the bedside then watches Mary's eyes carefully as he slowly tilts the object up until it is vertical, facing her face. Mary's eyes widen, brows furrow slightly, eyes cloud then clear again, her wrinkles ease, open out as at last she believes she understands and nods her head.

*

Thomas puts his airman's uniform on, regarding himself carefully in the full-length mirror then tells his mother he will be back in a couple of hours. The boundary to the RAF Kinburgh compound has changed since his day. It takes him half an hour of walking across fields and the narrow borders of rural roads without pavements until arriving at the long straight avenue across open moor towards the checkpoint at the entry gates. The two armed guards watch Thomas' progress from the lookout tower. Nobody approaches the gate on foot. Even a lunatic or a terrorist would have more sense. One of the guards radios for backup as a precaution and several closed-circuit cameras rotate to begin filming Thomas. As standard protocol, the senior of the two guards paces forward to intercept the visitor before he is even within striking distance of the post. *Can you identify yourself please, sir? This is Ministry of Defence Property so I have to stop you from proceeding any further.*

Thomas halts and the guard looks his antiquated uniform up and down with a mixture of confusion and revulsion. *Captain Thomas F Tellman, pilot. I'm here to report to the air base commander.*

Do you have an appointment? The guard asks mechanically.

Thomas reaches his hand into his chest pocket and the guard flinches, steps back, primes his rifle, while his colleague steps out from behind the gate. The three figures now form a triangle, with Thomas in the inferior position. The two rifles are not quite raised, not quite aimed at Thomas yet, but clearly could be in a second. The index fingers of their right hands are visible in the same posture, as training, just one step down from the trigger zone. *Easy, slowly, please sir. What's in the pocket that we'd want to see?*

My papers, military I.D, pilot licence and number. I am on active service, a member of squadron 576. I have been missing in action and wish to present myself for debriefing.

The second soldier back away and speaks into his walkie-talkie, his exact words hard to discern amid the noise. The first soldier appears to already know the answer to the question being relayed. *There is no such squadron. Is that uniform from a museum, a historical re-enactment club?*

Thomas shakes his head slowly, his arm frozen carefully, hand poised at the half-opened pocket.

We're not generally appreciative of practical jokes, sir. These guns aren't replicas, and they're loaded with live ammunition, as I do hope you understand. But if you want to carefully and slowly hand your documents towards me, then we might take a copy of them if you wait where you are for a few minutes. You realise that attempting to forge military documentation is a criminal offence? So if this is any kind of forgery, then again it won't be taken as a joke.

I understand, corporal. The documents are not fake, I can assure you... Thomas responds, impressing or perhaps unnerving, his interlocutors, with his unwavering gaze and extreme calm.

You American? The soldier asks, relaxing very slightly, but still not taking his eye off Tellman, while handing the I.D to the second soldier, who takes it back to scan at the sentry box.

Kentucky, U.S.A. But I joined the RAF about six years ago, when I was nineteen.

Sir, are you disorientated perhaps? Your uniform, nor you I.D, I suspect, are current or valid and I would almost certainly know you if you were on active service at this base. So you are potentially a hostile intruder wasting our time and harassing two guards at the south gates of Her Majesty's RAF Kinburgh. So I'm going to have to ask you now to turn around and walk away down this road and get a bus back into town.

My I.D. Could I have my papers back please?

I could also if you wish call the local police and ask them to escort you back into town, sir. Shall I do that?

No need, thank you. Thomas slowly shakes his head. *Once you realise my papers are genuine then I would like them returned, please. Good afternoon.* He turns and walks away the way he came. The guards visibly relax into a mixture of relief and dissatisfied confusion.

*

Curiosity and the thought of a couple of hours spare come together in Thomas' mind before he turns home towards Mary's house. Also wary of being belatedly followed by the surprisingly hostile military personnel, he changes direction and makes his way towards the town of Kinburgh, which was something much closer to a village the last time he saw it. He is shocked by the new roads, the speed and quantity of cars. He remembers how rich and fertile the fields and hedgerows were, compared to their depleted state now, poisoned by car exhaust fumes. He notices fewer insects and birds, constant noise, an air of death and retreat everywhere as if nature is being grievously wounded.

He passes an expensive-looking new nursing home with full-height windows, and notes the number of old people inside the main lounge, many lined up like schoolchildren in their chairs, some gazing vacantly into space alone or up at the distant television on the wall as if it is a religious icon, while young women dressed not unlike Mary's carers drift about the corridors changing sheets.

He reaches the new housing estates on the periphery of town and is appalled by their cartoon architecture, like stage-set copies of mansions twice the size, everything scaled down. But no shops or play parks, everyone hiding behind high fences. All hard landscaping for maximum area of car parking, no front gardens, flowerbeds, rockeries, trees or verges or hedgerows. Reaching the heart of the old village, he slows down and listens intently to overheard conversations, trying to rapidly assimilate how English useage has changed. He notices how the young and old have grown further apart into mutual distrust, reinforced by clothes, mannerisms, meaningless linguistic tics and catchphrases, neologisms.

He enters a café and buys a cup of tea with loose change from Mary's kitchen table, tries not to puzzle for too long over the unfamiliar coins, keen not to stand out as a tourist, but knows his accent will count against him. Sitting down at a table alone for an hour with a free local newspaper, he absorbs knowledge like a sponge, rotates his hearing from one nearby table to the next, picking up phrases, gradually surmising and interpolating meanings. When he leaves, he thanks the staff behind the counter and waves to them, but they don't even seem to notice him, which both disturbs and reassures him. But his turn of the head has blinded him to someone else coming in the door, an attractive young woman whose short skirt and revealing top almost alarm him, but she meets his eyes unabashed as they try to squeeze past each other. He understands the look she gives him, as if she could eat him like a cake, but is taken aback that she offers such interest in a stranger. In war time once, perhaps, but this is peacetime. Maybe this town bores her compared to the big cities where she might meet a wider range of men. He has no interest in whatever she wants, doesn't even turn his head once they've passed. Might like to hear her talk out of general interest, learn about her life, but understands the danger even of conversation, with someone sexually charged, the tensions it sets off in others around them. He is trying now to gather information without giving any out, but already suspects it may ultimately prove a losing battle.

On his way home he remembers the path to a stretch of slow-moving river he and Eleanor used to swim in on summer days. The clear pure water he remembers is now clouded with pollution, traces of domestic detergent, agricultural pesticides, by-products from local industry. The muddy banks are clogged with the silver skeletons of discarded supermarket trolleys in various stages of slow decay towards rust, roots and trees now growing through and around their frames. Withered fragments of plastic bags blow among the leaves and branches like some alien fruit, white flags of defeat.

Nearer to home he chances upon a waterlogged corner of neglected field where nature has had more luck: damselflies and butterflies flutter around his face, some landing on his shoulders. He kneels down to find tiny lime green frogs emerging from the water onto his hands. He looks up to see a blackbird perched on a wind-blasted old tree above him, sprinkling the air with bright notes of its joyous song despite nearby traffic.

07

He said it again on the phone this morning, Chrissy...
Magda says quietly in the passenger seat.

Said what? Chrissy replies as they take the familiar turning off the main road towards the Tellman house.

That he was Mary Tellman's father, not her son.

Did he indeed? That just can't be, Magda. It's not remotely possible. Self-evidently. I'll put him right if need be. Do you think he could be some kind of nut job, a crazy?

He seems to know her. And when her senses return she seems to know him, as if they have...

History?

Yes, a back story. Trust, affection. They do seem like family to each other.

Just not father and daughter, eh?

But I don't think he's crazy. He seems so calm and kind. His eyes look right into you.

As if you're naked, eh? Precisely what I don't like about him. Pull yourself together, Magdalena. You never can tell. Sometimes the truly bonkers can seem very convincing. I've seen all sorts in my time in this job. Mary Tell-me-my-name-again is a mild case compared to some. If this guy, this relative, is staying around for a while then we should tell the management soon, even the doctor. He could be designated her carer, if he's legit, take some of the strain off us.

They enter the house and are impressed to find that Thomas already has Mary up and dressed and sitting at the kitchen table. Mary turns her head and greets them with a smile, seemingly having run through her morning re-boot already. *Hallo ladies! Have yoo met ma faither yet? He came hame the day afore yesterday, richt oot the blue with nae warning. Ah wonder if the newspapers will want tae ken aboot it?*

Now, Mary... this man is your grandson, not your father. You're getting confused there again.

Pardon me, Ma'am. Christine, I am her father. My daughter is not confused about that.

Chrissy pauses, brow furrowed, looks at Magda for assistance. A fraught silence reigns for several seconds. She looks down at Thomas, her hands on her hips. *Now, come on, let's get real here. Ma heid doesnae button up the back. You're a young man. How old are you?*

Twenty five years old, I think, or maybe twenty six now.

Maybe? How can you not be sure? Well anyway, be that as it may, this lady, lovely Mrs Mary Tellman is eighty seven years old, so unless my O Grade arithmetic fails me, that means you'd have to be about at least one hundred and three years old to be her father. So you can't be her father, can you? Chrissy asks, frowning, tapping her right foot.

Thomas shrugs. *I can see your viewpoint, and I'm not going to argue with you, Ma'am.*

Viewpoint? Magda reaches a hand out to touch Chrissy's shoulder from behind, trying to calm her. *Explain to me, how you could be her father. I'm open minded, all-ears.*

Thomas sighs. *Very well. But may I suggest that we all pull up chairs and sit around my daughter's, Mary's, dining table for a few moments, and have our English tea and biscuits together like civilised friends?* Thomas sets the kettle boiling, but Magda insists on finishing the process, getting the biscuits out the cupboard.

Thomas puts his cup down and holds up the saucer only, side on to Chrissy's viewpoint, then says: *If I asked you to draw exactly the shape this object is, going only by what you can see of it, what would you draw?*

Shrugging, Chrissy reluctantly dips her pinkie in the tea and draws a long smile-shape onto the table top.

And if I turned it like this, how would you draw it then?

Chrissy draws a circle.

Now suppose I put a small mark on one side of the dish, and spun it fast, like this, how would you know how many times the plate had spun before I showed it to you again?

I couldn't. You've spun it far too many times, too fast to count. How are you doing that by the way? That's so fast, it's like a party trick.

The black dot looks like a line when I spin it fast enough, doesn't it?

Yes, but what's any of this got to do with how old you are?

Thomas stills the plate and puts it down and then produces a black and white photograph from his shirt pocket and holds it out for Chrissy and Magda to see. *The date stamp says 1948, doesn't it? And yet this photograph was only taken a year ago, from my perspective.*

Your perspective!? It looks like you, alright. But you haven't aged, which isn't possible. Why isn't it in colour?

You, Christine, you also Magdalena, Mary also, all of you are the black dot on the plate. The Earth, this planet, spins like a plate. All your lives you have been spinning very fast while I travelled very far away. From my perspective you appeared to stay still, but now that I've come back and the plate has stopped spinning, I see that it and you spun many times, many years have passed, while for me, the observer of the plate, almost no time has passed at all.

Chrissy closes her eyes for a few moments, opens them, drinks back her tea in a single gulp then stands up, exclaiming: *Right! Too deep for me! I'm out of here!*

Magda, standing up to follow her, tries to apologise, make excuses for Chrissy, tapping her watch. *I'm really sorry, but we're running late now, we really need to go. It'd been nice to meet you, Mister...*

Tellman, Thomas Tellman. Call me Tom. Perception is relative, is the point I was making. As is time...

*

Chrissy, Chrissy! Magda shouts in a hoarse whisper, catching up with her at the car. *We haven't even given her the pills yet! You've forgotten about her pills.*

Chrissy turns around and hisses at her like a cat over

the roof of the car. *I've not forgotten anything. We needed to get out of there. That man's clean off his head.*

Why? Didn't you understand what he was saying?

Oh I understood just fine. Are you sure you did? He's saying he left the flaming planet, flew off into outer space. He's some kind of impostor, a con artist.

But we have to give Mrs Tellman her pills. It's our job.

You go back in there then, Magda. I'll wait right here.

Going back into the hallway, Magda jumps again. Something about Thomas' smiling expression, his posture, how close he is already standing to the door. As if he somehow knew she would be coming back, knows all about the pills now even though yesterday he didn't even know who Home Care were. Walking back down the hallway she asks him: *how do you know Polish?*

I only know a little... she hears him answering as he follows behind her. *I picked it up during the war from the free Polish pilots that flew with us, over Europe. They were real swell guys. Too bad how things turned later with the Red Army taking over. Out of the frying pan and into the fire, as they say.*

As she pops the pills out of their blister pack and hands them to Mary Tellman with a glass of water, she notices that Mary is now holding a framed black-and-white photo on the table in front of her, and is tapping her fingernail at the face of the man in a pilot's uniform standing over her as a child. Magda too now, begins to feel giddy and uneasy, and almost runs back to the back door after making her goodbyes again. But as a parting shot, she forces herself to turn to Thomas and asks: *If you were watching the plate spin, could you see when Poland became a free democratic country again?*

He looks deep into her eyes and again Magda has the uncanny feeling, both comforting and vaguely frightening simultaneously, that he can read her every thought before she expresses it, and indeed whether she expresses it or not. Oddly, he now seems to answer an entirely different, more general question in response: *Fear is what oppresses people, but it can only last so long. Curiosity, kindness and joy are stronger emotions that will always win out in the end.*

Magda nods, blushes, head down, and hurries to the car.

*

Now Chrissy and Madga bicker and fight all the way back to Kinburgh. *I'm going straight to the police, Magda, that guy's well creepy.*

The police? On what grounds? Shouldn't we go to our supervisor first?

You mean Helen Murchison, unfortunately. She'll make some personal mileage out of it somehow, for sure. She always does. Tell everyone how she saved the day and we were a pair of diddies getting conned by a dangerous intruder or something.

*But what if he **is** her father, Chrissy? He certainly looks like the photo...*

Magda, stop. Just stop. Don't go there. That's crazy talk. We don't do fantasy in this car, on this shift, or in this job.

Why can't you even keep your mind just a tiny little bit open, entertain the possibility?

Waiting at the traffic lights, Chrissy closes her eyes in frustration and mimes thumping her head off the wheel. *Because, Magda, if I let go like that, even for a second, then I let go of everything else, can't you see that? Aren't you the same? Then ghosts you heard in old houses as a kid, premonitions your aunty Sally had, that mirror you broke that gave you seven years bad luck five years ago, not walking on the cracks between paving stones... all of it... all the crazy bullshit turns up at your door with its long black unkempt hair droochit in the rain, begging to be allowed back in again. And how would you stop it? Science and facts are all we have, Madga, that stop us from being a bunch of crazy cave women, witches stirring our brews.*

Magda frowns. *But miracles do happen sometimes.*

Human beings don't understand everything in creation, and probably never will.

Uh oh... this isn't a Roman Catholic thing, is it? Next you'll be telling me you saw an apparition of Jesus in your burnt toast this morning!

Don't bring my religion into this, Chrissy, that's out of bounds.

Out of bounds? Ah-ha! You see... how open minded are you then? We've all got boundaries, fences to keep our thoughts safe, haven't we?

Like sheep you mean?

Chrissy chuckles. *Well that's a Christian metaphor, isn't it? The Lord's my shepherd and all that, so you do understand. We're just debating where our fence posts should be hammered in.*

I don't like you mocking my faith. To me it is my truth, my light. Not arbitrary.

Oh Madga, I'm not getting at you, bless you, sweetheart. Chrissy changes gear as the lights change.

Don't call me that. I'm offended now. Magda sighs, winds the window down and gazes across the passing fields.

Chrissy glances quickly over at her, returning her eyes to the road. *I'm just talking about evidence. Belief is not enough, because people are easily fooled, all of us.*

But that goes for you too then. If your evidence is incomplete sometimes, then you can be fooled.

Yes, I accept that, reluctantly. You're pretty good at logic and reason. We both are. Let's hang on to that.

08

Mary Tellman wakes up and is again unable to remember where she is, what she is doing there, what age she is, or what living relations or family members she has to hand. Thomas runs through the usual reminder routine that the carers use with her, adept already. She silently digests this information for a few moments then speaks:

We should gie them a phone then, shouldn't we no? Ma son and daughter, Andy an Lou? Tae tell them their grandpappy huz cum hame agin, eh?

Thomas lifts the phone from its cradle in the hallway, puzzled at first that it lacks the cord that telephones used to, but – remembering seeing the carers on their mobile phones – brings it through to his daughter and hands it to her as she sits up in bed, rubbing her hands in gleeful anticipation.

Lou? Lou? Is that you? It's yir dear old ma' here, how ur yoo, sweetheart? Ah surprise eh? Weel, ah'm daen allricht but ah dinnae get the chance tae mak phonecalls sae often as ah did in the past. How are the weans? Guid, guid. Never? The bright wee chiel. Listen, listen, Lou, ah've goat a big surprise o' ma ain tae tell ye the nicht, ye'll ne'er believe it. Ah've goat yir grandfaither here, Thomas, ma daddy. The one yoo ne'er met. No, ah'm nae kiddin', doll. He's come back, wiz still dressed in his RAF uniform an everythin'. Ah'm nae kiddin'. Ah swear it, luv. He's stonnin' right here. Ah'll put him oan if ye like. Nae, really. Ye kin talk tae him yersel', ask him yer questions...

Hello? Louise? Yeah, I'm your grandfather. Yeah, the one who disappeared. The UFO thing. Well, hell, that's a long story. Eighty years long to be precise, so I'm told. But I'm not eighty, no, that's right. Einstein's theory of relativity. I've aged about a year, maybe less, I think. Incredible. Yes, incredible is the word. I sure wish I could disbelieve it myself. But every morning I wake up it's still the case, here I am, the man who shouldn't be here. Your mother is my daughter, but I'm younger than you. I know, it's messed up, isn't it? Look... let's be honest, I don't expect you to entirely believe me, not yet, how could you, how could anyone? But can you come up here? You're due up anyway? That's swell. That will be nice. Strange but real nice. I look forward to it. Want me to put you back on to her now?

09

Chrissy knocks on Helen Murchison's office door at Home Care headquarters. *Helen, did you get my email? It's about that Tellman man. I have grave doubts, suspicions, that I feel obliged to share...*

Oh really? Good morning, Christine. Please come in and have a seat and close the door behind you.

The view over Helen's shoulder is of the many tiled rooftops of the historic burgh, its cluttered blonde sandstone steeples and occasional domes vying for sky as if for the distracted attention of God. Noises drift vaguely from the street below: the beep-beep of a lorry reversing, of beer barrels being rolled into the cellar of a pub across the street, of street-sweepers clearing the remnants of weekend revelling from the granite indifference of ancient cobbles. Helen keeps writing notes and reading something on screen, making Chrissy wait in order to signal her authority over her. Irritated by this, soon Chrissy quietly starts talking anyway:

He came out of nowhere. It seems to me nobody knows who he is really, he could be anybody. Just walks into that woman's house and announces he's her long lost father or a spaceman or something. Shouldn't there be background checks? I mean, he could just be a homeless guy, a con man, who's figured out where to find a soft touch. An old woman with no memory but a decent Air Force pension and savings. How long until he starts stealing off her? I mean, does he have a job? Where did he actually come from? How will we know he's not messing with her pills, planning to bump her off or something?

Next of kin... is the key... Helen finally says, eyes still on her screen. *I got a phonecall from her daughter the other day. We're on it, as they say – thanks, Christine.*

But she's alone in that house with a stranger now, an impostor potentially.

Helen stops typing at last and finally turns her attention

to Chrissy, looking at her face, or almost through her, with a distant kind of focus, as if one of them is still not entirely present. *She doesn't seem to think so. He sounds harmless enough.*

But she's amnesiac, demented.

Not entirely or consistently, Christine. Her memory generally returns, as I understand it, after half an hour or so of confusion. It's not uncommon in these cases.

These cases? You get a lot of alien abductee returnee airmen then?

I meant elderly people living alone with intermittent short-term memory loss as a symptom of their progressive dementia, Christine.

You don't think his absurd claims of having jumped forward in time by 80 years are relevant then?

He's a young able-bodied man, the case notes now say, so not likely to be subject to the concerns of our department. There are proper channels for everything, after all. Social Work, the family doctor, and so forth. They'll all do their job in due course, if need-be. If this young man has any significant mental health issues then other professionals within the community will identify that, I'm quite sure. It's not your job, Christine.

Chrissy stands up grimacing, barely concealing her anger, turning around to excuse herself, then pausing at the door: *Well, bugger the proper channels, I'm telling you as a human being, that there's something wrong about that guy, dangerous even. On the record, Helen. If anything happens after this, I want it there in black and white that I flagged him up.*

Helen shrugs, head tilting to one side, one lip curling into the semblance of an enigmatic smile, her eyes returning to the green glow of her screen.

10

Helen Murchison, district nurse and senior supervisor, turns up a couple of days later to find Thomas mowing the lawn and clipping the hedges with rusted and antiquated equipment from the garden shed. *Making an early start, eh? I always say this is the best part of the day!* Helen announces cheerily, stepping out of her car, crossing the lawn to offer out her hand. *My name's Helen, the district nurse. Are you Thomas? Pleased to meet you. I'm told you're a long lost relation. Always good to have a man about the house. Could we possibly go inside and talk about Mrs Tellman for a few minutes? I need to ask you a few questions and update my notes.*

Well sure... go right ahead, Ma'am. Thomas answers, smiling warmly, wiping the sweat from his forehead. *You been here before? Know the way? You go have a look-see if Mary's awake yet while I throw some water over my head then I'll come join you.*

Finding Mary still snoring, Thomas and Helen retreat down the hallway to the kitchen, where he makes them both a cup of coffee. Paranoid questions rapidly flick through Helen's head as she watches him from behind as he deftly performs domestic tasks at the worktop. He seems so masculine and straightforward, but... she remembers reading something about vulnerable men idolising old ladies that remind them of their mother. Could he be some kind of confused drifter who's latched onto this woman somehow?

Where did you live before, Thomas? Helen asks the first of her questions after they sit down.

Here. This house. Like I said, I was, am, Mary's father. I lived in this house with her mother Eleanor until the day I went missing, and now I'm back. I know how strange it must seem to you and everyone else, but that can't be as strange as it is for me. For me: this is all I have, the truth, the reality, that I have to find a way forward from.

So you're planning to live here, indefinitely, I mean from now on?

Of course, at least I think so, to be with my daughter, the only family I have left. What father wouldn't want that?

Don't you have any family in America? What state did you say you were from?

Kentucky. Now just think about that. My little sister was two years younger than me, and she hadn't married by the time I disappeared. She'd be over a hundred years old by now, so quite probably dead. If she married, I have no way of knowing what name she took and what name her children have.

You could search on the internet.

Someone else mentioned that recently, one of the nurses I think.

One of the care workers you mean, I am a nurse, but they are merely trained and qualified residential carers.

They are kind and patient women, whatever you want to call them, Ma'am, to whom I am very grateful for the help they give Mary. But Ma'am, where do I find the internet?

Do just call me Helen, by the way. Why, you have a phone line here, a land line, don't you? Well whoever sends you bills for that, whatever company that is, will be able to give you internet access if you ask them. But haven't you a mobile phone?

Thomas shrugs, pointing to the phone in the hallway: *Only that one, that you called here on earlier.*

I see. You'll need some kind of computer as well, a laptop, tablet or PC. You really have been out of the swing of things, haven't you, Thomas, for a young man, 26 years old you said? What about employment? Are you going to look for a job? You'll have to register with the local doctor, local government, register to vote and...

I reckon I did, I had, all of those things, over eighty years ago, when I moved to Britain during the war.

Which is a very long time ago, Thomas, so whatever people or records you had, will be retired or out of date.

And your story is quite incredible, far-fetched I'm afraid many people will say, no matter what I think of it, which is in a sense neither here nor there. But you're going to have to re-engage with society, with where you came from, or believe you came from. The self-evident fact is that you are here, flesh and blood, and you need a place to live and money to buy food and pay bills with. I know your mother pays for a lot of that at the moment...

My daughter, you mean...

Well, as you wish, Mary shall we just call her? Mary is... Helen looks down at her records, *eighty-seven and isn't going to be around forever, whereas you have your whole life ahead of you potentially. But in the short term, it's good news for everyone if you are a relative who is willing to live here and keep Mary company, because my file indicates that Mary's loneliness is one gap we've identified recently in her care package. We were thinking of approaching what's called a 'befriender', local volunteers who come and spend time talking to old people in their homes.*

A package. A befriender. Is that commonplace?

Yes, it is these days. Is something the matter?

All this loneliness... Thomas rubs his face in anguish, furrowing his brow. *I'm beginning to see it everywhere now, since I've come back. It's grown like a silent disease, in every street, invisible, multiplying like weeds, choking everyone slowly. Mary should have family, community, neighbours and relatives. She should be at the heart of things, a valued old dame, not outcast here like this, like some piece of antique furniture nobody wants, cared for by paid strangers. I'm grateful for you and the others, all this 'care', and I certainly know Mary is. But can't you see that it's grotesque as well?*

Grotesque?

Salving of conscience, of guilt. Not really caring, but what society contrives to do instead of caring.

Oh that's a terribly sad and cynical way of looking at things, if you don't mind me saying so, Thomas. I've dedicated my whole working life to this field, to 'Care'.

I'm sorry. I didn't mean to show disrespect for your work, but in the world I left, care wasn't a career. It was a human emotion. Now you seem to be telling me that even the word itself has been changed, desecrated. If words become false, then life is false. Aren't words all we have?

Helen pauses, wide-eyed, unsure how to proceed. *I never thought of it like that. You said you were an airline pilot?*

I fought in the war, dropping bombs over Nazi Germany. Joseph Goebbels believed in changing the meaning of words I seem to remember, even if no one else still does.

I'm sorry now. Our conversation seems to have gone off course somewhat.

As did my aeroplane and I, I suppose.

Yes, quite, how apt. All I was trying to say was how positive it might prove for you to have come here to live with Mary and keep her company and assist with her... comfort, in old age. You could become her designated carer, and for that to happen your own well-being comes under the spotlight. Mary's daughter Louise phoned me and says she is flying up soon, and would like to meet you.

To check me out in case I'm some sort of impostor.

Well, anyone's scepticism is understandable under these highly unusual circumstances, surely? You're a complete stranger from her perspective, suddenly looking after her mother. Do you have a birth certificate for instance, an NHS number?

I left, disappeared, just before I've been told the British National Health Service was founded. But I should have a birth certificate, passport even, in some drawer about the house here. I'll look it out later. I even had my pilot's licence until a few days ago when the RAF failed to return it to me.

You've been to the local air base? Of course. How did that go?

Not well.

They didn't believe you were who you said?

Well, the goons on the gates didn't. But give it time. The penny may eventually drop with their superiors, and then they'll probably come looking for me. I'd put money on it.

If your own employers, ex-employers, didn't believe you, then I fear that doesn't bode well for the rest of society. You might as well start building a new identity for yourself all over again, I would suggest, Thomas. But what if the newspapers come looking for you, UFO fanatics and cranks?

I don't think that would be very good for Mary, do you?

No, very probably not. Helen pauses to think for a moment. Takes a long sip of her tea, staring into space, the glimpse of sky through the window over Thomas' shoulder, estimating possibilities and probabilities. *But suppose someone like me was to say that I believe you, even for a moment. Then what would you, will you, tell people like me about what happened to you, where you've been for the last eighty years?*

I'll tell them the truth I suppose, given the chance, the whole truth and nothing but the truth.

Which is?

Overwhelming, to most folks, most likely. Disturbing. But I reckon I ain't ready to talk about that just yet, to strangers. But I'll ponder on it, get my shit together ready, pardon my language, Ma'am.

Why overwhelming?

Are we nearly done here? Thomas puts his mug back down on the table. *You wanna follow me out to the garden and I'll show you something there?*

Back outside, Thomas kneels over a rose bush, smells its aroma, his eyes filling with something like tears. Bees, one at first, then several others, land on his bare arms and crawl up over his skin and clothing towards his face. Helen flinches, but Thomas lifts the little insects off onto his fingertips and hold them up admiringly, whispers to them as if he is addressing a pet dog or caged songbird. Several run through his hair, still provoking no reaction.

He turns back around to address her as she reflexively steps back:

Little pilots like me, you see? We're trained to observe in great detail, to pay attention to the slightest thing in the land or the weather from up there. You notice a lot of change when you look away for eighty years. The natural world is in failing health, Helen, as surely as my daughter is. But unlike Mary, this planet is designed to be self-renewing, effectively immortal, give or take a few billion years. Except that it seems clear to me it's dying now because of the pollution folks are doing to it every day. If only you knew how rare and precious all this is, this bountiful world, amid the arid expanses of space. These tiny creatures seem to know more about that than we do, don't you think? Do you know they're all female? It's true – each hive keeps only a few male drones for breeding and they never get out. Seems to me like the bees show more respect, do more to help repair our damage than we do. Maybe bees are really running the planet, not us. We only think we are. We're just the vandals. Maybe I'll tell people something about that, if they'll listen.

Helen looks at him in mild amazement at his sudden passion. *Well, Thomas, you should be a gardener then. That might be an easy job to start in. How's that for an idea?*

Well hell yes... he shrugs, hoisting a bag of chopped branches onto his back, *I suppose it might just be as good a place to start as any.*

11

Mary's daughter Louise arrives in a taxi outside the house, her heart beating fast as she pays the driver, her mind in turmoil over her fear and hope regarding Thomas. She has already spoken on the phone to Doctor McCaffrey, Social Work and Home Care, and is grimly prepared to identify and mollify a hopefully harmless lunatic in her mother's home, or... or what? The other possibility has no precedent or antecedent, no referential context she has been able to imagine other than problematic modern conundrums such as adoptees finding their real parents, and other similar anomalies that seldom go well.

Turning around as the car departs, Louise finds Thomas walking towards her smiling, almost laughing, introducing himself, taking her suitcase from her effortlessly with strong, fit chest and arms. The telephone conversation had somehow misled her brain to expect an old man, her grandfather after all. Or if some part of her mind had also grasped the notion of a man supposedly in his twenties, then for some reason she had pictured someone weedy and studious, gawky and out of touch. But of course, she thinks now, he is military; RAF, close-cropped hair, knows how to clean a floor in jig-time with a towel under his feet and other practical tricks, cook his own dinner, press his own shirts, maintain self-discipline and liberate Europe.

The family resemblance! But your name... he is suddenly asking her, stirring her from her dreamlike enchantment at his unexpected youth. *I wanted to ask you before Mary's within earshot. How come Mary's still called Tellman?* he taps his finger on the brass nameplate outside the door, *...if she married and had two kids, one of which is you?*

Louise's brain snaps back into shape for a moment, thinking: Wow, asking me the questions like I'm the surprise. If this guy's an impostor then he must have come straight from Hollywood. Her eyes meet his again at the door and she has the irrational notion that he has just heard her thoughts inside her head. *Divorce...* she answers him. *Mum's married name, my maiden name, was MacPherson. She changed hers back to Tellman after the divorce. Some people do that, for acrimonious reasons. But with Mum I think it had something more to do with...* Louise nearly says 'you' but stops herself, *waiting for her father to return. Which we all thought was a mythic quest – as did a few psychiatrists. Until now, perhaps. Are you for real? I'm sorry, there's no other way to phrase it.*

Honesty of course, Thomas answers as they enter the house, *is a trait I'm very glad to see in my granddaughter, the granddaughter I never knew I had until now. I feel pretty real to me, I can tell you.*

She looks at him again, perplexed, hesitant, part of her wanting to believe, but unable to negotiate the profound strangeness of the situation. Then her reverie is suddenly broken by the sound of her mother's voice calling from the bedroom.

Mary's morning amnesia seems about to proceed along normal lines as they both enter the bedroom, Louise carrying flowers in her arms, but very quickly something changes in her eyes, as her daughter embraces her. *Lou... Lou...!* Louise almost sobs at the relief of being recognised so soon. *Huv yoo twa been introduced?* Mary sputters over Louise's shoulder. *This young man...* she begins and the phrase hangs on the air for a moment as they both look towards her... *is ma faither.*

Louise picks up the black and white photograph from her mother's bedside and brings it across the room to Thomas and holds it up, rests it against his chest. He laughs as she flicks her eyes up and down again repeatedly between photograph and person. *It is remarkable, isn't it? But how can it be possible? No one's going to believe you, you know, except the cranks and nutters.*

And you, maybe? Thomas asks, allowing himself to

look momentarily downcast. *I've been looking through other photographs today – there are several albums of them in the bureau in the study. Can I show you?*

*

Louise and Thomas sit either side of Mary's bed and flick through old black and white photographs of the 1940's, then a few in colour just before the time of his disappearance. *See, I remember this day clearly...* Thomas prods the page with his finger. *Mary must have been about five years old, the war in Japan not long over. Sonny was just two, the most difficult age, and we went on holiday to Prestwick, down on the west coast, where Eleanor and I first met when I was posted there in 1940. Ordinary little town I guess, but it had romantic associations for us. I wonder what it's like now, changed much? I should go visit, maybe take Mary, if I can get my driver's licence updated. Or maybe the memories would hurt too much. What do you think, Mary?*

Yer lucky tae huv memories, Daddy. Ah cannae recall ah thing aboot Prestwick, except mibbe a big sandy beach.

Or maybe you're lucky to have lost some memories, sweetheart. Like the days after I went missing. That must have been damned hard. I can't tell you how bad I feel I wasn't around.

She often talked about it... Louise intones, resting her hand on her mother's. *Didn't you, Mum? A hard time, lonely and bewildered after... Thomas... went missing.*

Och aye, lass, nae doot aboot that. A sair fecht it wiz, and all they newspaper blokes speering awa' wi a' their questions.

Eighty years ago... Louise sighs, almost to herself.

Not to me, it isn't. Thomas corrects her. *To me, I left a year ago.*

Left?

Was taken away.

Can you talk about it? Louise asks, sitting on one side

of her mother's bed, brushing her hair back over her ears, looking up to where Thomas now stands in the light from the window. *You're going to have to, if you haven't already. Can you remember? And why, how, did you get back here at last?*

You wanna know about the little green men, eh? Flying saucers? Thomas chuckles.

Well, there has to be an explanation, doesn't there?

Space travel is no surprise, is it? People landed on the moon while I was away, so I'm told. I just went somewhere different.

But where and with whom? If you don't mind me asking.

I went into the future, Louise, but so did we all, if you think about it. It's just that I went quite a bit faster. I went with beings not dissimilar to ourselves, just with a technological head-start over us of many thousands of years. There's a lot of stars up there in the sky. Surely you didn't think we were alone, or the smartest, or the furthest ahead?

I don't know. Louise muses, eyes far away in thought. *I didn't think much about it most of the time. Most people don't, they have enough on their plate just trying to cope with their own lives here on Earth. I suppose it makes sense that there would be others up there... but it's just too big, too frightening a possibility to compute.*

Compute?

I suppose that's something else that took off while you were away. Computers. They were based on something the British built at Bletchley to decode the Nazi enigma machines. They eventually became huge then small again, and now they're in everything, our phones, our cars, our coffee machines for all I know. Machine intelligence, extensions of our brains.

I've been reading about that.

Where?

The local library in town, it's been becoming like a regular home from home. We're supposed to be getting the internet delivered here next week then maybe I can leave those poor librarians alone again. But I can't say I've noticed the internet making people smarter, their brains bigger. More like the opposite maybe.

Ain't that the truth.

Ain't? That's another thing I've noticed that's changed. The way people speak here, their figures of speech. It's less like English now, more like American. I don't reckon I sound so out of place as I used to, in some respects.

But these alien beings you say you went away with… they must have computers and then some, right?

Something like them, once, long ago. Now they engineer themselves, if you can get your head around that.

Genetics you mean? The genetic code was also cracked while you were away.

That's a first step, but so was splitting the atom. We are a precocious species you know, like babies playing with a box of matches.

Like we shouldn't be left alone?

In point of fact, we haven't been and we aren't.

You two are losing me, makin' ma heid spin noo. Mary finally intercedes. *Lou, have yoo showed yer grandad pictures o' yer weans yet? Daddy, wait 'til ye see. Yer no jist a granda but a great granda. Kin ye believe it?*

When Louise produces the photographs on her phone, Thomas's eyes cloud over then well up with tears. *If only Eleanor was here. Did she live to see her grandchildren?*

One of them, yes. Me, although I was too young to remember much. Louise suppresses an unexpected urge to reach out and put her arm around him, but stops herself, everything still feeling so new, too strange. An idea comes to her. *Have you been… oh maybe you wouldn't want to, but you must. I'm sorry to be morbid. But the graveyard in town. Granny, Eleanor is there, and so is Sonny, or Uncle Orson as we called him.*

I would like that. Thomas says quietly and sombrely, looking at his feet for a moment then looks up again with feigned brightness: *Mary, would you want to do that? Come with us to the churchyard, pay our respects to your mother and brother?*

Mary's eyes narrow and look far away. *Ye'd need a taxi widdn't ye? Mibbe some ither time when ye hauv a cor tae drive.*

But we need to get you out now and again, Mum, on your feet more often, the doctor says so. Louise counters.

Aye, och mibbe next time though, lass. You two should gang alang tigether wi oot me. Ah'd jist be in the way.

*

Kinburgh's old graveyard sits on a sandy plain of whispering dune grasses, just above the beach, just beyond the old town walls. Thomas and Louise walk there in the afternoon, leaving Mary to her afternoon nap. *A curious place to put the dead...* Thomas reflects aloud, *as if mediating between the land and the sea, the realm of the living and the waves of eternity.*

You speak like a poet, not a pilot, sometimes, Thomas.

A dramatic effect spoiled only by a neighbouring golf course.

Was this here when you left? Louise asks, prompting Thomas to laugh.

God yes, Lou, golf is a good deal older than I am, even from your perspective. But I've never played. It never interested me so much as being the ball, as it were, the thing doing the flying.

Reaching Eleanor and Sonny's gravestone, the conversation peters out, the sound of the breeze and the waves takes over, the distant voices of golfers and children on the beach fade as if passing into a dream. Thomas kneels down and closes his eyes, runs his fingers over the carved words on the stone, as if questioning their reality. He seems about to stand up again, but collapses back into a seated position on the grass, just staring ahead at the grave. Louise feels uncertain whether to look at him or away, so turns to gaze for a minute over the top of the dry stone dyke enclosing the graveyard, to watch the white froth of waves forming and dissolving endlessly in the distance, the silhouette of a small child flying a kite at the water's edge.

After a while, Louise finds she has voiced her own thoughts, almost without even intending to: *I feel so guilty, leaving Mum here each time I go back to London.*

So do I... she hears Thomas answer to her surprise, and feels compelled to go over and place her hands on his shoulders at last. *The guilt I feel, I can't hardly express. It was all my fault. I should have followed orders and returned to the air base. My oxygen was running out, I was going too high. I knew what I was doing was dangerous. But what I saw, what I was trying to see and catch up with. It seemed more important than anything else. The idea that there was something bigger than us, some meaning to it all, like angels watching over us. Is that why I kept on flying like a fool, like Icarus going too near to the sun? But what I left behind was more precious, more important. What a fool.*

On an impulse, Louise kneels down on the grass beside him, where she now sees the tracks of slow tears working their way down his face.

My wife and children, left alone, abandoned, widowed and orphaned. Because of what? All for what? I was young and excitable, bursting with curiosity. But this is what it all comes to. Fate's like a mirror. What I find is what I left behind. What I find is this.

Louise reaches out and touches his exposed right arm, momentarily noticing something odd about his skin that she will only remember and ponder over later. *You're still young.*

On the outside, maybe. But not inside, not with all I know now.

You regret it, the greatest trip maybe any human being has ever had?

I regret everything, Lou. It's what they call the human condition, isn't it? You think you want to know the meaning of life, maybe everyone does, but it carries a price. One most people are lucky enough never to have the chance to pay.

And what is it? she can't resist asking as they stand up, he the younger man with suppler joints assisting her, a woman in her late forties.

You don't wanna know, Lou, not the bulk of it, not yet at any rate... he sighs into the wind as they pace towards the ruined church at the center of the churchyard, look back towards the many other spires punctuating the stage-set silhouette of the town seen from this viewpoint. *Once you know it, you start to see it everywhere. This steeple for instance. It's all there: the yearning to escape gravity, the hand reaching up for help towards the sky. The stone made to look weightless. Here...* he says picking up a pebble at their feet, *I'll show you some fun stuff though. Hold this stone in your hand and feel the weight of it. Memorise its weight, if you can, right?*

Louise stands there squinting in the afternoon light, with her hand out, not sure what to expect next.

Now give it back to me for a moment. As she watches Thomas briefly puts the stone deep into his jacket pocket then brings it out again. *Here, hold it again, weigh it now.*

Louise gasps. *Oh my God. What did you just do? How's that possible? It's like balsa wood now, like it would float on water.*

Thomas smiles a little sheepishly then looks around himself to check they are alone. *I shouldn't do this, but that was nothing.* He takes the stone back into his pocket again, for a little longer this time then hands it back once more to Louise.

She nearly cries out in shock, drops the stone. Or tries to. In fact the stone is now so weightless that it remains hovering in the air where she held it only a moment ago. *Oh no, no, this can't be. Is this...? Can I touch it again?*

Thomas nods again, guardedly, looking around once more.

When Louise nudges the hovering stone it slowly drifts off to the left, but with no apparent sign of slowing down, until she stops it with another touch. *It has no weight now at all. That's fucking unbelievable. That's... witchcraft, devilry, you're... you're frightening me now.*

Thomas takes the stone back into his pocket, shakes it and returns it to her with its normal weight restored. *I'm shocked at your language. Polite British women didn't use words like that in 1948, except maybe in intimate situations.*

Louise laughs, the sudden tensions easing off her a little. *Jesus. You're relaxed with a stone defying gravity, but shocked by a woman swearing? How messed up is that? I think I need to sit down for a moment, that made me feel quite queer.*

They walk north for a hundred yards then sit at the edge of the sand dunes, gazing at the long beach, just outside the cemetery, its tumbledown wall behind their backs. *Is that something your... captors... taught you?*

Let's call them my teachers, yes. What I did just there is terrifyingly easy once you know how. Electric light would have amazed a medieval peasant in a similar way, got you burned as a witch. At any given moment, human beings and their scientists always kind of assume that they know all there is to know about everything. Despite our famous monkey curiosity, we're incredibly arrogant and complacent a lot of the time, for whole centuries in fact. I know that now. There is no magic, only technology based on physical laws one doesn't understand yet.

The earth is enormous compared to that stone. Louise furrows her brow. *Surely the mass of the earth should outweigh everything on it, including us?*

You might think so... Thomas responds, *but every object, including each of us, has its own invisible electromagnetic field around it. Gravity is just one property of that field, a property that depends on how sub-atomic particles are firing around it. Think of it like a dance. Like the Dashing White Sergeant or Strip The Willow.*

Showing your age there, Thomas. No, I'm joking. Scottish people still dance those at weddings and ceilidhs, although I'm not sure kids are still being taught them at school since I teach down south.

Well, all you need to know how to do, is tell the

particles to switch to the Canadian Barn Dance, if you get my drift. Then pop goes the weasel. The stone's field becomes as significant to it as the Earth's one is to the Earth, and they cancel each other out.

Louise stops walking and thinks and thinks until her head hurts. *My mind might be blown, Thomas. But I'm not sure that's a good thing. If what I just saw is possible then what else might be? How do I know you're not an alien? You've appeared out of nowhere, and I have to decide whether you are to be trusted living in the same house as my aged mother, looking after her. I don't need you to make her float, or fly her to Venus. I just need you to not kill her, just bring her food from the fridge and help change and clean her bedding.*

Piece of cake, Lou. I understand what you're saying, I really do. From my perspective though, Mary is my daughter and you are my granddaughter. I know that's difficult to imagine, but even more mind-blowingly, as you put it: in a sense I only lost Eleanor, my beloved wife, your grandmother, and our young son, a year ago. Or maybe I only really lost them a few minutes ago, when it finally sunk in. What would be my motive in being here, in putting myself through this, all this pain, other than if I were me, this place being where I came from, where I needed to return to? It's hard to express what I'm feeling right now. I might understand miraculous quirks of physics obscure to you, but human emotions are still no clearer or easier for me than for anyone, no different than they were before I left. No less painful to experience.

As they turn to go, Thomas pauses at the point on the beach where the barbed wire of the M.O.D military testing range begins. He stands and stares through the wire. *What are you thinking, Thomas?* Louise asks him.

This was just an RAF base when I left.

Munitions Testing range. There's dozens of them all across Britain, it's nothing personal where Kinburgh is concerned. We used to hear them rumbling guns and tanks around when we were kids, but not so much now.

Practising for all those wars, eh? Korea, Vietnam, the

Falklands, the Balkans, Iraq, Afghanistan.

You've been catching up with your homework then?

It's the most depressing thing to discover in the future, this amnesia regarding war, its repetitive futility.

My mother's amnesia is altogether more benign in comparison.

Yes. Human history is like giving Mary a machine gun.

Incredibly they both start laughing at that, lightly embrace for the first time, then head home.

*

A full moon rises up out of the sea that evening, that Thomas and Louise glimpse above the dark green pine woods surrounding the house, before they each turn in for the night to their rooms. Unable to sleep, Louise gets up at 2am and is puzzled to notice a dim white light emanating under the door of Thomas's room. Standing in the kitchen watching the moon sail above the trees, she suddenly realises that a window in the garage off to the left is reflecting Thomas's bedroom window, in which she can dimly see his dark silhouette sitting as if also unable to sleep, but with two strange glowing white spheres the size of apples floating around the room like tiny captured moons. Moments later she sees Thomas' shadow move and the curtains being drawn as if he had just become aware of her.

12

Two nights later back in London, Louise phones Doctor McCaffrey, who was her childhood sweetheart about thirty years ago, Kinburgh being a small place. *James... Let me know how the medical goes. I persuaded him of how important it is, I think. What do I reckon? It would be ridiculous enough if he was an ingenious impostor, wouldn't it? Truth is though... I think maybe the truth is even more ridiculous. I think he's who he says he is, James. Although the implications of that are beyond me. But James, the reason I'm phoning is... I've been looking through old photographs of him, of my grandfather, Thomas, just before he disappeared, and I've got one on screen now, zoomed right in close. I've noticed something strange. In the photo he has hair on his arms, even a little on his chest. Big deal? But Jimmy, you'll find out for yourself, tomorrow. I can't be sure, but Thomas, this Thomas, has no hair on his arms at all. I suspect he has none anywhere, other than on his head. Not uncommon? Maybe it's nothing, but I felt I should mention it. Yes, thanks again, good night.*

Doctor McCaffrey puts the phone down and finishes brushing his teeth before retiring to his bedroom in his pyjamas, where his wife Emily sits reading a paperback by the light from her bedside lamp. *Who on earth was that, Jimmy, at this hour of the night?*

Just Louise, you know, the Tellman girl, the daughter. A bit neurotic I think. Old school friend so can't be too impolite. He climbs into bed and reflects for a moment. *I'll resort to the answering machine if it starts happening too frequently. You know, nip it in the bud. Nothing to worry about.*

*

Half a mile away, Chrissy puts her young daughter to bed and comes back through to the kitchen to pour herself a gin. *Can you believe it, Kenny? That bitch Murchison took me off the Mary Tellman shift today, because I've been making too much noise about that freaky American bloke claiming he's her father. Says I've been obsessing about it...*

Aye, maybe she has a point. Kenny chuckles. *I'm sick o' hearin' about him too. Anyone would think you fancied the cunt or something.*

Right! See you! Shut the fuck up! Chrissy snarls, throwing Kenny's cup of tea over his own face. He pauses, fazed for a moment, looking down at his stained T-shirt, then lunges at her and they fall to the kitchen floor, fists flying wildly until they clamp into a mutual head lock, trying to make no noise to wake the baby, their blood slowly staining the linoleum floor.

In the fish tank in their hallway, two goldfish swish back and forward in eerie green electric light. Meeting and re-meeting each other forever in their miniature world of artificial coral and shipwrecks, imprisoned but saved from insanity by short-sightedness and amnesia.

13

Doctor McCaffrey looks up from his desk at the surgery. Over his shoulder he retains a cluttered but wistful glimpse of the sea seen across the mish mash of the old town's roofs and turrets. *Come in Thomas. I've heard a certain amount about you, I must confess. I won't say a lot, but a certain amount, from Mary Tellman and her carers and the district nurse. We're a small community you know, where people know each other – know far too much about each other sometimes, sceptical outsiders might say, but there you have it, it is what it is. I'm told you're new to the area and want to register with this practice? Well as you may know, for that we just need to carry out a short medical examination of you, nothing heavy, and ask you a few questions.*

No problem. Your predecessor, Doctor Matheson, did the same thing you know, in 1942, when I was first posted here. I was just a lad, a green-faced yank, wet behind the ears, no idea what Europe had waiting for him.

Doctor Matheson? Well, that name rings a bell, I think he was in charge then, although I could check our records.

And a Doctor Clark and a Doctor Guthrie, I seem to recall, and a couple of nurses, one called Annabel and the other one Mavis. One of them took a shine to me, I seem to recall, in a motherly sort of way you understand.

Why, that's quite remarkable, Thomas. Do you mind if I write some of that down, take notes?

Go right ahead. In fact, Doc, if you really do still have those records somewhere then I'd suggest you take very good care of them, cos' I've got a feeling they might become mighty significant soon enough.

Oh? How do you mean?

As proof of course. Proof that I'm who I say I am.

But you're Thomas Tellman.

Sure, but let's not play daft, Doc. If I was 25 in 1948, then that would make me 105 years old now. As a medical man, you're going to find that harder to swallow than a horse pill.

McCaffrey laughs. *You have an amusing turn of phrase. Well, I have an open and inquiring mind, Thomas. If I think you're mentally deranged, I'll tell you, don't worry, or some other specialist will. If you're not then we'll leave you be, to claim anything you like about the details of your past, provided you obey the law and fulfill a role as healthy normal citizen in this town. Young people like you are still leaving here too often to go off to the big cities. Frankly, sometimes my job feels like archaeology, the number of old people I have to treat. I hope you settle, find work, even start a family. No one wishes you harm, I can assure you, and if you're going to look after your mother...*

My daughter, Mary...

Yes, quite so. Then you're going to be doing her and her family good...

My family...

Yes, forgive me again, quite so. If you're going to be looking after Mary and keeping her company then that will be a very good thing. Loneliness in the elderly is the thing no one seems to be able to treat, I'm afraid.

If you could, you'd have a cure to being human, Doc. Don't people want to be human anymore? I feel like I've returned to a world of robots.

Doctor McCaffrey, after rolling up Thomas' sleeve, pumping away to take his blood pressure then pressing a stethoscope against his chest, sits back down for a moment and gazes at Thomas wide-eyed. *Robots, eh? I've wondered that myself recently. If you're who you say you are, which I must admit seems implausible, impossible even, but if you were, then I'd be very interested to hear all your other observations along those lines.*

That's mighty kind of you to say so, Doc. You're not the average country quack, are you? Something of a closet philosopher, I'd say.

Right! McCaffrey laughs a little uncomfortably and

clears his throat. *Just who's examining who here? Thomas, finally I just need you to take your shoes and socks off, your trousers down and unbutton your shirt fully. Can you do that for me please?*

14

Mary wakes up confused again, and Thomas hears her from the kitchen so saunters down the corridor to say good morning to her. Her memory start-up routine has subtly changed over recent days: *Daddy! Whaur am I? Whit's wrang with me? My legs feel awfy tired, and ma haunds are a' wrinklet.*

Mary, Mary. Everything's all right, don't worry... Thomas pleads soothingly, crossing the room to take her hands in his. *You've just lost your memory for a moment. It will come back in a short while. You've aged. You're 87 years old.*

Na! Awa'! Whit ye oan aboot? Ye huvney aged a day, Daddy.

Well now, I must confess you have me there. I went away, Mary, for a very long time, for eighty years as it happens, except that I was travelling through space close to the speed of light so my biological clock was dramatically slowed by time dilation.

Time whit?

Time dilation in accordance with the predictions of Albert Einsteins's theory of special relativity. Would you like a cup of tea?

You went into space and you came back for me?

Sure. You are my little girl, after all. Sorry I didn't make it back sooner. I won't leave you again now, I promise.

Keys sound in the front door, and the carers come in. This time it's Magdalena accompanied by her new shift-mate Annie Bevans. In the hallway, Magdalena introduces Annie to Thomas and something happens. Something Einstein never devised an equation for. Their eyes meet and glimpse something in each other. The floor momentarily turns to glass, beneath which waves break in the light of other days. Their hearts lift as if some cosmic curtains were being unexpectedly pulled aside. As if their eyes could become further corridors beyond this one, leading to hidden worlds, other suns rising and setting over other oceans. As if they could somehow be children and parents to each other in some uncharted annexe of reality, repairing all the damage and missteps of time. As if these two strangers could contrive the mysterious hope of taking care of each other some day, protecting and inspiring each other. As if they could belong. To the world and to each other. Become each other's retrospective authors through the process of admiration. History long written in their blood seems to know at least it's always worth a try. Always more important than any of any day's other business.

Please to meet you, Thomas. You're the rocket man, they tell me, the pilot who came back... Annie is shocked at herself, already saying more than she planned to, but more surprised still at feeling no shame or awkwardness, because of his eyes, his countenance, to coin an old-fashioned phrase, the way her own gaze is returned.

Magdalena feels compelled to apologise for Annie as she busies herself with blankets. *I'm sorry, Thomas. But it's inevitable I suppose, to some extent. Word will get around sooner or later about who you say you are.*

It's quite all right, Magda. I have only myself to blame. He answers, still not taking his eyes away from Annie's. *I'll go make some tea for everyone. Do you take sugar and milk, Annie?*

*

Later Magda turns to Thomas and says: *Our supervisor Helen was telling me you might be looking for a job, Thomas, is that right? She also said she'd seen you working wonders in the garden.*

Annie parts the bedroom curtains and peers out. *My, come to think of it, things are looking very tidy and trim out there since I was last here. What is it you're good at, Thomas? Mowing, pruning, trimming? You trained or just a natural?*

Well, beggars can't be choosers I guess. I'll turn my

hand to anything. If you fly away for eighty years you gotta accept going to the back of the queue when you return. Queues... a fine British invention.

But you could go on telly, become a celebrity if you wanted. Annie beams.

Thanks but no thanks, as I believe they say. I've had enough of being the centre of attention and being experimented on. I've returned to my own species in order to blissfully vanish and blend in, not stand out.

And we're not British, we're Scottish now, hasn't anyone told you? We have our own parliament.

Sure, but Britain is the name of the island though, the land mass. Sorry to be a stickler for geography. Pilots are big on maps, and how things look from the air, where some borders turn out not to exist at all, except in people's minds. You also learn about the impact of cultivation up there: how much folks growing crops and gardens changes the entire appearance of the Earth. Gardening strikes me as a noble craft, having flown over so many deserts.

Annie nods her head. *I've flown to Spain and Portugal on holidays, looked down flying over the Alps, probably small beer compared to you.*

It's significant enough I would imagine, for a sensitive person. Looking down on the patchwork quilt of fields and roads. Airlines are comfortable I believe, like sitting in your living room, but they came after my time. I've only ever done it the dangerous way, in a little tin can, paper-thin, with Germans firing bullets up at you.

Wow, that's mental.

Mental?

You know, wild, crazy, daring.

Yeah, well I could have done without it. I envy you your peaceful well-fed life, your good health, your grounded upbringing, without a barking dog on the radio harping on about racial purity. Joke is we could speak German in my family, growing up in Kentucky. The Tellmans were German Jews who crossed the pond in the 1900's.

My upbringing wasn't all that grounded, I'm afraid.

Annie sighs. *Father with a drink problem. Mother who left him.*

Ah... in friedlichen Zeiten der kriegerische Mann greift sich selbst an. In peaceful times, the warlike man attacks himself.

And we still have fascists, I'm afraid, even in governments.

Particularly in governments... Magda chips in as she swirls past, carrying a fresh duvet. *They're just more coy and clever about disguising themselves.*

15

Chrissy walks into the local police station. She is determined to continue to make trouble, her pride hurt, her paranoia pricked into imagining that her colleagues were laughing at her for her stance on Mary Tellman's mysterious house guest. Detective Inspector Hugh Drummond wearily opens his black notebook, already suspecting from her hectoring tone that this woman is, despite the respect afforded by her uniform, a time waster. *So what evidence do you have that this man is embezzling from Mrs Tellman?* he asks.

Evidence? Isn't that your domain?

Are you trying to be humorous? Like you think we manufacture evidence?

No, no, I just mean, it would take time and bank records and paperwork and stuff to prove he was robbing from her, I wouldn't know how to get that.

And neither could we, the police, unless we had reasonable grounds to suspect that a crime has actually taken place. Shouldn't all this be a matter for her relatives rather than you? She does have children and grand children, doesn't she?

Yes, but they don't visit very often. She's awfully exposed out there at that isolated house on her own.

But she has you, right? Local authority carers?

Exactly. Which is why I'm here. Because I have concerns about some crazy guy who's appeared from nowhere to claim he's been a spaceman for eighty years. Doesn't that concern you?

Mrs Nevison, in my job I regularly have to deal with people who think they're still on Jupiter, never mind whizzing around it, swinging bottles at me and trying to jab my officers with hypodermic needles choc full of hepatitis. If this Tellman bloke pays his taxes and leads a life of exemplary non-narcotic sobriety whilst helping an old lady that he may or may not be related to, then he'd get my vote if he ever runs as a councillor. In fact, if he's not related to the old dear then he's even more of a hero, isn't he? In fact, if he takes enough dosh from her wallet from time to time to pay for his food as well as hers, then I'd probably turn a blind eye, frankly. But if you see him driving around speeding in a hot hatch and doing handbrake turns in the station car park, be sure to let me know. Or dealing dope to school kids or waving his dick at them in the park then likewise. Otherwise I'm glad he's here and hope he gets a decent job to make use of his youthful brawn and brain.

You're not interested then? she says, standing up and reaching for her coat.

Oh, I'm interested in everything and everyone, Mrs Nevison. The eyes and ears and nose of the law, and all that. I just want everyone to lead a nice quiet life and not leave their blood and vomit all over our lovely cobbled streets. A good day is when I'm not interested in you, if you get my drift.

Chrissy halts at the door: *I'm not sure that I do, actually.*

Explaining euphemisms also constitutes it. Wasting my time. Good day, as I said.

16

Magdalena and Annie pull up outside the house to find the red van of a broadband provider parked there and Thomas inside on his knees in the hallway unpacking a computer and monitor. He looks up at them, laughing: *Any of you two got the slightest idea how to work this magic box?*

Now, now, don't play dumb, Thomas, we know you're Einstein and you've mastered the one at the local library already. Magda answers.

Just pretend it's a space ship and take it for a spin around Saturn... Annie quips, then worries her tone was too cheeky. *My wee boy is a wizard with computers. They all are these days. You'll manage fine.*

That's good... I think. Thomas mumbles, switching on the power and pulling up a seat.

Oh Thomas, Magda calls out to him from his mother's room, *we have some news for you. There's a wealthy lady on Anderson Avenue we visit, says she's looking for someone to get her garden into shape. We told her you might be up for it, that you're fit and keen, lean and mean, as they say.*

Why, Magda, that's incredibly thoughtful of you. Thomas exclaims. *I wanted to finish getting this place in shape first though.*

It would only be one day a week at first. You could still get lots done here. It was our Annie's idea. Trying to help you find your feet. So you can earn enough lolly to take her out to the pictures.

Annie whacks Magda's head with a pillow case as they change the sheets.

What? Thomas calls back, confused, eyes on the screen. *What's lolly?*

On the way out the door, Annie comes to look over his shoulder and points to a few icons and websites, explaining their meaning, the Urban Dictionary particularly, her blonde hair falling over his shoulder, the pleasant aroma of her breath and skin wafting across his face. *Oestrogen...* he says aloud.

What? She turns to look at him, perplexed.

They didn't have any perfume like yours in space.

I'm not wearing any perfume... she laughs.

17

Arriving later that week, Magdalena happens to see, at a distance, Thomas taking his shoe off in the garden, emptying out some dirt he's inadvertently raked onto himself from a flowerbed. She freezes for a second at what she notices. The light is bright on his skin, enough to challenge her eyes from the shadow of the house, but the lurch in her stomach, the sweat instantly breaking out on her brow, tells her she was not imagining anything. On the way back in the car, she feels compelled to share her strange misgivings:

Annie. I have something to tell you. I saw something by accident back there this morning. Thomas, his naked feet. He has no toes.

What? Oh be serious, Magda. He wouldn't be able to walk without them. Unless it's a war injury I suppose, prosthetic toes... but it doesn't sound right does it? Where did you see what? Are you sure you didn't misconstrue something?

No, no, I don't mean missing as in chopped off, I mean his foot was like... all one... all toes, like, like.... like a flipper. It was in the garden this morning, he took his shoe off, garden clog or whatever it was, for a moment, and I saw his foot was all one thing, a fused fleshy flipper, like a hoof or something.

Annie laughs long and hard as she drives. *Oh Magda, don't be ridiculous. You mean like a mermaid, a mer man?*

Yes, a little bit I suppose. In Poland we have legends about such things, stories we are told as children.

So does everyone, everywhere, I think. Is it not meant to be based on people in the past seeing seals at a distance? How human the cries of their pups sound on the beach? My mother is from the Isle of Lewis, the Gaelic legends there often feature Selkies, Kelpies and Waterhorses. Selkies were meant to be half human, half seal, that could be lured into relationships with humans by hiding their fishy skin or something. Kelpies were darker though, horse-like water monsters who could assume human form apart from some telltale sign like black hooves.

Or flippers? In Poland we have the Sea Bishop and we have the wicked Wodnica, who asked a foolish young man for a necklace made of stars. And we have the sleeping knights-in-armour under the Tatra Mountains, who an angel will tell when the time has come to awaken. We have angels all the time in legends, who come down and help or set tests. But we also have demons who deceive.

Nice. And come to think of it, Annie continues, *that thing about sleeping knights is really dreamy. Gaelic legends are riddled with stuff about people being abducted by faeries and coming back fifty years to later to find that everyone they knew are old or dead. And what is that American story about a guy who falls asleep in the mountains? Rip something?*

Rip Van Winkle.

That's it. It makes you think, doesn't it?

Think what?

I don't know. Like maybe our Thomas is a phenomenon. A recurrence. You know, like Halley's Comet. Something that comes around again and again, whose meaning no one ever quite manages to grasp.

I think you'd like to grasp him.

Magda! I'm shocked at you!

Well, if you ever come close, see and get a look at his feet and tell me that I was wrong, if you can.

Is this some kind of a dare? Like, how would I go about getting a glimpse of Thomas Tellman's feet?

I'm sure you'll think of something, Annie, a resourceful woman like you. I reckon he has an eye for your resources.

Oh stop it, you wicked wod... what did you call it, the Polish mermaid demon?

Wodnica.

You wicked wodnica, you!

18

Chrissy walks into the local newspaper office. Janet McComish, Editor of the Kinburgh Herald greets her, and Chrissy immediately finds herself wrong-footed by her power-dressing, her quirky personal fashion choices involving a crimson neck scarf pattern co-ordinated with the wallpaper on the reception focus wall. She clutches a pet pug in her arms which she hands to her secretary to go give a bowl of water. Janet hears Chrissy out on an electric green sofa, but not for the reasons she expects. *He says what? That he's the same Thomas Tellman who was abducted by aliens eighty years ago?*

Yes, but no, I mean. That's just the point. He's not Thomas Tellman at all, he's a fraud.

Oh... Janet suddenly looks downcast. *How can you be so sure though?*

Sure? How could he be? That's crazy talk for cranks and nutters.

Well... Janet laughs, *I have to say it would sell a lot more newspapers if it were true.*

Your readers aren't UFO nuts, they're ordinary folk like me. They're interested in crime, threats to the community.

Yeah, well... Janet yawns, *I'm not sure I am after ten years of stolen tractors and foot-and-mouth outbreaks. An alien abduction might be quite exciting, rather welcome really.*

Well, I'm sorry to disappoint you then. He's not the pilot who went missing in 1948, he's some creepy conman with an American accent...

Janet's ears prick up. *American accent you say? Maybe we could interview him... have you got a number we could call? Where did you say the house was...?*

Oh forget it. Chrissy stands up. *I thought you were a serious newspaper. I can see I better just go to the Press And Journal.*

Chrissy re-emerges raging onto the street, her face creased like a used bed sheet.

Back in her office, Janet's pug, Griselda, jumps up onto her lap where she can admire the dog's bulging eyes and compacted breathing passageways in absent-minded wonder.

19

Thomas digs all day in the garden of the elderly art collector Annie told him about. He sits down at one o'clock after pouring water over his head, then takes out some lunch from his haversack. He hears a car pull up behind the high hedge and a moment later Annie's head appears around the side of it: *Oh hi there! I thought you might want a lift back to Mary's house.*

Being half way through a swig of fruit juice, Thomas takes a while to swallow then answers: *Thanks, that's very thoughtful. I was just planning to walk back. I'm bushwhacked now, was just sitting down to some lunch. D'you want some? Here, I'll share this with you, why not? It's a chilli tortilla, two wraps as it happens – one for you, entirely unplanned.*

Well then, I can hardly refuse can I? She laughs sitting down at his side. *Made by your own fair hand.*

By a fair hand for a fair maid. She looks at him strangely for a moment and blushes slightly. He smiles. *You allowed to do this? You not on duty or whatever you would call it?*

Taking my lunch break early, hardly a hanging offence, I'll log it as such, I've got time. You enjoying working here? I can see you've made a difference already.

Yes, and thank you again for being so kind to recommend me. I could do with the cash. I've a lot more chopping to do yet though, as is now apparent. I feel a bit bad being away from Mary so long though.

It's just a few mornings a week, and she has us carers, coming and going – she's in safe hands. You can't stay there all the time. Like I said before, you're still a young man. That new funky wardrobe I helped you order arrived yet? You need to get out and meet people.

To fit in, eh? But that's exactly what I won't do unless I keep my trap shut.

About what?

Oh, you know. All the UFO fandango.

Annie laughs and lies back on her elbows, letting the sun fall on her face. *I kind of know the feeling.*

You do?

Sure, as you would say. Like not mentioning my little boy. Single mother. All the societal judgement kicks in. Eligible woman with ineligible complications.

How old did you say he was?

Eight.

And his name?

Bruce.

A good Scottish name. I can see you love him a lot, right?

Mmmm... Annie nods her head.

You're divorced, right? How long ago?

Formally, paperwork and stuff, three years ago. It finished long before that, we only lived together for about four years, all in. Frank, Bruce's dad, was a nightmare.

All these names... Thomas sighs, almost to himself.

Sorry?

All these people, all these names, all these mistakes, so many human beings on the planet. Except it's never a mistake is it? Nothing is. You have young Bruce.

Yes. It's just messy, that's all. Never the way you planned. Never as good as you'd thought and hoped. Never easy.

How do you manage to do a job and look after him at the same time?

Well, school helps, and my shifts can be rotated around, but you're right, I still need a lot of help from my dad, bless him.

He lives with you?

Not quite, no. He lives a couple of blocks away though, and drops by when he's required. He's an excellent granddad to Bruce. A bit of symmetry there, eh? Me with my Dad and you with... she pauses awkwardly.

With my daughter, yes. Except that I'm younger than you. You getting used to any of this yet?

It's you who has a lot to get used to, partner. A world gone astray for eighty years without you. Is it a worse or better place do you think than the one you left?

Thomas sighs and closes his eyes and thinks hard. *I left in 1948. A time of recovery and hope after a world war, there was a feeling of us entering upon a bright new future, that mankind had sorted itself out and everything would be better now. Although the Cold War was already starting, to be fair. But what do I come back to? Oh it's a future alright, but I'm not sure it's a brighter one. It's darker if anything, more cynical and complex. More fragmented. As if nobody is at the steering wheel anymore. I mean where's the U.N. got to? It feels like a dangerous, brooding world to me, one always on the edge of fractious rage about something, but I'm not sure what. That internet you showed me, seems at the heart of it somehow. Like every mind on the planet has been wired up together, except that there's no filters on it, people live on it, sleep on it, share their nightmares and unconscious fears on it. As if there's no self-control or self-discipline anymore. Only vanity and some petulant, childish sense of universal entitlement, as if being born is enough, like some kind of lottery win and you don't have to get off your backside and do a thing about yourself from that moment forward, just let it all come to you. As if when they wired everyone up they thought they'd get one big giant super brain, but what they got instead was one giant sewer, with everyone's faces strapped in to it, face-first, and now everyone's caught cholera.*

Wow, Thomas. You should be on telly, have your own show.

No, Annie. We've gotta resist that, for as long as possible.

Why?

Oh, never mind. You'll see. Fate and destiny and all that. These are the good times... he says, reaching out to brush her hand lightly. *We gotta make the most of them.*

We?

You wanna go to the pictures or something sometime?

Annie laughs out loud. *Oh you're so funny, Thomas, what a hoot. The cinema here closed about forty years ago. The nearest one's in Inverness or Aberdeen.*

Gee. That's a bummer. But they still make films don't they? I've seen trailers.

On the internet, yes. People watch them on that, on TVs and computers in their houses.

Really? How dull and claustrophobic. I'd rather go for a walk in the rain or a forest or along a beach than that.

Well, there's a place for everything I suppose. You rested now? Ready to head home?

*

On the way back in the car, Thomas asks: *What went wrong between you and Frank? If you don't mind me asking?*

Maybe I should mind, but for you I'll make an exception, you being a space man and all.

Lobe die Welt dem Engel…

Sorry?

Praise the world to the angel. Show him how happy a thing can be, how innocent and ours. Rilke. German. I'm sorry I bombed them now that I've learned the thoughts of their great minds. Go on.

You're so strange, Thomas, you should be televised. Nothing went wrong with us, just with him, Frank. He became a heroin addict and overdosed eventually. A long story.

I'm sorry to hear that. That's so sad. Why, why throw your life away like that? Turn your back on a beautiful wife and child?

His father rejected him at a very young age. He thought he'd got over it, but it was like a time bomb ticking in his head. Lack of self-esteem, paranoia. Some damage lasts a lifetime, if it happens when you're young.

Now that makes me think, I'm afraid. About Sonny, my son, Mary's brother. Lou, my granddaughter, and Mary when her memory is up to it, tells me he died single and lonely and they didn't know why, and that maybe he was never happy. All that troubles me a great deal to be honest.

Go on... Annie says quietly, as she turns into the single-track drive to the house.

The thought that my disappearance might have damaged him emotionally, psychologically.

You didn't disappear on purpose though, did you?

No, but maybe I let curiosity get the better of me, flew too near to that damned thing.

What was it anyway, the UFO?

My home for a year, as it turned out. A lift, a bit like this, but with much stranger drivers.

As they get out the car, she stops him and says quietly: *It wasn't your fault, you know, Thomas, about your son.*

How can you know that though?

Maybe I've spent more time with Mary, post-disappearance-Mary, than you have yet. Thought of that? What happened was fate. And yes, give me a call sometimes, and let's go for a walk in the rain or something, I'll write you out my number.

20

The Reverend Desmond Baliol comes to visit Mary at home. Thomas is working in the garden when the car pulls up. Not usually so bold with his faith when meeting strangers, the minister is surprised to hear himself calling out to Thomas in humorous greeting: *the Lord God had planted a garden in the east, in Eden; and there he put the man he had formed.*

To which Thomas smiles and answers, leaning on his spade: *Genesis.* Then says in sudden inspiration, his voice slow and strong and clear as the minister stops dead in his tracks, listening: *And he showed me a river of water of life, bright as crystal, proceeding out of the throne of God and of the Lamb, in the midst of the street thereof. And on this side of the river and on that was the tree of life, bearing twelve manner of fruits, yielding its fruit every month: and the leaves of the tree were for the healing of the nations. And there shall be no curse any more.*

The minister comes over to see Thomas at close quarters, eyes wide. *Revelation! Bravo!* he continues, laughing in joy. *My word, you said that beautifully, and word perfect I believe! How uplifting! My goodness, it's not often these days I meet a layman so fluent in scripture.*

My ma and pa made me learn it by heart back in Kentucky, Reverend, when I was a small lad. Repeating it recalls them to my mind. I often recited it when I was… in my captivity shall we say.

For there our captors asked us for songs, our tormentors demanded songs of joy; they said, 'Sing us one of the songs of Zion!' How can we sing the songs of the Lord while in a foreign land?

Thomas chuckles. *I so knew you were going to say that!*

Well, it's a good script we're running through, isn't it? Captivity you say. Were you in prison, my dear chap?

No, not really. I was with the angels, you might say. Mary will explain to you, no doubt.

Oh yes? Has her memory improved of late? Are you one of her nephews perhaps?

You know, Reverend, come to think of it, I think she might have improved a bit. We all benefit from company. Yes, I'm family. Her father, once removed, one might say. It's a little complicated.

21

Major Leslie J Kelsington, base commander at RAF Kinburgh, presses the buzzer on his desk and a moment later the senior of the two sentry guards who questioned Thomas Tellman, is ushered into the room. *Corporal Webster, isn't it? Take a seat please.*

Webster is nervous. He has only been summoned directly to this room on two previous occasions, and never alone, and is somehow further unnerved to see that the Major isn't alone. Kelsington explains, with a slight gesture of his right hand towards the man in a black suit seated two metres back from the Major's desk as if he is some kind of observer or regulator: *This gentleman is with the Intelligence Services and has come here from London today to assist us with something very unusual that has come up. You and sergeant Chisholm questioned a man who unexpectedly approached the south gates two weeks ago, and identified himself as one Thomas Tellman. Is that correct?*

Yes, sir.

Can I ask why you didn't detain this man, but instead let him go, even urged him to?

He wasn't under arrest, sir, and as far as we knew at that point had not actually broken any rules, any laws or byelaws. Anyone can approach the gates, although we discourage it without an appointment, as you know.

Yes I do.

Was he a forger then, sir? The I.D. he gave us, did it prove false?

I believe I'm asking the questions, Corporal.

I do apologise, sir. Webster lowers his head in shame, almost blushing, eyes to the floor. *I was just curious. It was a very odd incident.*

Well now, that is interesting. Webster allows himself to look up again, surprised. Kelsington continues: *Tell me about it. What struck you as most odd about it? We've watched the CCTV footage, but what was he like, this man, in person?*

He was so calm, sir. I don't know what he could have wanted or expected. In an old-fashioned uniform and with a weird American accent. Was it ...? We wondered if it might have been some kind of prank. But he was so serious, and unfazed by our reaction. It puzzled me. If we had been told, if evidence or orders had been reported back to us, that his documents were forged, then of course we would have apprehended and detained him, sir. But no word ever came back to me, until now that is.

Did this man who claimed to be named Tellman, look 26 years old to you, Corporal? The secret service officer suddenly addresses Webster, almost making him jump.

Yes, around about that I suppose, quite possibly.

And did you see him leave or arrive by any kind of vehicle, or simply walk?

He walked, only walked, definitely. Which struck us as weird, saying as how far we are from town or a bus route. I watched as he went away for as long as I could, and no one was waiting for him, he just walked away along that narrow pavement on the main road, with cars driving past him, as if he had no lift and wasn't looking for one either.

The Major and the secret service officer glance at each other in silence for a brief moment then the Major says: *That will be all, Webster, thank you. You can tell Chisholm to come in next if you pass him outside. Oh and corporal?*

Webster pauses, half turns, before he reaches the door.

You repeat nothing about this to anyone, if it is ever brought up, particularly by civilians, newspaper reporters, etcetera. Do you understand?

22

Thomas steps off the train in Aberdeen and walks up through the grey granite streets towards the university. His wardrobe looks more contemporary and suitably nondescript now after the postal delivery inspired by Annie's advice. He enjoys blending in, not being noticed. Reaching the campus he walks through the sequence of quadrangles, the pleasantly mowed lawns, with a sense of pleasure and respect, even a little awe for the hallowed atmosphere of knowledge and learning. He smiles at the Gothic architecture, the undertones of medieval religion, the idea that ideas themselves might be worthy of devotion, rather than all the broken idols of centuries of tribal primitivism. He spots some black cloaks and mortarboard hats lingering for photographs, late graduations after re-sits. He dislikes the whiff of ritual, uniform, dogma, but knows there is a fire of ethos driving it, something he can get at and kindle.

He finds an ornate doorway of weathered stone, old painted planks and decorative iron hinges in floral forms, and presses the buzzer, then is allowed inside. An academic in casual clothes out of term, corduroy trousers and open shirt, greets him halfway down musty stairs redolent of Victorian dust. *Professor Radim Hromádka? Dobré ráno. Jak se máte? Děkuji za souhlas se setkáním se mnou.*

You speak Czech?! The professor exclaims. *I left there forty years ago!*

Only a little. I picked it up during the war from some fellow pilots, the 312 squadron. Otto Smik. Miroslav Štandera. Brave, brave men.

The war? What war?

39 to 45.

But you're not a pensioner. What are you talking about? Time travel? The man laughs light-heartedly, turning as they both ascend the stair again to his office.

Well... Thomas muses, entering the room and being

offered a heavy hardwood seat to pull up opposite the professor's desk. *The internet tells me you were born on 16th May, 1972. About 34 weeks before that, your heart would have begun beating inside your mother's womb. From that moment forward you have been a time traveller, have you not? As are we all. You got the equations I sent you?*

Yes... Hromádka answers, wide-eyed. *And they were strange enough.*

Only strange? Then why am I here?

All right then. More than strange. Extraordinary. I've never seen anything like them. Where are you an alumnus of? Harvard? Stanford? M.I.T? Where did you get your degrees in Physics and Mathematics?

None of them. I don't have any degrees. I was educated somewhere else. Do the equations make sense to you?

This is all somewhat bizarre, I have to say, with respect. But yes, they made some sense, enticingly so. If they're original and you are their author, then you have a command of your subject at a high level, coupled with original ideas. They cry out for some empirical research to back up their implications however. But why have you contacted me in particular? Do you wish to join the Post-Graduate course, teach even? Or maybe you're from industry, some multi-national concern looking to sponsor placements, a new avenue of applied research? You really need to tell me more about yourself.

Thomas laughs heartily. *Well stone me, Professor, I seem to have hit some kind of jackpot, inadvertently.*

I wanted to meet you in person, out of curiosity, I must confess. But who exactly are you and what do you want?

My name is Tellman. I was trained in aviation. But think of me as a messenger, who has had the subject of those equations explained and demonstrated to him in depth.

Demonstrated? But by whom?

By a hidden group of scientists whose knowledge far exceeds that of anyone else around. They are impartial. They work for no government or business or special interest group. They work only for themselves and for the betterment of mankind.

Philanthropists, then?

You could call them that. Who I am doesn't matter all that much. Knowledge is knowledge. You've already anticipated the next part yourself, as it happens. I'm looking for someone to carry out experiments, to develop practical proofs of what the equations imply, namely that gravity can be manipulated by controlled processes at the sub-atomic level with relatively simple materials and equipment.

But do you realise, I take it you do, that scientists have been working on this for decades? Anti-gravity. It was only a fringe interest back in the 1980's. Laithwaite's infamous gyroscope experiment at the Royal Institution in 1973... condemned as some sort of sensationalist heresy at the time. But since then numerous avenues have been explored, becoming gradually more mainstream. It's widely accepted now that a range of anti-gravity devices have generated angular momentum without violating Newton's laws of motion, but invariably not enough momentum, not enough energy to levitate anything substantial and be of much use in the wider world for transport and so on. But, well, I see by your nods that you do know all this already of course. Sandy Kidd of Dundee University in 1986, Ronald Evans of BAE's conference in 1990. But what about the Abraham Force and the Biefield Brown effect? The Boyd Bushman effect? You seem to be side-stepping and superseding all of that with the elegance of your equations, if their meaning can be replicated in the real world. But what would you say is the essence of what's new in your approach?

Regulation and pattern. The prototype generating its own electromagnetic field needs to have a sensor built-in that can match the pattern of its field to that which the Earth's magnetic field generates around it. It's like tuning a radio. It can all happen in a second, a millisecond, but the device needs to modulate itself by trial and error essentially, in a flash, to find the moment of correlation between inner and outer fields and then tune to it, home in on it and develop its resonance. When the fields cancel each other out, terrestrial gravity ceases to apply, and after that even the slightest angular momentum generated internally becomes a very substantial force. The cancelled field zone also eliminates all friction and other physical side-effects of thrust, sonic-booms and so forth, although in fact the propulsion system needn't make any noise in the first place.

But if that's true, if that's possible... it would transform the world, traditional transport systems would become obsolete almost overnight.

Which is why it is so urgent.

Urgent?

Fossil fuel consumption for mass transport has brought the global eco-system to the brink of collapse, right now.

Who else have you, are you, or are you planning to show this to?

Everyone. The patents will be open-source. But you're the first, a head start of a few months. Enough for your name to go down in history, if you begin soon enough. Your greatest challenge will be getting hold of metamaterials. They exist already, but at great expense. You won't need them in the early stages for demonstrations, but for large scale transport vehicles you'll need metamaterials, nanocomposites employing zirconium, yttrium, praseodymium, rare earth metals, each atom programmed one might say, to re-heal its bonds to its neighbours in the event of collision or explosion. The good news is once a hull like that is built it will be truly indestructible. Once your prototypes are working, you'll probably have a queue of companies competing to offer you the metal, hence costs should come down.

But you seem so confident all this works, as if you've seen a prototype or demonstration yourself, in which case why not share that, and then why would you need me?

You need proof I see. Here, watch. Thomas takes a silver sphere from his pocket and rolls it sideways across the desk until it rolls smoothly off the end, where instead of falling to the floor it keeps on rolling for two feet before coming to a standstill, hovering in space.

Hromádka gets up then drops to his knees, his mouth agape, and takes his glasses off, reaching his hands all around the sphere in wonder. *Who made this?*

The philanthropists, as you call them.

Probably an inner and outer shell with a charged field in vacuum in between? What's holding it up?

Nothing. The question's wrong. It's just that Earth's gravity isn't acting on it. As if it's floating in outer space. I could also make it move, if you like, or indeed you could. Go on, just give it a tap.

Hromádka taps the sphere and it glides through the air back towards Thomas's side of the desk, where he smiles broadly, stands up, puts the object back in his pocket, and walks towards the door. *I see that I've achieved my objective. You'll help me with this then? We'll work together? I'll guide you with occasional emails.*

Potřebuji pivo! I think I need a drink. A fucking beer. Hromádka collapses back into his chair with his white hair fluffed up in comic disarray and an expression like a man who's just seen his own ghost. *Yes of course, of course. I'd see you out, but you can probably walk through walls if you need to. I'll do everything you say. Let's stay in touch.*

23

Over the phone, the priest and the minister agree to get together to talk about the stranger in the community and the peculiar allegation that he might be a demon with cloven feet. Now the Reverend Desmond Baliol smiles broadly, feeling magnanimous, uplifted by his own hospitality, as he stands at the open door of his vestry watching Father Seamus O'Hara walking up the cobbled driveway towards him with the sun at his back throwing yellow rays like a sign of God blessing their inter-faith rapprochement. He welcomes him in and sits him down with a cup of tea in a room of rich oak-panelling and many books on shelves, some of which they excitedly discover a shared enthusiasm for. *Thomas Aquinas! Marcus Aurelius! My word! Oh, and tut tut, The Secret Commonwealth, Robert Kirk!*

Well now though, there's a thought, old chap, the faeries... Baliol runs his hand through his thick grey hair, *that's what Kirk was on about in that one, veritable lunatic though we must presume he was. But that stuff goes back deep into Gaelic culture and many others around the world, as you doubtless know.*

Oh yes, Reverend, in Ireland even more so, to be sure, Tír na nÓg, the land of the young, the voyages and adventures, the echtrai and the baili, the feast of Goibniu, the metalsmith of the Tuatha Dé Danann, which granted immortality. Allegedly!

You're with me then? Like Rip Van Winkle, the legend always goes the same, the young man who falls asleep or goes astray in some way or other and is rescued by supernatural creatures who take him to a fabulous land, only to return him a century later when all his kin are old and dead.

Quite so, quite so. Not to mention the changelings. Whether what comes back is human at all, or an elf or a troll in disguise and so forth. But you said you've met him in person, while I have not as yet. Would you say he

82

is a good man, a man of God even?

A man of God?! How few of those you and I must truly meet these days, I might venture, especially among the young. But there was the surprise. He knew the scriptures well. We even exchanged quotes from them such as you and I might do among ecclesiastical colleagues.

Remarkable. And what age you say, 26?

The two men sigh wistfully for a moment, wishing for a world with more such company, poised upon the brink of silence in those learned surroundings, before the priest continues: *There's a problem though, nonetheless. One of my flock has confided in me, claims that she saw with her own eyes that the fellow has webbed feet or some such.*

A deformity perhaps. What of it? We're not medieval superstitionists surely? Does she think we'll burn him as a witch?

Not at all. She is a bright soul. All this in confidence between us, you understand of course. Not given to hysteria, but adamant of what she saw, although...

Go on, Father.

Curiously, at the same time she attributes no evil or superstition to the man. Just this doubt, this fear she has that he is something otherworldly, demonic even, who may be fooling everyone around him with a velvet tongue.

But to what aim? We must judge each man by his acts and words, must we not? And as I understand it, he has proved exemplary thus far on both these counts. What else is there?

His thoughts? His soul?

We may guess at both of course, but only our divine father knows truly of those.

Quite so... The priest muses, his fingers caressing his lips. *We must wait then. I believe the archaeologists call it a watching brief.*

Do they indeed now? Watching and not witching? Well it strikes me that already this strange man has done some good for us both by inadvertently bringing us here together in this confabulation. Will you join me in a little glass of brandy to toast that hope of closer intercourse between our churches? Let us watch him together. For if God has sent him, it is only as he sent us once also, to be tested on this earth. We test each other, as Christ tests us which is to say he does so through love and the help afforded by his teachings.

You are most generous, Reverend. There is always a purpose in things, and often a hidden one that we only see months or years later. Maybe fear is the test. I need scarcely cite Hebrews 13:2, so obvious is its relevance here, regarding strangers.

Ah yes of course, how apt. The Reverend smiles, unstoppering his decanter, its crystal facets throwing light around the room and across the spines of his books in fabulous diadems like a merry-go-round. *That we must not be inhospitable to them, lest they be angels in disguise.*

24

Thomas and Annie's first date together, begins at Mary's house, from where he suggests they simply take a walk, in the rain if need be. He is taken aback to see her in different clothes, no longer the shapeless blue trouser suit, her hair let down, colourful T-shirt, quirky second-hand leather jacket and boots. *Wouldn't it be humorous if that was a flight jacket?* he teases her lightheartedly, *I've got the real thing back in there.* In the flat ground around the house, Annie notices rectangular outlines. Thomas notices her looking at them and answers the question in her head before she voices it: *Those are foundations. There were five other houses there once, just like Mary's, same size and shape. They were still there the day I left. For the other airmen like me, Americans who chose to re-settle here during the war. Louise, my granddaughter, tells me that after I left they wanted to demolish our house too, re-house them elsewhere, but Mary wouldn't stand for it. Just in case I came back, so she'd be in the same place. Kind of moving, huh?*

Annie's eyes fill with tears at that, and she reaches out to stroke his shoulder as they stroll through the strange hinterland of self-sown woodland where saplings have grown through the hard-standing that was once the pre-fabricated homes.

Kind of cold too. Thomas muses. *Those houses were only every meant to be temporary, but ours has lasted for about four times its intended lifespan already. Ramshackle flotsam. Held together with love and hope. They probably stuck us out here because we were Yanks, how we sounded and how we looked. In case we contaminated the town. I remember the other families. The Joneses, the Montereys and the Jeffersons, and I wonder where they and their descendants are now. If only Mary could remember more.*

Why did you leave Kentucky, Thomas? Do you think of going back now at all? Annie asks as they walk towards the woods.

Well they murdered a preacher called Martin Luther King while I was away, didn't they? And meanwhile, I see everyone grew up here in the sixties and seventies and eighties watching American television pumping out that white patriotic crap about the land of the free. The land they stole from the people they called Indians so that no one would call them Americans, that being what they truly were, more so than us. I'm glad to learn there's been civil rights movements, but I know it won't have changed much, the real America, the one they never show even now. The poverty, the racism, whole districts of cities no-go areas that whites just drive-through in a state of terror between their nice suburbs, in case their gas runs out. Ghettos where everyone is black, disabled, driven to drink and drugs and violence through lack of hope, dealt to the bottom of the pack and with no means to drag themselves up and out. When I came here as an airman, I was afforded respect. A man was a man, no matter where he came from, or so it seemed for a moment, against the background of Hitler and his fascism. The shared enemy did us all a favour for a while: showed us what we needed to be the opposite of, the values we need to cherish. America's still too far away to learn those lessons deep enough.

Annie looks at him wide-eyed. *You sound quite angry, Thomas.*

Well, the America I left was a fascist country really, of the very sort I found myself dropping bombs on here. The Ku Klux Klan never went away. My mother saw them driving by in trucks with lit torches. She knew decent folks who had unspeakable things done to them on account only of the colour of their skin. It's so goddam banal. The colour of a person's skin. The legacy of slavery has never been addressed in the States, because it would mean tackling inequality, and inequality is the engine of the so-called American dream. The poor being colour-coded is just too valuable a gift to a system like that, for it to ever give it up, except by force. And who wants another civil war? I stayed on here in Britain after the war because I never felt so alive and useful, so safe and free and valued in Kentucky, as I did here. Europe doesn't shout about it so much as the States. But you've got something here, in terms of peace and democracy, something worth fighting for. Not that I want to fight anyone or anything anymore, except with words. I'm sorry. That was a rant. I go on too long.

Not at all... Annie consoles him. *I love to hear you talk when you're inspired like that. You have such a melodious voice.*

Melodious? He stops and laughs. *Hell, that's a pretty word for a man's accent. It's just that I sound different, is all, maybe. It's an unfortunate facet of human consciousness, how quickly we get bored with everything familiar and commonplace, and run it down in favour of the exotic.*

Exotic? Annie clasps her hands together. *Ooh... that's an even better term. An exotic accent. Do you know where we're going?*

Sure, Thomas answers, *this path leads through the woods, more or less straight to the beach, from where we can even stroll as far as the town if we wish.*

If we wish? She playfully mocks his sometimes archaic use of English. *Do we wish?*

Oh, we do, we do. I think.

In the densest part of the wood, they stop and stare up towards a halo of light between treetops, leaves swaying around it, and listen to the swishing silence where the breathing of the sea and the trees merges and becomes indistinguishable from each other. Annie looks down at the dark green mossy carpet that covers everything underfoot and the texture of the tree bark, deeply pitted like hills and valleys seen from high above. *Look!* Thomas gasps, as an osprey flies right across the window of sky framed by the trees. *Who needs a trip to the cinema when we have all this?*

When they emerge onto the beach they are thrilled by the size of waves starting to break there. *Can you believe I once saw waves like these made of liquid mercury, breaking on a beach of sulphur, under twin red suns?*

No, are you crazy? How could anyone get their head around that? Did you take any holiday snaps? Can you make sandcastles in sulphur? Wouldn't that have been a bit smelly, like eggs or something?

I had breathing apparatus on of course, the atmosphere was saturated with chlorine, among other things. The sky was green, gradated from lime to emerald, all day long.

Doesn't sound as nice as Earth. Annie smiles, picking some sand up in her hand and crumbling it between her fingers.

That's because the Earth designed you to enjoy the Earth.

Can a planet design people? Even though it can't talk? she asks, looking out to sea, towards the tiny silhouette of a distant container ship slowly crossing the horizon.

But it can talk. It's talking right now, through you. That's what you're for.

You're so strange, Thomas. Where is God in all this?

He's never left us. He or she. That's just a word for everything around you, the thing that is creating life here.

What is it though? Annie asks, picking up a length of seaweed now, turning it over in her hands.

Life is life, a kind of virus, a positive contamination, slowly spreading its roots and tendrils across the universe.

To what purpose though?

Oh, don't we know that already? The same reason you're here, the reason you got out your bed this morning, the reason you and I are interested in each other. Call it curiosity, joy. The quest for knowledge. The universe wanting to know itself, to become awake and aware. When I say design, of course I'm talking about evolution, and that only works through birth and death.

And sex?

Yes of course. This discussion, this getting to know itself, is how life improves and refines itself, getting better all the time in each generation, reaching for the stars. It's all accumulating, the feelings, these words, all the words of everyone everywhere like grains of sand. Nothing is lost.

Well I just hope it's all getting better all the time. I wish Britain was as good as you seemed to imply in that rant of yours. But the British Empire's legacy is just as poisonous as America's... Suddenly an RAF jet speeds overhead, leaving a sonic boom in its wake, making Thomas flinch considerably more than Annie.

I wouldn't mind a shot in one of those. You're used to that? he exclaims.

Annie nods. *And it made my point right on cue. Warmongering nonsense that and the nuclear subs, at enormous expense while families live in poverty. I was about to say this beach is so quiet, I never knew it was here. I should bring my wee boy here sometime, is there anywhere to park?*

Thomas smiles and shakes his head. *It wouldn't be so quiet if cars could get here, would it? We should come again together. I'm good with kids, just ask Mary.*

Ha! You sure you want that? He's a bit of a handful, my wee Brucie.

Once they're past the nappies and projectile poo stage, they're a cinch.

Cinch! There's a word I've not heard in a while, I don't even know how to spell that. Annie laughs delightedly.

It's derived from something to do with leading horses on a rein I believe.

Pretty appropriate then.

Kids all want to be adults, and don't want to stand out too much, to be like others. The trick is to slow them down from becoming adults as much as you can, and to encourage them to be unlike others, the way I remember it. I doubt that's changed, or ever will. They want to be like us, while we would do very well to be a good deal more like them. Regard every day as play, and everything as adventure and an opportunity to learn. We all get so blunted. They're here to teach us, not the other way about all the time.

Dark spots of rain begin to appear in the sand at their

feet and Annie says: *I reckon there's a storm coming soon.*

Thomas claps his hands together. *Let's walk to Kinburgh then, it's only twenty minutes along the beach.*

We could have driven there. Annie looks uncertain.

But we didn't. Relax. We'll get the bus back, I know the timetables, then you can get your car back at the house.

She takes his hand and they set off at a pace.

*

It is just starting to rain heavily by the time they run up from the sand onto the cobbled streets of Kinburgh's old town, holding Thomas's jacket over both their heads by way of makeshift umbrella. To her amazement, he appears to very quietly break the lock on a boarded-up old grain store, and they rush inside for shelter. They climb up stairs to the top storey where they can look out through a dust-caked window, its view uphill towards the rest of the town. Occasional raindrops fall intermittently from the sagging roof above them. *It was sunny earlier on, still relatively warm up here, we're lucky.* Thomas says as he puts his arms around her and they both feel something ancient in the posture, looking out from where nobody knows to look for them.

It's a beautiful old town, isn't it? Annie sighs. *All that medieval history. Not as famous as it once was, like a faded rock star or something.*

Rock star? Thomas looks askance at her. *For a moment I thought you were talking astronomy and geology. Apart from Elvis maybe, that whole era of musicians being hailed as gods was pretty much after my time I'm afraid, or before it now, however it is one might phrase it, but you know what I mean.*

Jesus! Her eyes widen. *So you've never heard Neil Young, Bob Dylan, Abba, U2?*

I've seen the names amid all the reading I've done recently, but not had time to listen to all the music that's been and gone. How could I unless I was superhuman? Are they good?

Annie resolves not to be shy or blush, and sings quietly of Dylan as Jesse James knocking on Heaven's door as a long black cloud comes down, laying his guns on the ground, who hasn't the heart to shoot them anymore. Of Neil Young crossing the ocean in search of a heart of gold that eludes him in everyone and everywhere he goes, as he feels his youth escaping him.

They're both so sad... Thomas says, smiling and applauding. *Do you know any Billie Holiday? Let me sing some for you:*

> *Those pretty clothes madam wears*
> *Cool cotton comes from where?*
> *Who slaves long hours in burning sun*
> *So that at madam suitors stare?*
>
> *In parties in white villas of the gilded south*
> *Where madam spins and pouts her mouth*
> *Lauded by young men who bow and sway*
> *Fathers give their daughters away*
>
> *Two by two as Noah's ark*
> *The master chooses, listens, hark*
> *On whom life's freedom to bestow*
> *To whom to offer hope or woe.*
>
> *Yet from the prison of the fields*
> *No black son or daughter leaves*
> *How cruel, cool cotton that weaves*
> *So many pains and never yields.*

As he sings, a middle-aged couple passing in the street below pause under their umbrella for a moment and squint up to try and work out where the music is coming from.

Boy oh boy, that's dark, isn't it? Sinister, even. Annie finally remarks into the silent aftermath, wiping tears from her eyes. *I don't think I've heard that before. You sang it beautifully. I thought you were going to sing something cheery to counteract my sad stuff?*

Nope, 'fraid not. The occasion and strange surroundings seemed to call for melancholy. Sometimes you have to just go with it. A good cry is good for you, you know. My mother sang it better. There's another grave I'll have to go find I guess, and say a few words over. Why do people keep dying on this stupid planet?

Annie looks at him in silence as his words die on the air. Drawn by a tear in the corner of her eye he leans closer until they embrace and kiss at last. Annie's back pressed against the dusty glass, the pigeons taking flight from the window sill and roof, cast out for a moment from their habitual abode, the abandoned spaces of the town that men and time have overlooked.

When Thomas opens the dust-caked window, Annie is amazed to see a goldfinch land on his arm, then two sparrows. She jumps back in fright when he turns towards her, scared that they will be unleashed to beat their wings in distress around the ceiling, but they remain curiously docile, as if in some kind of spell, before he gently shakes his arm and sets them free again, showing her the handful of seeds the trick required. She pinches herself, feeling for a moment as if she is in some kind of sleepwalking trance.

When the rain goes off, they buy fish and chips wrapped in newspaper and sit down to eat together on a park bench in the war memorial park, whose brass plaques Thomas takes a keen interest in. *Several names I recognise here, boys I remember who never came back. I feel like I'm one of them sometimes...*

How do you mean? Annie asks, passing him her bottle of Irn Bru.

I mean like I'm a ghost or this is all some kind of dream and I'm not really here.

You're here alright, she says, running her fingers through his hair then putting her hand inside his shirt. *I can feel your heartbeat.*

Shucks, a romantic dinner for two, as the sun starts to go down. I should take you to a restaurant next time, once I've saved up some more smackers.

You sure know how to treat a girl, eh? This was just fine, pilot. There's not a hell of a lot of choice in Kinburgh. The Indian, the Chinese, or a couple of pubs selling scampi and chips.

Hey, chips are good. French fries we called them stateside. But we can cook for ourselves, indoors, where the town spies can't plot the course of our romance on their wall charts.

Annie looks around over her shoulders. *You think everyone's watching us and gossiping eh?*

Someone will be, sooner or later. Military intelligence.

A contradiction in terms.

What's that?

An old joke, like me, I must be nearly four years older than you, you know, a baby snatcher. What time's the next bus then?

Ten minutes, from outside the bakers.

How do you answer so fast without a phone or a watch? You memorised the timetables?

Yup. And there's a clock over your shoulder on that Gothic monument there. No magic. You ready to go?

On the bus back, Annie says: *I don't think I've caught a bus in about 15 years you know, it reminds me of being a school girl. Where were you when I was 16 then?*

Thomas strains his neck to look up at the cobalt evening sky beginning to appear behind golden clouds. *I was up there, on my way back from Alpha Centauri.*

What's that like then? she asks dreamily, resting her head on his shoulder for a moment.

A triple star system. Complicated. A celestial ménage à trois...

Like you, me, and Mary.

Like you, me, and Bruce.

No, really, seriously, what's it like?

Depends what planet you're on. Four of them are habitable. Very complicated orbits around three stars, three suns in the sky, can you imagine it? Years of constant daylight. Rare dark regions that creatures migrate to, seasons of storms to equalise the temperatures. Whole underground cities to escape the heat. Gas giants where animals swim under the orbit of moons they use as parasols, cooling depths beneath their shadows.

Bus timetables must be complicated.

Indeed.

The man on the seat in front of them gets up to get off at his stop and looks over his shoulder at them in semi-hostile amazement. Once he leaves the bus they laugh together until they cry.

Back at the house, Thomas invites her in, but Annie insists on getting back home before it's her son's bedtime. After their farewell hug and kiss before she gets into her car, they stare up together at the stars again. *Will you go back?* she asks him.

We're all going back, sooner or later... he answers, cryptically.

25

'Rookie' reporter Lesley Crawford turns up at Mary Tellman's house, nervous. She suspects her bosses have sent her on this one as a practical joke, to keep her out their hair for a few hours – that there's no real story here. Unluckily or luckily, she arrives at a rare moment when Mary is alone and out of bed, having made her way to the kitchen, after an afternoon nap in which she has, as usual, blanked her memory banks. She answers the door.

Lesley leans in enthusiastically: *Oh good afternoon. Mary Tellman?*

Aye, weel, pleased to meet yoo, Mary, whit can ah dae fur ye? the old lady answers.

No, no, sorry, my name's Lesley, I'm asking whether you're Mary Tellman or not?

Ah dinnae ken, ah mean ah'm nae sure, lass. Dae ye want to come in like while you wait fur her?

Wait for who?

Fur whoever ye said ye wur lookin' fur.

Oh I see. Maybe you're her cleaner or home help or something, or a relative?

Aye, that'll be richt ah suppose. Wid ye like a wee cup o' tea ma dear?

Oh thank you, Missus... I'm sorry, I didn't catch your name?

Lesley.

Mrs Lesley? Really? Well, what a coincidence, that being my first name too. Lesley says, brow furrowed, closing the door behind her and following Mary into her kitchen. *Yes, tea please that's very kind, if you're having one yourself. Just milk, no sugar. Thank you. Well, Mrs Lesley, maybe I can just ask you a few questions before Mrs Tellman gets back, how would that be?*

Aye, fine lass, on you go.

I was wondering if you'd heard anything about rumours going about that the pilot, the airman who disappeared 80 years ago chasing a UFO, Mrs Tellman's father, had come back?

Come back ye say? Come back frae where?

Well I don't know, from outer space I suppose, from inside a flying saucer.

Saucer? Did ye want a saucer, lass, for yoor cup o' tea? They young folks dinnae bother wi' that sae much these days.

No, no thank you. I'm just fine like this. No, I meant flying saucer as in aliens. You know, little green men? Lesley lifts up Mary's saucer and swishes it through the air to demonstrate.

*

When Magda and Annie turn up, they are surprised to find the newspaper reporter behind the door, in the midst of making her goodbyes to Mary Tellman. She introduces herself quickly and exclaims: *I'm just going. Mrs Tellman's housekeeper Mrs Lesley has just been kindly telling me about the little green men with glowing spades she's seen visiting Mary in her garden, who arrive by flying saucer, who her father chases away by juggling with his balls.*

Really? Magda furrows her brow. *That's quite long-winded for a newspaper headline, isn't it?*

Annie pokes her head over her shoulder, smiling broadly: *Might be better putting that in the Classifieds, doll.*

26

As Thomas finishes his morning's work again at the art collector's garden, and Annie turns up to give him a lift, the collector's daughter Sylvia greets her from the back door and invites them both in for a cup of tea. Stepping into the spacious depths of the dimly lit hallway, Thomas is immediately stunned to see art he recognises. *Holy smoke, is that a Marinetti? And that there...* he spins around, *is a Severini, and down there at the end of the hall... that's a Carlo Carrà isn't it? Italian Futurism.*

Wow! Sylvia and Annie look at him agape, but Sylvia more so. *You're the first tradesman to ever walk in here and say that.*

Are you Italian? The Futurists were such a seminal movement. Look at the aeroplanes in that one, the spotlights, the trains and cars, the excitement of machinery and the dawn of a new age, so they thought.

Bravo! Sylvia claps her hands in delight, then caresses the string of pearls around her neck as she continues proudly: *Most other people only ever ask what the weird pictures are. My bed-bound father upstairs, who Annie and the other carers have been so kind as to attend to, grew up in Genoa and became a successful art dealer in Milan. He married my mother who was a fashion designer from Edinburgh and they retired here, the sunniest part of Scotland, she lied, but at least it's by the sea. But how come you know about Italian art, are you an artist yourself?*

Thomas seems lost for words for a moment, wrong-footed by his own enthusiasm, still muttering about the colours and brush strokes as his eyes scan the surface of the canvases. *No, sadly. I was trained as a pilot. I was imprisoned abroad for a long while, but I had access to a library, where my parched mind absorbed a prodigious amount of information. I found the arts to be the most wonderful solace to the human soul in captivity.*

How eloquently put. Goodness, a war hero.

Afghanistan or Iraq presumably? You were lucky not to be badly wounded.

Gosh, look at the time on that big grandfather clock! We need to be going soon... Annie intervenes, tapping her wrist watch theatrically.

*

On the way back in the car, Annie breathes a sigh of relief. *That was an excellent bit of improvisation there, Thomas, well done. For a horrific moment I thought you were going to tell her you were abducted by aliens. How come they taught you about modern art? I wouldn't have thought stuff like that would have meant much to green bug-eyed monsters with dangly tentacles.*

Thomas laughs. *The irony is you're both right and wrong about that. They no longer have any of their own, since science and art has fused for them. But they take great interest in the art we created in our past, not in the aesthetic way we do, but in an anthropological sense because of how it embodies and expresses our history and culture, which fascinates them because it is so at odds with our savagery. The library I referred to was a five-foot-diameter floating sphere of circulating data streams that I could stick my head inside to absorb knowledge. I didn't lie, really. I just left a lot of stuff out.*

Well, it strikes me as an art form you're alarmingly adept at. Do you think you could adopt – adopt and adapt – some of that technique with my dad?

Why, are we going to meet him?

No, not today, not intentionally if I can help it. But this is a small town. We're bound to run into him one of these days. And when we do I'd like you to lie or improvise or leave stuff out or whatever you want to call it. Oh shit.

What?

I don't fucking believe it, this is truly supernatural. There he is coming out of the grocers and turning this way right now. What are the chances? He's never normally down here this early. He's bound to see us in a minute and wave. Oh fuckity fuck fuck fuck. I'll have to offer him a lift.

What do you want me to do? Thomas asks, knuckles whitening, gripping his seat.

Shit, I don't know. Charm him, pilot.

Oh hi there lass! Her white-haired father clambers down from the pavement to lean his head in the window.

Annie leans across Thomas to smile up at him. *This is Thomas, Dad, a friend of mine I'm giving a lift over to the east side of town, d'you need a lift too?*

Well, ah wouldnae say no, Annie, ah wis thinkin' o' goin' oot tae Davie's. Is there room in the back?

Of course there is, just shift some of the jackets and blankets side, this old chugaboom needs a bit of a clear out.

Thomas and Annie's father shake hands as Thomas helps him into the back seat, and they set off again down the main street. *Yon's some military crew cut ye've goat there Thomas, what d'ye dae fur a livin' like?*

I'm a pilot, sir.

Commercial airlines an' that, like?

Out of work at the moment, sir. Looking for a new job.

You Americans are sae polite. I'll bet you saw some unco things when you were a pilot.

How do you mean? Thomas turns around to look at her father, his brow furrowed quizzically.

Oh ye know. Weird things, unexplained lights. I saw a program oan the telly aboot it the other night. The car comes to a jolting halt as Annie nearly overshoots the traffic lights, her eyebrows raised high in incredulity, glancing at her father in the rear mirror. *They've held a few public enquiries over the years aboot near misses at airports and that. Damndest thing. Naebuddy seems tae be able to explain it, the speed o' they things, and whit the blazes they might be.*

Yeah, I saw a few things, Mister Bevans. Most pilots do after a few years service. There's definitely something out there. More than we know or understand. Annie drives off as the lights change, brakes almost screeching.

Oh here's Davie's street oan the left coming up, sweethert, ye kin jist droap me here and get oan yer way. It wiz dead nice meetin' ye, Thomas. Ah'll mibbe see yoo tomorrow nicht, Annie, if the wean's needin' mindin' like. Awrabest!

Jesus... driving off, Annie laughs until she cries and Thomas chuckles deeply, finding the wheezing sounds she makes infectious. *God's having a laugh isn't he? Now, of all times, my dad comes out as a frigging UFO nut. Who knew? I've only known him all my life. You were a class act there, pilot. Cool as a cucumber. You could leave-stuff-out for Scotland.*

27

Annie brings her son Bruce along in the car, and she takes him in to meet Thomas and cheer up Mary. *Oh lass, whit a lovely wee bairn! He looks jist like ye. Ur yoo ganging tae the beach thi day, wee fella? Huve ye goat yer bucket and spade wi' ye? Ur ye gonnae mak sand caistles like? Splendid. Never tae auld fur that. Man, if a wiznae sae waurn oot these days and git up oan ma sticks and come doon tae thi watter wi' ye.*

There's a wheelchair there in the cupboard we haven't tried yet, Mary, Annie beams. *We could give it a go with you if you want?*

Naw, naw, lass, dinna be daft. Ah'd jist be a muckle burden. Jist yoo and Daddy and the wean heed oan doon tae thi beach an huv a braw time fur me. Shaw me some pictures aifter ur somethin'. It's sae nice tae see a young un' aboot this place efter aw these years.

*

On the way through the woods, Bruce asks Thomas what it's like to travel in a spaceship. Thomas looks at Annie who only smiles and shrugs. *Hold on tight and I'll show you...* he says, hoisting the boy onto his shoulders and climbing up the trunk of an enormous tree while Annie sways below in a state of semi-terror, hoping she can catch anyone who falls. A moment later Thomas leaps back down onto the soft pine-needle covered ground below and release the boy in a fit of giggles. *That answer your question? Terrifying, exhilarating, like being a bird? All of the above?*

All of the above, all of the above... Bruce sings all the way to the beach, taking a model aeroplane from his rucksack and flying it in his hands between the trunks, making swishing noises as it passes close to the rough bark, tilting its wings.

What are you thinking, Pilot? Annie asks, noticing

Thomas seems deep in thought.

Well, all this reminds me of Mary's brother, Sonny, who I last saw when he was five. Never to see him again as it turned out. All those years when he was like this, that I missed out on. But also I'm thinking how Mary lit up in his presence back there. How cruel it is the way society seems to keep very old people and young children apart as if ageing and death are some kind of contagious disease.

I know, Annie squeezes his hand. *Life is a continuum though, isn't it? Like a forest, like those tiny green seedlings you can see all around here. Gradually they'll catch up while the old trunks fall, letting light down, leaving a space they can reach up through. The dead wood decaying back into compost in the soil. The forest is immortal.*

If only it was, Annie. It probably would be if it wasn't for human beings. Our ancestors got all this, everyone's ancestors did, in every culture around the world. The need not to take too much, to preserve the source. How can we have gone backwards in that regard, while moving forward in so many others?

I don't know, Annie smiles as she starts to break into a run towards the beach, which Bruce is now running across open-armed. She turns around, raising her voice: *But I know it's not too late, it must all be part of the scheme of things.*

*

Is it true you flew fighter jets, Thomas? Bruce asks Thomas on the beach, holding his model aeroplane up to him. Thomas takes this one carefully in his hand, while Bruce lifts up another so they can have a dog fight together while making suitable zoom and swishing noises.

Not quite, Brucie. He answers. *I flew propeller-driven planes, Spitfires and Lancasters and then a Hawker Sea Fury after the war.*

Do you have it with you? The boy asks.

Shhhh! Thomas puts a single finger to his lips then looks over his shoulder to where Annie is splashing in the waves. *Yes, I do, but don't tell anyone.*

Where have you hidden it? The boy asks.

Somewhere secret. The last place in the world anyone would ever think to look for it. But you won't tell anyone, will you?

Bruce shakes his head, sombrely. *When will you bring it out and fly it, Thomas?*

Soon, Brucie, soon. When no one is expecting it, just to give them all a big surprise.

What's that light flashing in your pocket, Thomas? Is that your phone?

I don't have a...

Annie returns to find Bruce engrossed in his aeroplanes on his own, and Thomas sitting next to him cross-legged, engrossed in something else that she's never seen before: a glowing sphere of light the size of an apple, resting in the palm of his hand, with moving pictures in it.

What's that, Thomas? She stands over him, trying to make out the moving images playing upside down on the globe. *Is everything all right?*

It's Mary, he says tensely, standing up. *I need to head back to the house. Someone's trying to break in.*

Break in? There's no burglaries out here.

They're not from here, Annie. They're from London.

What is that thing? Some kind of camera connected to the house?

In a way, yes. I've gotta go!

We'll come too then, we'll catch you up.

*

Disappointed that the door is locked and Thomas apparently isn't in, the first agent tries to prise open the key box and gets an electric shock for his trouble, strong enough to send him rolling backwards, howling in pain, his arm jolted like the kick from a horse. The second agent then attempts to lever the kitchen window open, which is unfortunately also metal framed and which duly dispenses a similar shock to him, from which he recoils more efficiently, now prepared for the voltage. They both scout around the house, peering in through the net curtains, glimpsing Mary inside sleeping. Returning to the front door, the smarter of the two, who seems in charge, says aloud: *The door's wood, and wood framed. This is our best bet – get me the jemmy from the car, will you?*

Inside, they advance on tip-toe, made very wary by the defences encountered so far. The doors to both Thomas's room and Mary's room lie open, encouraging them to relax a little. *Who's there?* The old lady calls out. *Is that you, Daddy? Is it time fur a cup o' tea?*

Putting her glasses on, she spots one of the agents standing at her door: *Eh? Who the deil ur yoo? A peeping tam? Git oot ma house ur ah'll batter yer lugs, ye wee scallywag!*

Shut up, you old bag. The agent addresses her and attempts to walk into the room but encounters an invisible barrier that he bounces back from. *What the fuck?* He tries and fails again, then draws his gun.

No! The smarter one shouts, but too late. The bullet behaves like a snooker ball striking a cushion, angle of incidence equalling angle of reflection, and shoots the tip off the other agent's shoe. *Too close, you muppet...* he winces, rubbing his foot. *Don't shoot at that again.*

Mary however is now on her feet and hobbling her way across the room, clutching a chamber pot. The agent at her door smirks, saying to his colleague: *Well at least she won't be able to get out.* Just before Mary and the chamber pot connect with his head and the old lady emerges into the corridor showing every indication of wishing to follow through on her kill. She stops as the other agent raises his gun towards her, standing eight feet away. *This will kill you if I fire it. But we're only here about Thomas. Tell me which room is Thomas's. Is it this one?* He nudges his shoulder towards his right. Mary says nothing, simply slowly nodding her head, her eyes watching his, coldly.

I thought so... he sighs. *Now get back into your bed and lie quiet, old lady, behind your personalised flash gordon force field or whatever the fuck that thing is. No one's getting hurt today... apart from bonzo there on the floor. We're just taking a look around, so relax.* Mary nods again and reverses into the room with her chamber pot, while the first agent sits up on the floor, rubbing his head. The second agent strides into Thomas' room and is immediately bounced back with enough force to throw him across the corridor and wind him, his gun dropping from his hand.

Just then the alternate shift of carers, Becky and April, come in the door and stand at the end of the corridor, looking puzzled at the scene of two men in black suits lying on the floor, drowsily picking themselves up and hurriedly trying to conceal things that look suspiciously like guns in their pockets. *Who are you guys?*

Surveyors. The smart one says, standing up and dusting himself down. *Thomas Tellman phoned us to come out and survey the place for dry rot, wet rot and woodworm. We've been examining the floors, but we're nearly done now. Doesn't look too bad actually.* He helps his colleague to his feet. *We've taken a few photos and some dampness readings. We'll go back and type up the report and post it out for Thomas, if you want to tell him that when he gets back.* They both sidle rapidly down the corridor, heads down, before turning momentarily at the end. *That front door was just hanging open by the way, when we arrived. You might want to fix that, from a security point of view.*

*

When Thomas returns to the house, Becky and April meet him at the door on their way off again – they tell him they chased away two rather suspicious men ten minutes ago, who they told that Thomas Tellman had just gone away travelling for a month. Thomas smiles, slightly out of breath: *Good thinking, ladies. I am indebted to you. Is Mary okay?*

Just fine, Becky reassures him, *says she doesn't remember a thing about them. Aren't you going to go in?*

Not yet, he grimaces, pointing to the woods, *just waiting for Annie and Bruce.*

As the carers pull away in their car, and Annie and Bruce arrive at Thomas' side, he squeezes the sphere in his hand and a rapid sequence of small percussive bangs ring out from inside the house. *What was that?* Annie and Mary ask simultaneously, from different ends of the building as Annie, Bruce and Thomas step into the hallway and close the door behind them.

Here... Thomas says, bringing a black rubble sack from the kitchen, – *let me just carefully pick up all these little presents. Mary! I'm home! Everything's fine, sweetheart.*

Annie watches Thomas bag a series of tiny smoking black tangles of wires fallen from the ceiling at various points throughout the house, coaxing the final remnants of some down with a kitchen knife. *What are those?*

Bugs. Eyes and ears. Theirs, not mine.

*Who are **they**?* she asks nervously, clutching Bruce's hand, leading him into the kitchen to get some biscuits.

What was that Bob Dylan song you sang the other day? The long black cloud is coming down. They never knock, those boys.

28

Mary vomits twice during the night and is too weak to get out of bed in the morning. Thomas does his best with her, Magda and Becky likewise who fail to get her to take much food and report their concerns around lunchtime, so that Doctor McCaffrey comes out to visit in the late afternoon. Thomas greets the doctor warmly at the door but with an expression fraught with a certain anxiety that his daughter's age is going to take her away from him again, irredeemably this time, when he's only been back for so short a duration.

Doctor McCaffrey greets Mary and kneels by her bedside with his stethoscope. Thomas pulls up a chair for him, as he examines her eyes, takes her pulse, blood pressure and heartbeat, all the time asking her questions. *Ah'm ah oan ma way oot, doachter? Gie it tae me straight, like. Full barrels blazin'...*

Well, you're certainly rather weak, Mary. I'm not convinced you've been eating properly recently, and that urinary tract infection I gave you the antibiotics for seems to have taken its toll on you. The problem when you stop moving around and lie in bed too much at your age, is that we enter a vicious circle where your muscle tissue starts to waste and your skin gets sores.

Aye, ah get it, Doachter. If ye dinnae use it, yoo loose it, as they young uns say. Och ah've hud a fair innings noo anyhoo.

Nonsense, Mary. Look at Thomas, your s... your father there, only just got back so recently. You need to stay alive and well for him. You're still sharp and these limbs of yours were working wonders only a few weeks ago. You need to stay strong in your spirit. You're in better shape than a lot of my other patients, as long as you don't give up.

McCaffrey takes Thomas quietly aside in the kitchen afterwards, but Mary quickly shouts from the bedroom: *Whit ur yoo twa whispering awa' aboot?! Ye've nain tae hide frae auld Mary that she cannae tak. Ah'm nae shrinkin' violet!*

Moving outside to talk next to McCaffrey's car in the slanting evening light, the doctor says: *I'm sorry, Thomas, but I might have to recommend, if she isn't any better tomorrow, that we move your mother into hospital for a while.*

Well you say a while, Doc, but from what I've gathered from the carers, once an old person goes into hospital, they often never return home. They die or go off to some impersonal nursing home and then fade away. And Mary has told me repeatedly, in no uncertain terms, that she wants to go on living at home and die at home when the time comes.

Of course, of course, Thomas, I understand. I wish you were misinformed in what you're saying, but sadly the statistics bear you out. Personally I wonder if it's actually the house as such, and not rather the people – alive and dead – that are associated with a house, that helps keep an old person alive. We are profoundly social creatures, all of us, and without others around us we lose our meaning. In hospital and care homes, there are too many strangers and too little personal history, and then the sense of self ebbs away.

Now you sound against the idea of hospital, Doc.

Well I am, long term, Thomas. What I'm doing is promising you that I will use my influence at the hospital, such as it is, to ensure that Mary comes back home here as quickly as possible. But unfortunately, my professional opinion, that I am duty bound to share with you, is that if she doesn't improve tomorrow and we don't then send her to hospital, then she may die within a week or two. A stint in hospital should stabilise her while they carry out more tests, and all being well extend her life for months, maybe many months, even years.

Well that's no choice at all then, doc. I trust you completely. Let me know your judgement tomorrow.

Do you have a mobile phone I can call you on?

I don't use mobile phones, Doc, they mess with my

electromagnetic field. But I'll be here, or at Annie's, and this is her mobile number here on this card.

Annie?

Anne Bevans. One of Mary's carers.

You and her are…

Close friends these days, yeah.

That's good. I remember Anne, nice girl. I hope that works out for you both. Good night, Thomas. Oh Thomas? Thomas turns back from Mary's door to catch the doctor's afterthought: *I was thinking about our last discussion at our surgery, your philosophical insights, and I wanted to share one of mine with you.*

Oh yeah?

We keep assuming that Mary's memory loss is just decay. But what if we were to view it as disengagement from time? Like the teeth of a cogwheel lifted out of the chain? What's the difference between memory and time travel at the end of the day?

That's very interesting, Doc, thank you, very interesting indeed. You're no ordinary quack, that's for sure.

29

Annie and Thomas sit around the dining table at Annie's flat, drinking coffee and gazing out from the little kitchen window onto the cramped and crooked old streets below, the mercat cross, the to and fro of country folk, farmers and estate workers, distillery employees, tourists, shop assistants, school children taking the long way home. There's a knock at the door and her father and Bruce come in and Annie insists they all sit down together.

Thanks for taking care of him today, Dad. You remember Thomas, don't you? Did you two have a good time together?

Aye, we did that, Annie. Afternoon, Thomas. Ah'm Bobby, by the wye, ye never coat that last time. Is it Tommy, Tom or Thomas ye like folks tae cry ye?

Bruce interjects: *Mammy, we went fishing up at the loch and granddad caught a trout, it was flapping around like mad.*

I was called Thomas by my mother, but in the Air Force everyone called me Tommy. Since I got back here, people are calling me Thomas, which I kinda like for the novelty, but it's no big deal.

Did you not bring us a fish for our dinner then, boys? Annie teases.

'Fraid not, lass. These days, ye huv tae fling them a' back, by law. Stocks huv been dwindlin' a' ma life. They conservation fowk are scared we'll lose the lot soon. There were tonnes o' them when I wiz a wean. Ye couldnae eat them fast enough back then. We had nae idea, never thought aboot it. Ye dinnae ken how precious a thing is 'til it's near gone, dae ye?

Annie's phone rings and she stands up to answer it then passes it to Thomas who excuses himself to go and use the phone on hands-free in the hallway.

Is everything a' richt there? Bobby asks quietly as they lift their tools to eat.

His mother's not so well, she's quite old and frail. Annie answers.

Thomas returns to the room and sits down again.

We wur jist talkin' aboot ye', Tam. Sorry to hear yir mither's poorly.

Thomas and Annie exchange a meaningful glance, as Thomas hesitates to reply. *Mary... yes. That was the doctor saying he wants her to go into hospital tonight, for a short spell. Until they get her weight and her blood pressure up. He's ordered an ambulance for a couple of hours from now. We've been feeding her all we can, but she's been getting anaemic, he reckons.*

I'll run you back over later, to see her off... Annie whispers.

Aye... Bobby nods his head. *There but for the grace and a' that. Annie wiz tellin' me she's seldom oot her bed. It's gey hard when they reach yon stage, tae keep thi bluid ganging aboot. Ah hudnae realized ye bided aroond here yersel', Tam, whit wi' yir accent and a'.*

Yeah, I raised a young family here on my RAF wages. But my wife died.

Aw, ye've hud some sair fortuin, son. But yer young. Time mends awthing, stock n' brock. Ye'll prosper yet.

Thomas has flown in spaceships, granddad, and strafed the Luftwaffe! Bruce pipes up.

Noo is that so, wee fella? Ah hope yoor nae plannin' ganging intae orbit yersel onny time? Yer mither here needs ye tae look efter her, and this wee toun needs ye tae stay an keep it chirpin'.

30

Chrissy stays on late at Home Care headquarters, even hiding in the toilet for fifteen minutes with the lights out, in order to dupe her colleagues into thinking she's gone home. Unfortunately neither has Helen Murchison, who chances upon Chrissy ten minutes later, on her knees in the archive room, with Mary Tellman's file in one hand and a sheaf of photocopies from it in the other.

What are you doing down there, then, Christine. Waiting for a bus?

I was just about to head home, when I remembered some paperwork I needed... Chrissy mutters, red in the face.

Needed to photocopy it and send to someone else... who I wonder? Helen stands over her, frowning. *What is your obsession with that poor man? Well you can go home and stay there now. You're suspended. I don't want to see you back here again until the disciplinary committee call for you. Is that clear?*

31

Thomas catches the train to Inverness to visit Mary in hospital. The town seems three times the scale of how he remembers it, a wide unruly sprawl of roundabouts, industrial estates and schemes of miniaturised houses on cul-de-sacs, having blossomed around it in the post-war decades. The morning is bright at first, but with a dark body of cloud slowly building up to the west promising rain from mountains inland. Something about the towering form of the modern hospital building intimidates Thomas, its beige brick ramparts resembling a taciturn castle designed to withstand seige.

Thomas asks to speak to the ward doctor, then walks down the long modern corridors with flowers and black grapes in his hand and some shortbread, Mary's favourite. Doctor Yasin Khatib comes to speak to him while Mary is still asleep in bed with her mouth open, head thrown back, pale and frail in a way that reminds Thomas uncomfortably of the dead. Not his mother, his daughter, everything inverted in a way that no one else can understand.

Are you the grandson? Yasin asks, over his white clipboard, and Thomas has learned by now to simply nod his head in acquiescence to this recurring torment of a question. He leads Thomas to a side room before continuing. *The prognosis is not very good, I'm afraid. Your grandmother is very weak and her blood pressure is very low. We're not entirely sure why in her case, we'll have to do more tests and keep her under observation, tests for internal bleeding and so forth. But really, this kind of anaemia is not uncommon in people of this age.*

What's the cure then, doctor?

Cure? Well, I'm afraid when someone reaches their late eighties and beyond, it's really just wear and tear. There is no cure. The organs are all winding down, just at different rates. All we can do is manage someone's health and try to make sure their pain and discomfort are not intolerable for them. Manage them, with the help of their families, towards a dignified death.

What is it that's worn out though, Doctor? What organs?

Well, her kidneys I suppose, her liver probably the most, then her heart. She never smoked did she? Her lungs are doing alright so far.

I'd like to get her back home as soon as possible, Doctor, and I know she wants that, once all your tests are done.

Yes of course, I understand. No point being here any longer than necessary, especially if there's nothing more we can do. We'll do our best to get her strength back up with the hospital regime of regular meals, see what the tests say, and let you know how things are going.

Thomas returns to Mary's bedside, and puts her flowers in a vase and places her grapes and shortbread on her bedside cabinet. After sitting for a further hour, listening to her breathing, he realises she is not going to wake up for a while longer, and decides to go home. Outside in the car park, dwarfed by the fortress of indomitable health he stops to look up into the now completely clouded sky, feeling the first fat drops of rain on his face.

32

Relucant to return to the empty house, troubled by the thought of losing his daughter, Thomas gets out at Kinburgh station and goes up through the winding lanes to knock on Annie's door, but finds there is no answer. He assumes she is away for the day with Bruce. Walking away, he runs into Bobby in the street who insists on dragging him into the pub for a game of snooker.

Whit will ye huv tae drink, Tam? A pint o' lager, heavy?

Whatever you're having Mister Bevans.

Ah tellt ye, son, it's Bobby, jist Bobby, nae need fur a' that Yankee hankee pankee here. Next ye'll be tellin' me tae huv a nice day.

And are you?

Ah will if ah can thrash ye at snooker, son. But Jesus, that was a good shot. An that wan tae. Whit the bloo blazes, where d'ye learn to play shots like that? Gonna gie a chance tae the auld yin sae he kin git his cue in edgewyes?

It's just geometry really, isn't it?

A young man watching their game places some coins on the edge of the table and Thomas reacts as he walks away: *Oh, wait, excuse me sir! You've left your money behind on the table!*

Tam, Tam, shhhh. Bobby prods him. *Ye're missing the sketch there. Whaur ye been fur thi last hundret years? That lad's put his coins there cos' he wants a game, wants tae play the winner like, which is lookin' like it's gonna be yoo.*

The young man, apparently drunk already in the middle of the afternoon comes back and faces up to Thomas: *What's the game mister, is there a problem?*

Bobby jumps in: *Nae problem at a' son, our freend's just not from aroond here, disnae ken the ropes. Are yoo sure ye want tae play him though? He's bloody good, son.*

Aye, nae worries, auld yin... the young man replies, looking insulted.

When the new game starts, the young man quickly becomes infuriated by Thomas's skill, the humiliation of not getting a shot in. *Yer cheating, ya Yankee cunt! Yoo touched that ba' with yer paw there, I saw ye!*

Naw, he didnae, ya dafty... Bobby laughs nervously, *he disnae need tae.*

Who asked yoo, auld yin, eh?

Very well... Thomas smiles. *Let's say that points goes to you. The next shot is yours. Oh... too bad.*

Yoo put me aff. Yoo shook the table there, didn't ye?

It's you that's shaking.

Whit?! Come here and say that tae ma face ya bla...

Thomas, who has suddenly reached out and put his index finger into the right ear of the young man, now carries him over, with the help of Bobby holding the other arm, to sit him down on the nearest sofa while Bobby orders them a fresh drink. The lad regains consciousness to find himself weeping profusely while spilling his heart out as if Thomas is his long lost best friend or father confessor. When Bobby returns from the bar, Thomas looks up with his arm around his unexpected companion, saying: *This is Micky, Bobby, from Lossiemouth – he was just telling me how his father went off to work on the oil rigs and separated from his mother when he was only ten. His stepfather was hostile to him, and he failed all his exams at school because his homelife was disrupted. He drinks to forget and make himself feel better. And he adores that barmaid with the brown hair, but hasn't found an excuse to ask her out yet, because his self-esteem is so low. He had a chance of a good job at the brewery but blew it after two weeks because of his excessive drinking. Maybe a job on a remote farm and couple of months teetotal will sort him out, like the opportunity his uncle offered him recently. Now go home, Micky, and have a good long sleep and things will look better in the morning.* Micky stands up obediently to go, his head down, shaking Thomas's hand and thanking him for helping him so much.

Bobby sits back beside Thomas for one last pint together. *Woof. That was uncanny, Tam. Whit did ye dae tae that boy's heid? Ah've ne'er seen a hard nut dissolve sae fast. Yoo some kind o' hypnotist or somethin'?*

They teach you a few tricks in the forces. First one being don't start anything you don't mean to finish, and that one would have finished in hospital for sure, which is where I was this morning and right now have no desire to send anyone or myself back to the casualty department thereof.

Och, ah clean furgoat aboot that, lad, ah shood hae asked. Hoo wiz yer mither? Annie was saying ye were frettin' ower hur.

You know… Thomas smiles mischievously. *The doctors were talking like she's dead already, but I've got a very strong intuition that she's going to astound everyone and make a very sudden and spectacular recovery.*

Aye? Hoo kin ye ken a thing like that then? If she kin play snooker like yoo though, then ah widnae put onny thing past her. Ah hope yir richt. Yoo not feelin' tipsy at a'?

Tipsy. Drunk? No, should I?

Yer made o' strong stuff, Tam. Annie's sic a nice lass, sae bonnie, but she seems to aye hud shite luck wi' blokes. She'll ah tellt ye aboot yon junkie she was mixed up wi' fur tae monny years.

Yes, she did. Sounds very sad. But Bruce seems pretty well-balanced. You and she did well to bring him through that undamaged. Time to go now, eh? I better head off. Tell Annie I dropped by and I'll call her tomorrow.

Aye, tea time noo, lad. Jist yoo gang easy oot there mind, keep yer peepers peeled, ye never ken when some crazy young cunt's gonna jump ye in a back alley whaun yer magic spells wear aff him.

33

Returning to the hospital ward two days later, Thomas finds Mary's bed empty and looks around in confusion. A nurse spots his lost-looking posture from her station and calls out: *Are you here for Mary Tellman? Didn't the doctor phone you? She's up and about. Through there in Ward F, physiotherapy, follow the signs.*

As he passes alongside the nurse, she smiles up at him and nudges him. *We've never seen anything like it. What a lady. Even the surgeons are puzzled. What did you put in that shortbread?*

She ate it all then? Thomas laughs.

God, aye. She'd have eaten us this morning if we'd run out of toast.

34

Believing Thomas to be alone at his house, Annie drives over to see him. They immediately start kissing in the hallway. When Annie wakes up an hour later, she sees Thomas is sitting up in bed reading a book by a dim blue lamp on his bedside cabinet.

Don't you ever sleep, Pilot? What are you reading? Annie asks Thomas, reaching her hand out to stroke his shoulder.

Poetry... Thomas answers, taking her hand in his. *William Blake. Who would have thought it? I never bothered with it much before I went away. Had to study a couple of classic ones at school of course, as every kid does. Walt Whitman, Robert Frost. Of all the things for a journey through space and time to give you a taste for. Maybe because it's so emotional and irrational. So human, compared to the wilderness of space.*

I can't imagine any of that... Annie sighs. *I suppose I'm gradually growing to believe all your chat though.*

One day early on, in the silver room, when I was scared and naked and alone, and uncertain what would happen next, uncertain of where I was going at all; my hosts put a blackbird, also taken from Earth, into the room with me. I can never describe to you the joy that blackbird and I took from each other's company, because we recognised each other and knew we were from the same planet and had breathed the same air. When he finally sang his beautiful evening song, sitting on my shoulder, my heart broke a hundred times over, so much I almost thought I would die.

Later they took it away and brought a deer in, one with horns that might have hurt me, but again instead: our joy, our longing to overcome our loneliness through smelling and caressing each other, overtook everything. I became afraid for a while that they might put in something deadly next time, like a wolf or a tiger. They never did of course, but what dawned on me was that even if they had done, I wasn't sure what would have happened. We, whatever fellow creature and I, would have loved each other at some level, because in the end, amid the blackness of space, that's all there ever is to do with each other that is of any use, any help, and of any meaning.

Annie strokes her hair back over her ears and rolls a cigarette, cross-legged on the bed, listening to Thomas continue.

I think maybe they were trying to teach me something. That was the moment at which I knew that the ceaseless wars of humankind will come to an end one day, because they must, because it's like a rule of physics, a tendency of all organic matter to come together and make itself better. That hope, that knowledge, sustained me through many days thereafter, as they finally ushered me out of the silver room, and does so still. Here, Annie, you have such a lovely soft Scottish voice. Would you read this aloud for me?

Annie, eyebrows raised, takes the poetry book from him, clears her throat and slowly reads a verse:

Tyger Tyger, burning bright,
In the forests of the night;
What immortal hand or eye,
Could frame thy fearful symmetry?

Thomas reaches out a hand to stroke her cheek, and a tear appears in her eye as if responding to the touch of his fingers. He sighs, and without breaking their gaze recites the next verse from memory to her:

In what distant deeps or skies.
Burnt the fire of thine eyes?
On what wings dare he aspire?
What the hand, dare seize the fire?

They embrace and kiss passionately as he stops speaking. He runs his fingers through the sun-like curls of her blonde hair, his own eyes beginning to water with emotion. She runs her hand down across his chest, and he stops her, bringing the book back into the space between them and saying calmly: *Read the next verse.* As she does so, he runs his fingers gently over her neck and kisses her ears. Her voice begins to shake:

And what shoulder, & what art,
Could twist the sinews of thy heart?

He joins her in reciting in unison the next two lines from memory, their voices intertwining with the resonance and ritual of a prayer:

And when thy heart began to beat,
What dread hand? & what dread feet?

Thomas takes the book back, as Annie caresses his shoulders, marvelling at the beauty of his dark skin and muscle tone. He embraces her and they lie down facing each other, Thomas reciting again from memory as he gazes into her eyes:

What the hammer? what the chain,
In what furnace was thy brain?
What the anvil? what dread grasp,
Dare its deadly terrors clasp?

They rotate around each other naked, laughing and unashamed. Thomas kneels down before her golden form, shining, rippling with life, bathed in the muted yellow evening light from the drawn curtains, and kisses her stomach, presses his nose into the fragrant curls of hair between her legs. Shaking now almost to the point of incoherence, Annie reads the final verse, before letting the book drop to the floor with a thunk:

When the stars threw down their spears
And water'd heaven with their tears:
Did he smile his work to see?
Did he who made the Lamb make thee?

What are we? Who are you? Blake's poem is a question. An unanswerable one perhaps, but one they now continue to wordlessly ask of each other's bodies in the language of gesture, of ballet, of dance and caress. Annie and Thomas make love in slow motion, as if in a dream. Nothing needs thought out. Each moment begets the next with total fluidity. They live in the pure moment with the grace of animals. The white sheets they draw from the bed rotate, like a slow torrent beneath them as they twist and turn. Like the skeins of matter around two colliding galaxies, like nebulae in the interstellar medium: the birthplace of molecular clouds collapsing under their own weight to give birth to new worlds, or later, the death-throes of giant, short-lived stars.

35

Doctor McCaffrey turns up unexpectedly at the house to find the door unlocked and a strange tangle of wires draped at head-height along the walls. Looking closer he sees that they are not conventional electrical conduits but something stranger: white and silver filaments, seemingly metallic, but also corroding and effervescing in the surrounding air. Also, stranger still: they are, even as he watches, becoming colonised and entwined with something like ivy and Russian vine reaching into the house from the garden along the pathway created by the wires. Unable to believe or understand what he is looking at, McCaffrey follows the wire-tendril pathways along the walls to find what it is within the house that they are linked to. He holds his breath, for reasons he is not entirely sure of, walks on tiptoes, opens doors with the stealth of a thief, the beating heart of a frightened but guiltily enchanted child. He finds the wires lead through a perfect circular hole the size of an apple into Mary Tellman's room. Entering the room he makes out in the dim moonlight how the wires fan out and are linked to various nodes on her body, her forehead and temples, how she seems not just asleep but hooked up to some kind of decantation or transfusion process, twitching.

He turns around and follows the wires to their next apparent destination, noting how the colonisation process by green roots and tendrils has now accelerated further, as if in weird symmetry and parody of the house's 1950's style floral wallpaper. He reaches out to almost touch the network and sees how it is giving off a faint blue glow of light, how moss is now also being propagated by it, spreading across the wallpaper and plaster as if it is a fertile growing medium.

In the next and final room that McCaffrey enters he finds Annie Bevans naked on the floor, her form almost lost and buried beneath the frenzy of wires and tendrils, technology and nature, that are weaving around her, like motorway interchanges, spaghetti junction, mainlining into her womb. In time to Annie's breathing, two white globes hover and rotate within the room like moons, each small enough to be held in the human hand. The whole house, McCaffrey now realises, hums as if with electricity, shakes as if it is a powerstation, a nuclear reactor. Looking up, vaguely feeling as if he is being watched, McCaffrey sees that Thomas Tellman is asleep on the ceiling, lying on it as if glued to it, as if gravity has been inverted. But he notices he is transparent, almost invisible, as if he is made of molten glass.

McCaffrey wakes up, crying out, almost screaming, waking his wife in bed at his side. *Jimmy, Jimmy, calm down!* she croons, her hand on his forehead, wet with sweat. *You were only dreaming, darling, having a nightmare, whatever's the matter?*

36

When Annie wakes up after dark, and looks around for her clothes to get dressed, she is surprised to hear muffled talking from somewhere else in the house, then horrified to realise that Mary Tellman has been home and in bed in the next room the entire time she has been here, while she was making love with Thomas. Unable to even face Mary, she bangs a door then gestures furiously from the hallway to Thomas to follow her so they can have a blazing row outside before she jumps into the car and speeds off, brakes screeching.

Later he pleads with her on the phone: *She was asleep the entire time, Annie, sedated in fact, and both doors were closed. What's the problem?*

You just don't get it, do you? Are you some kind of alien? Don't answer that. I mean… it's just not what anyone does. Certainly not, you know… the first time. It's icky. It's weird. Don't you get that? I need you to be human, Thomas, not some weird alien performing experiments on me. I thought what we did was sacred, but now it feels like some circus side show, a freak show. You've freaked me out, big style.

37

Doctor McCaffrey decides on an impulse whose logic escapes him, to drive out to Mary Tellman's house. On the way, he has to pull off the single-track road as Annie Bevans speeds past him in her car, her facial expression curiously hard and frozen, seemingly so engrossed or distracted by something, that she appears not to see or recognise the doctor. He arrives at the house and goes in to check on Mary and talk to Thomas.

How's the patient doing then?

Not bad at all, Doctor, remarkable even. She was sitting up this morning and even asking for her slippers, wanting me to help her stand and walk.

No? That wouldn't be advisable at all, Thomas. She must take things slowly. Mary! McCaffrey exclaims arriving at the door to her room. *You look rather perky! Thomas tells me you've been planning a nine mile hike. We'll have none of that nonsense. Rest and small steps only for you, until you make a gradual and thorough recovery.*

Gradual, Doachter? Ah've nae goat thi time like tae footer aboot. There's roses tae sniff and shoartbreed tae cook and thi cheeks of wee grand weans tae pinch and kiss. Ah'm sae glad tae be hame.

Mary, you're a soldier, a targe, a battle-axe as they say, but I insist you defer to the wisdom of your learnèd physician. McCaffrey looks up and winks at Thomas.

Aye, aye, ah hear ye, Jimmy. Daddy there will keep me richt, dinnae ye fash yersel'

*

Talking outside at the car again as the doctor is departing, Thomas says: *I've been meaning to say, Doctor. The locks on the doors to your surgery, front and back, I'd advise you to upgrade them.*

Oh really? We occasionally have a few problems with

methadone-crazed addicts sadly, the products of Kinburgh's own little micro-ghettos of social despair, but generally nothing the police and I can't handle.

That's not what I mean, unfortunately. We had some shady types sniffing around here least week, MI5 or 6 or whatever they call themselves this year. They are interested in me. I'd strongly suggest you take my medical records out of the surgery, photocopy them, and keep them and the copies somewhere else and safe.

My word. You're serious, aren't you?

I'm afraid so, Doctor. They won't use them on you, but they do carry guns, so don't aggravate or challenge them if you encounter them. They tend to wear plain clothes, black suits, like business men.

But whatever do they want?

To take me in, I would imagine, supposedly for questioning, but I doubt anyone would ever see me again if they do. Something about my story and my telling it frightens them, evidently.

McCaffrey shakes his head grimly, looking down at the ground. *I don't know what to think, Thomas. All that sounds quite ridiculous. But I shall take the precautions you suggest, just in case.*

38

Detective Inspector Hugh Drummond gets a call from his Superintendent, suggesting he interviews the head surgeon at Raigmore Hospital in Inverness, who has made an unusual initial statement to the police concerning vital organs going missing from the Transplant unit. Drummond turns up and is met by a Doctor Yasin Khatib, who shows him around the unit in sterilised gowns, face masks and gloves. *I thought organ transplants were still quite rare, no?* Drummond asks.

Not really... Yasin answers, as Drummond follows him down the corridor to his office. *Four thousand a year roughly on average at present in Britain, which translates to about 11 a day. Science and medicine have steadily moved on over the years, something that once seemed risky and radical is now relatively routine.*

I seem to remember that rejection of the organ by the new host was the biggest problem in the early days when I was a kid. Drummond ventures, as Yasin offers him a seat in his clean, compact room with a single window over an inner courtyard of dismal modernity.

Rejection by immune system, yes. But we have developed drugs to mostly overcome that, immunosuppression therapy. Hearts are the hardest things to transplant, they do not like being frozen very much. You've got about four hours to harvest a heart and get it into a recipient's chest, after that the likelihood of cell failure and organ malfunction rise rapidly. The heart needs blood supply the most, but the kidneys are surprisingly tough. They can last for a day to a day and a half in cold storage. Lungs will be good for six to eight hours. Liver lasts about twelve hours.

Crikey, you make this place sound like a restaurant kitchen from hell. So what happened on... when was it... Drummond checks his notes, *Friday night?*

That's correct. Well we don't really know. I mean,

don't know how it is even possible. But some organs went missing.

Why so impossible? You just showed me the freezer storage systems, didn't you?

Yes, but these organs did not go missing from there. They disappeared from inside a body.

How do you mean disappeared?

A patient had died, one hour beforehand, before the... incident... must have occurred, and when we opened up their abdomen to perform an autopsy we found the liver and kidneys had already been removed, which means someone took them out during the four hours of down time when the body was left alone.

That would have to be a surgeon that did that then?

Yes, in theory. Except that they must have been a very skilful one.

Why's that?

Because they left almost no scar on the body, just the thinnest of hairline incisions on the abdomen, no other traces, no blood.

How's that possible?

It should not be. I do not understand it.

This body, the deceased person from whom the organs were... harvested... as you call it.

Taken, stolen, I suppose I might say in this instance.

Really? Well, had they given their assent to donate organs after their death?

No, as it happens. They had opted out. They were carrying a non-donor card.

Well, wait a minute then. What crime was actually committed here?

Desecration of the body of a deceased person, I suppose.

I'm sorry to sound dumb, Doctor, and even a bit crude potentially, unprofessional even. But how will anyone know?

The body went to the mortuary a couple of hours ago, and should be claimed by the undertakers acting for the family some time in the next forty-eight hours. I don't want anyone pointing the finger at us, so I am telling you about this, straight up, as they say.

Do they say? If it's a cremation no one will notice, am I right?

Maybe, maybe not. Those guys are paranoid these days about pacemakers and other implants exploding when they turn the flames on. I'm no expert on mortician's contemporary practice, but I would imagine they use X-rays and scalpels, open bodies up to tidy things up sometimes, just like they certainly do for burials, drain the blood and replace it with embalming fluid...

Alright, alright... no need to go into that, sounds queasier than surgery, I get the picture. So we're looking for an over-eager junior surgeon to charge with desecration, right?

You may never find him of course, but it needs to go on file in case it happens again. Such a person could be extremely dangerous. The lack of respect coupled with extraordinary surgical skills. It makes me uncomfortable to think of, if I am honest.

Could it have been one of your own staff, a medical student, or an outsider?

I cannot see it being any of mine, frankly. Between you and me, none of them are that good. Yet. The building isn't designed to be Fort Knox, it is only a hospital.

You're thinking some kind of criminal gang? Stealing organs to order?

They would need refrigeration equipment. Specialized vans that are not ten a penny. Things like that might show up on the CCTV for the car park and roads around here.

*Yes, we'll check all that, but tell me, Doctor, help me to understand, why would someone go to the length of stopping people using their organs to save other people's lives once they themselves were dead as a doornail? Shouldn't **that** be a crime?*

Yasin smiles with a reserved sadness. *Above both our pay grades, Inspector. Write to your MSP.*

39

Chrissy and Magda agree to meet for coffee in a Kinburgh café. Magda misses her shift mate, and has been surprised and appalled to hear she has been suspended. Delayed by five minutes and hurrying past the café's shopfront to reach the door, she sees Chrissy sitting there alone and is struck by the pensive and aggrieved expression on her face, and feels a pang of Christian charity.

Good to see you, Chrissy, the cakes are nice here, aren't they? Have you ordered yet? So sorry I was late, Becky and I had to stop for petrol on the way back from Newfield. How have you been?

Opposite the window in which they sit and talk, a cobbled street leads down towards the beach, and over the green tops of the Scots Pines the deep cobalt of the sea can be seen in the distance, resolving itself into a string of foam, twisting in the wind where sand meets water on the next peninsula up the coast. White doves fly to and fro from their purpose-built nooks in the old medieval tower of Kinburgh tolbooth, while crows swoop down onto the pavements between waves of shoppers and phases of traffic lights, strutting with the demeanor of guards, pecking at crumbs with a curious air of domination rather than subservience to the schemes of men.

Inside the café, Chrissy's eyes widen, while her brows furrow, a seeming contradiction, achieved with uncharacteristic grace, culminating in her mouth falling open. *You saw what?*

His feet, Chrissy. I don't understand it, but I swear it. Or one foot at least. His toes were fused together, you know, like a flipper.

What do you make of that?

Well, I don't know. I didn't know what to make of it. But it got me thinking about all the things you said and…

And? Chrissy asks, lifting up a square of Rocky Road towards her mouth as a strategic distraction, brow still furrowed, then deciding to put it back down and dissect it.

As if maybe he's not all he seems, just as you said.

You mean a conman, stealing from the old lady?

Or something else maybe, like a supernatural being, a demon.

Chrissy sighs, puts her knife down. *Well I can hardly use that in my defence at the disciplinary hearing, can I? I was photocopying classified personal files because Magda told me Thomas Tellman was a cloven-hoofed demon? I'd sooner believe in flying saucers than that sort of bunkum. At least UFOs probably obey the laws of physics, if they exist at all.*

But how do you explain it?

His toes? Do I need to? By you needing a trip to the opticians maybe? Or him having had a car accident and reconstructive surgery after third-degree burns? How would I know? And how would it matter?

I'm sorry. I just thought you'd be interested, was all.

I am interested, Magda, Chrissy reassures her, placing a hand over hers for a moment. *It's just I was hoping for something a bit more concrete. Evidence of wrongdoing, weirdness, to suggest that my misgivings were not unfounded. You can't go to jail for not having your toes differentiated.*

Well I'm not always out there, you know, we rotate our shifts around with other teams, but I'll ask around for you.

Discreetly, remember, very discreetly only, Magda, but thanks, I do appreciate your support.

Look! Magda exclaims, *There he is! What are the chances of that? I better wave.*

Don't you bloody dare! Chrissy rasps back, *Or I'll hide beneath this table top.*

Thomas hurries past, clutching a bouquet of flowers wrapped in fresh newspaper. The wind catches his scarf and he spins around, splashing himself in a puddle. The crows in the street, paused but unimpressed, stare after his dwindling figure with a look of ancient weariness in their eyes.

40

Thomas turns up at the door of Annie's flat with a bunch of yellow flowers in his hand: sunflowers, statice, asparagus fern and bupleurum. *My second bouquet in a week, I have to confess, although Mary slept through the grand presentation ceremony when I took her hers in hospital.*

You silly sausage... Annie sighs, shaking her head. *They cost money those things – that you don't have. You're so old fashioned.*

I've got a pretty good excuse for being old-fashioned though, if you think about it.

Better than most... she nods, arms folded, *I must admit. You bugger. I don't know whether to admire you or pity you. Or pity me. How do you do this to me?*

Isn't all love pity, ultimately?

There you go again. Can't you try to be a little less interesting? You know, like other people.

I would if I could, believe me.

Fuck it, come in and I'll make you coffee. You look like you've been rained on again.

41

The morning is bright and clear, but with a premonition of autumn about it, that slight yellowing and weariness of the quality of light, a certain wistful frothing of the high clouds, which late August tends to bring. Doctor McCaffrey's receptionist, Sarah Henderson, walks through the pleasant cobbled streets of the precinct on her way to work, noticing a few squirrels scarpering between the rowan trees and the overfull bins. Arriving at her usual time to unlock, she discovers that the door to the surgery is hanging open with the locks and bolts twisted out of shape. Large splinters of wood lie on the ground beneath where the door frame looks to have been levered with an iron bar. She takes her mobile phone out and calls the Doctor immediately.

Make sure you're alone then phone the police and ask for Hugh Drummond, Sarah. McCaffrey replies. *I've been half expecting this. I'll be there in an hour after I've finished two house calls in Milltown. Just stay at the door if you can and turn everyone away. The police should be there in under five minutes I'd think.*

Sarah makes the call then gingerly takes a few steps inside to check the place is empty and picks up some packaging tape and paper and pen with which to close off the door opening to patients. A squirrel runs up the lane and stops on its hind legs to look up at her quizzically for a moment, as if awaiting further instructions.

*

Doctor McCaffrey and Inspector Drummond arrive at the scene almost at the same moment, nodding to the two policemen at the door then going in to join Sarah inside.

Druggies, Jimmy? We've started dusting the place for fingerprints but it looks like gloves, oddly, so I don't hold out much hope... Drummond begins, disappointed in the situation but always pleased to see his old friend again.

Opting for a brief fatherly hand on his back rather than an inappropriate handshake.

Not addicts. Not a chance. Just made to look that way. McCaffrey replies dolefully.

Sarah chips in: *We always put the methadone and such like in the big safe and make sure that they see us doing it, Inspector. Just so they know, there would be no point trying it. They do talk to each other. Someone tried it about ten years ago. It's well known to be a hopeless endeavour.*

Ah, like life itself, eh? Drummond sighs. *But what was the real motive then? You sound like you have a theory, James?*

MI6 would be my bet. McCaffrey folds his arms. *Do you have any contact with them? I was tipped off they might be after the medical records of a patient of mine.*

Oh yes? I'm all ears. Drummond sits on the edge of a counter.

A former RAF pilot mixed up in some UFO business. You're nodding your head I see.

I don't know if they're MI6 or have got some other moniker, but I've been surprised over the years how much interest they show in certain UFO cases – ones near military bases particularly. I suspect the big secret they want to keep is how little they really know about what those things are. No more than us, has generally been my impression. I'd have thought they could just demand to see medical records though, if they produce a reasonable justification.

No doubt that will come next. They probably thought this would be easier.

They didn't get what you think they wanted then?

I'd hidden the relevant records off-site, as a precaution.

Oh dear, I've got a feeling we'll both be hearing from them soon then. You might be right, from what I've seen. We'll do a report of course for your insurance, but this looks like a professional job to me, made to look amateur. Spent all their time at the filing cabinets, then a final two minutes at the drugs, trying to look desperate and clumsy. Got away with all the aspirin they could handle.

When do you reckon then, Hugh?

I'd give it no more than 48 hours. Synchronize watches. Maybe they'll pull us in together. I'll try to swing it that way if I can, if they call me first.

Thanks, Hugh, I'd appreciate that. I'd rather not be alone in the custody of people who justify this sort of thing as a modus operandi.

42

Louise pulls up outside at her mother's house, in a car hired from the airport. This time she embraces Thomas wholeheartedly where she finds him standing to greet her in the open door, smiling broadly. *Look!* he says, turning around with a dramatic sweep of the arm, *Look who's back on her feet again!*

Mary hobbles down the hallway, fully dressed in skirt and blouse, her hair brushed and swept back, even her make-up done, leaning only on her old hardwood walking stick. *Lou! It's yersel, petal. Hoo ur yoo? Huv ye naw brought thi weans wi ye this time?*

Oh Mum, Louise collides with her and talks over her shoulder, wrapped in a long bear-hug of an embrace. *I tried to persuade them, but they're both at that difficult age now, sulky teenagers, wanted to stay and play with their computers.*

Ah ken, ah ken, darlin', dinnae hing yersel, it's aw been alike since thi dawn o' time – ye wur a sulky wee bisom yersel' once, right enough. Noo let me look at ye! Aren't yoo jist fine?

Aw Mum, never mind me, what about you? What a turnaround. Thomas tells me you've found a new lease of life and the hospital can scarcely account for it. Is it true?

Weel. Ah dinnae ken hoo lang it micht last, lass, but I say we gang tae the beach thi day while we kin.

We could take the wheelchair along just in case, Lou... Thomas says, putting his arms around them both. *I know you don't like it, Mary. But it folds up and I reckon it would fit in the car. What do you think?*

*

Sea spray, the taste of salt. Diadems of twisting sunlight, glittering on waves. Tiny fragments of shell and wet sand running between toes. Mary lifts her dress above her knees in comic playfulness as she saunters into the waves, whooping out loud for joy as the seagulls swing down as if somehow joining in, arcing over her and Louise and Thomas, birds like winged mime artists giving physical expression to human thoughts. Thomas thinks of the triple star system of Alpha Centauri, the three suns on intersecting orbits: the peculiar symmetry of Mary orbited by both her daughter and her father for these precious hours, their ages inverted, he a traveller forward in time, seeing like a ghost sees; a world unleashed beyond his era.

Mary soon tires however, in the walk up the wet sand, feet sinking, then floundering in the dry and shifting dunes, heading back up towards the old esplanade. Sitting down on a park bench with ice cream cones, Mary and Thomas share memories of the stalls and fairground rides that used to be there in the 1940's. *Dae ye mind yon shooting gallery an' thi Punch n' Judy, Daddy? An thi candy floss, an when a fell an' skint ma knee commin' aff thi dodgems? An Mammy winnin' that wee sun hat that wiz sae perfect fur Sonny? Ah mind like it wiz yesterday.*

To me it was yesterday, Mary. Thomas muses. *Or only a year ago, to be precise. But to you: eighty years. Like you went for a spin on the merry-go-round while I stood aside, watching.*

You know, Mum... Louise laughs, *I don't think I've heard you remembering so much all at once in a long, long time. This is a rare treat.*

I guess they don't hold fairs anymore, not here at least. Thomas sighs. *Now here we are together on a ghost esplanade, watching all the ghost rides and stalls in a ghost fairground. What a cruel magic trick time is, eh? I look away and hey presto – my daughter has a daughter old enough to be my mother, and is old enough to be my grandmother. It could make your head hurt.*

Aye, an' yer hairt, Daddy.

Och stop it, you two, being so morbid. Just be grateful we're all together. You tired now, Mum? Time for the dreaded wheelchair? Thomas will push you, it will give your pins a rest.

Aye, ah could dae with a rest darlin'. All these imaginary fairgroon rides are fair makin' ma heid spin. Stap thi wurld, ah wannae get aff, and a' that.

The three of them walk along the pier side, Thomas pushing Mary in her chair.

Who the devil are they? Louise asks, nodding towards two men in black suits emerging from a car and pointing at the trio, then hurrying along the pier towards them. Halfway there however, they slow down as if in disappointment and start looking around, peering down into the water and over the harbour wall. Coming level with Mary and Louise and examing them up and down, one of them remarks in a London accent: *Motorised wheelchair? You want to be careful letting her go so near the edge on her own like that, luv.*

Louise looks at Thomas in puzzlement as they hurry away. *What was all that about then? A threat? The wheelchair's not motorised.*

Thomas laughs quietly. *No, it isn't. But if you couldn't see the person pushing it, you might assume it was.*

Louise furrows her brow, changes the subject, as they return to the esplanade and push Mary under the arched stone gate through the medieval town wall: *I hear you've got yourself a girlfriend, Thomas. But you're no ordinary granddad I suppose.*

My, my, news travels fast in this little town it seems, even for those 600 miles away in London.

Louise laughs, enjoying herself. *Ah ha, I have connections, wired into the jungle drums. Somebody nice?*

Yes, she's very lovely. But I'm a bit rusty on the old romance malarkey. Bit like Mary's legs: as in take it slow, one step at a time. Love's changed a bit since my day. Or maybe died and come back as something more recreational.

You've changed, Thomas, already. Do you realise that?

Thomas stops and looks at Louise, as they near her parked car. *Really? You think so? How?*

Yes. You're getting more human. More humorous and

ironic. I guess it's what we use as armour, our personal space suits, here on Earth – or in Scotland at least. Slag ourselves before anyone else does. Hides the insecurities. You're good company, granddad. You'll make some girl very happy. Wouldn't it be funny if she was an air hostess, eh?

Aw, Lou. My sides are aching. I'm learning 21st century humour from you every minute. Now let's get Iron Mary here disassembled and flat-packed in the boot, shall we? Has she nodded off to sleep? That'll be all that rich sea air and ice cream.

43

Annie is surprised by the extent to which Thomas and Bruce can play together, potentially for hours. Thomas never seems to get tired or bored, as if he can enter more fully into the mind of a child than can most self-conscious adults. But she knows Bruce needs to play with children of his own age, begins to even worry he is getting too attached to Thomas, tries to subtly curtail their time together, their endless games with model aeroplanes, kneeling together on the living room floor. She hears him telling Bruce of daring aerial exploits over Germany in 1944, and wonders what is fact, exaggeration or pure fiction.

Well, Brucie, want me to show you how to really make that aeroplane fly? Unassisted, I mean. Thomas lodges a magnet inside one of the lighter of the planes, then places a circle of eight dark grey steel bricks, about the size of small chocolate bars, around where the plane sits on the floor.

Where did you get those, Thomas? Annie asks, looking over her shoulder, as she puts the dishes away in the kitchen cupboard. *Are they expensive?*

I made them myself, back at the house, from scrap metal in the garage. Charged them up. Electromagnets. Easy when you know how. Watch.

Annie and Bruce both marvel, as the toy plane lifts into the air, its slow shaking trajectory controlled by Thomas pulling or pushing a brick here or there, in and out of its alignment within the circle of the invisible field.

44

Mary wakes up confused. *Whaur ah'm ah? Is that yoo, Daddy? Hoo did ah get here? Whaur's Mammy?*

She passed away a long time ago, Sweetheart... Thomas sighs, sitting down at her bedside. *It's just you and me now.*

Whit's wrang? Why can ah nae move, Daddy? Ma legs are sae sluggish, ma back aches. Whit's happened tae me? Hoo cum ah kin hardly move?

Look at your hands, Mary. You've aged. You're old now. I know, it's like a very cruel magic trick, but it's real, and irreversible. Time and ageing, it comes to us all.

But Daddy, yoo look the same. Yoo huvnae aged a day. Hoo's yon possible?

I sometimes wonder. Maybe I'm just a dream you're having. But it's not for any of us poor mortals to question the games of the gods is it? We just have to live in the moment, as Lou said – be grateful for each other while we're here. Do you think you could manage some breakfast? Soup and bread? Cup of tea?

At that moment, Magdalena and Becky arrive at the door to assist, just as the phone goes. *Oh that reminds me,* Becky shouts as Thomas walks back down the hall, *there was a phone message the other day while you were out, Thomas. I wrote it down. Did you see it? Someone phoning from a company called M.I.T, whatever that is. Thought it might be telesales or a scam or something, but I took a note of their number.*

Thomas nods to her in response with his hand over the receiver, then takes the call: *Thanks for phoning back, Professor. You got my equations then? Good, that's good. Out of the question, I'm afraid. We'll have to make do with email. I have someone else working on a demonstration, I can put you in touch with. Yes, go on...*

45

In the playground at school Bruce gets teased by a group of older boys for not having a father. As the ring leader turns away, Bruce lobs a magnet at the back of his head, hard enough to knock him over, but recalls it to his pocket too rapidly for anyone to see. The effect is like tossing a yo-yo with no strings, dense mass and momentum, but no weight.

The boy sits up from where he fell, rubbing his head, looking around incredulous, as Bruce continues his game, seemingly engrossed, kneeling on the ground playing marbles with his friends.

46

What do you say I give you a driving lesson, Pilot? Annie asks when he next arrives at her door.

But I can drive, I told you. Thomas answers, coming in a while to read the paper while she gets ready to go out.

Yeah, but what are the chances of an 80 year old driving licence cutting any mustard with the West Highland Constabulary? And things might have changed a bit since your time. I wonder if you've ever even seen a roundabout. Not to mention a speed bump. You'll probably have to take another test, you know.

Well, what do you propose I drive and where?

That old banger of mine will do I suppose, provided you don't bang it. We'll go find some remote and deserted car park or something. You up for it?

Bit late isn't it? It will be getting dark in an hour or so.

Night driving. All the more for you to practice. You see, I'm thinking if you can pass a driving test then you could make yourself useful, pick up Bruce now and again from his karate lessons and friend's houses while I'm working. The council give me a car to drive when I'm on shift anyway, as you know, so this thing lies empty, and my Dad doesn't drive on account of his epilepsy.

What form does his epilepsy take? Thomas asks, as Annie locks up and they head out to her car.

Fits of shaking and dimmed eyesight. He's not had a bout in a few years now, but it's not worth the risk.

What causes that?

We don't know. Maybe the job he used to do. He was an electrician and got a couple of bad shocks towards the end of his career, always somebody else's fault. Annie says, unlocking the car, sitting down and starting the engine.

Human thoughts are carried on electrical impulses in the brain. Strange idea that all our thoughts are travelling around on electrons like train commuters. My hosts mastered how to transfer all that out of the brain and into a kind of computer I suppose we'd call it. A kind of crystal filled with flickering points of light. They showed me crystals that were the preserved minds, or souls if you prefer, of revered citizens who died centuries before.

That's sounds pretty creepy... but rather handy I suppose. Annie reflects as she drives through Kinburgh, most shops now closed apart from a handful of takeaways. *No need to guess what Einstein or HG Wells would have thought of something, when you can just go ask them. Are they really alive then, those crystals? Are these like immortal people, aware that they've lost their physical bodies?*

I believe so, as I understood it. Thomas says, winding the window down as they near the edge of town. *But they were changed of course, by not having bodies. It wasn't so much them, as the next phase of them. You know, like a sequel. Potentially stagnant without all the fresh stimuli, the joys and horrors, that living as a physical being among other such beings brings.*

Fascinating, Pilot. But tell me, did these beings have sex? Have gender even? How did they reproduce?

Oh, they pretty much gave that up thousands of year ago. They used to be male and female like us, but opted to become both and neither. Now and again, they revert a few couples voluntarily in order to create new children, or for research purposes.

Aren't they dying out without new babies coming along? Annie asks as they reach the dual carriageway and pick up speed.

No, because most of them live for many centuries of our time, some even for millennia. They replace internal organs and any body part really that becomes worn out or diseased. So there's no need, and no room, for many babies to be born.

That sounds horrible and boring and lifeless to me. Didn't you find that prospect dull, the reality of it soul-destroying?

Yes and no. We're primitive beings, we're always going to be repulsed at the thought of anything wildly different from us that questions our fundamental principles. At the same time, you chanced upon a significant issue there. Their genetic material was petering out, becoming run down and depleted. A bit like in-breeding.

I'll bet. I don't like the sound of these aliens and their alien life all that much, Thomas. Is that why you came back?

How could I not come back? I belong here. As me and the blackbird realised together in the silver room. We are extensions of the Earth.

Don't these aliens miss sex in terms of being a sublime metaphor for the union of two souls? Annie asks, laughing, winding down the window, letting the breeze play across her hair.

I guess they achieve that union more effectively by rubbing two crystals up against each other, or interlacing two brains through and around each other in a shared neural network. Maybe that's much better than sticking each other's fiddly bits together in a sloppy slurpy way. Who knows?

They didn't let you try it then? Alien brain sex?

No. That would have been like being unfaithful to Eleanor.

Annie laughs out loud, then stops herself, wondering if she should have. As they drive over the causeway across the Firth, with the colours of sunset reflected in the calm water all about them, Annie sighs and shakes her head. *Thomas, sometimes I don't know how to take you. So we shall presume seriously. Do you miss her? It's okay to say. I still miss Frank, despite all the years of torment when he was on the way out. I miss the good Frank, shall we say, and am increasingly forgetting the bad. That's the handy thing about dead people; they can't let you down anymore.*

Unless they've left a tell-all memoir in the attic I suppose. Or come back from the dead, like I have. You know, I've never thought of it like that, the other way around. Maybe I am a disappointment to Mary compared to her golden memory she had of a father she idolised.

Annie glances at him with interest. *Her golden memories were thin on the ground by the time you came back, just in time to top her up with some fresh ones. How is she today anyway? That's quite a comeback she made from the jaws of the hospital system.*

Not so good actually. Louise and I took her to the beach yesterday and she had a great time, but she's been exhausted ever since, like maybe we overdid it. And to answer your question, belatedly. Yes, I do miss Eleanor, and Sonny, very much. Maybe at some level, you and Bruce are a substitute. A way to numb the pain and overwrite the old memories with new ones. Like maybe it's not just Mary that needs to do that.

Well, I don't suppose I can be jealous of the dead, or either of us can.

*

Arriving at the remote car park Annie had in mind, half way up a mountain, they change seats to let Thomas practice driving, the basics of which he quickly appears to be adept at. *No stopping you, Pilot. Reckon you could drive us home safely?*

No problem. Maybe you're forgetting I was away for one year, not eighty, Annie.

How can I forget that, when you're not hobbling around on a Zimmer?

Right – before we go, let's step out for some fresh air here and admire the view with the last of the light.

Thomas and Annie go to stand at the edge of the clearing, holding hands. *Look at all the lights down there across the water, of Kinburgh and Inverness in the distance. Just like a neural network, an alien brain eh? Laid out like some kind of mirroring of the stars above, an invitation to communication.*

Shut up and kiss me... Annie laughs.

But Thomas tenses and gestures to her to be quiet. *Do you hear that?*

What? Just bird song at sunset isn't it?

No, listen. There's a pattern to it. They're saying there's something coming this way, through the woods.

You can speak bird language? Don't be ridiculous, Thomas.

No, it's nothing complicated. It's just a sound sequence that means 'threat on the ground'. It's obvious once you know to listen for it. Right, if you don't believe me, come over here and let's stay still and quiet for a few minutes. Whatever it is, is probably coming for the water of that pool there, just wait, trust me.

Sure enough, three minutes later, by listening and positioning themselves carefully, they are able to stand within a few feet of two hinds and a fawn stepping out of the woods at twilight. They kneel down and watch them sauntering over to the slow-moving stretch of burn to drink. To Annie's amazement, Thomas then slowly walks over to them without them noticing, getting close enough to stroke their backs, like pet dogs. When Annie takes one step as if to join him however, all three immediately notice her, freeze for a moment, then bound away.

Not fair! she laments. *How did you pull that off?*

I cheated, he chuckles. *They couldn't see me, and I was downwind.*

It's getting a bit chilly now. Let's get back in the car for a hug.

*

Thomas drives on the way back down, giving Annie the chance to marvel at all the tall pine trees densely packed on every side. She thinks she sees the full moon coming up above the top of them, remarking on it, then notices that it rises up too quickly until it gets brighter above them, even keeping pace with the car.

That's not the moon, is it, Thomas? What is it? She leans out the passenger window to crane her neck up to try to see it more clearly. *It's awfully bright. A helicopter?*

Thomas keeps driving calmly, his eyes glancing at the

wing mirror occasionally, the intensifying light source above and behind.

There's no sound from it at all, Annie muses, *It's not a helicopter either, is it Thomas?*

Nope. He answers, shaking his head, gaining confidence at the wheel, speeding up. Fantastical shadows of mature trees fall across the reflective bonnet of the speeding car, stroboscopic, kaleidoscopic. As the woods to the left begin to clear, the dark waters of the sea loch below glimmer dramatically.

Is that them? Your friends? Annie asks finally, raising her voice over the sound of the car engine.

Think of it like the deer and the birds. Thomas answers. *Fellow creatures just being friendly, keeping an eye on us.*

Were they watching us back there? When we... you know?

They're not much interested in that sort of thing, Annie. They have more important fish to fry.

What though? Why are they here?

Isn't it obvious? To save us from ourselves, of course.

Who are they?

You wouldn't believe or understand if I really gave you that answer.

Try me.

They're us, Annie, ourselves.

How do you mean?

We're being remembered by them. This is how they remember us. We are their memories. They're like Mary, in a way, trying to recover what was lost. Time is a circle, a closed loop. We can't be destroyed.

Thomas, that spaces me out. I both do and don't, know what the hell you're talking about.

Of course. The difference between the conscious and subconscious brain. In a dream, you know exactly what all of this means.

I know I'm tired now, and would like to get home to my bed in one piece and without being abducted or having experiments performed on me. Can you tell your little green friends to go away now?

They're going anyway. And they're not green, by the way.

What colour are they? Annie retorts sleepily.

You ask **me** *that?* Thomas laughs, good-naturedly. *What colour are humans? Pink? White? Black? Brown? Red? Yellow? Or grey mostly, when they're old?*

47

Are you Thomas Tellman?

Yup. Thomas has just answered his door to a young man he's never seen before, dressed in Gothic black T-shirt and jeans, with multiple piercings, a splash of white make-up and eye-liner.

I mean the Captain Thomas F Tellman, pilot, who went missing in action in 1948?

Yup. What about it?

Oh wow, man. Totally cool. Sorry, this is so awesome. Did you, like, travel inside a flying saucer?

Who are you, may I ask? Thomas frowns, leaning on the door frame. *And how did you hear about me living here?*

Oh sorry, I should have explained, but I'm a bit star-struck. Star struck, eh? Good one? I'm Jeff Prentiss, editor of UFO Watch Magazine. I heard a rumour. A friend of a friend, then I did a bit of digging.

Editor, eh? Thomas chuckles. *How many staff do you have?*

Well, oh, two I guess, although one of them's part-time. And the other one's me. But we do sterling work, I can assure you. Much respected, for keeping the dream alive against all the sceptics. Have you ever... read, seen us?

I was kinda busy getting abducted for the last 80 years, to be honest. I've got a lot of reading to catch up on. A 'TBR' pile, I believe it's called.

Could we interview you by any chance?

Thomas sighs. *I don't think so. Not yet.*

Aw, how come, man? You're the real deal, big news. The world needs to know, to learn about what you've seen. I mean, what are they like, what planet are they from? Are they benign or hostile? What are their plans for Earth?

*What are **your** plans for Earth?*

Sorry?

You seem so desperate to find out about life from other

planets. But where do you think such knowledge will get you?

I don't know, are you serious? It's just the most fascinating and exciting idea ever, isn't it? Just to know there's other life out there and we're not alone.

Is it? But what does it change? There is alien life out there, I've seen it and met it. There, I've told you. How's that? Feeling better? Ahh... anti-climax perhaps?

You got any pictures? Of what they look like? Drawings even?

Sure. Lend me your phone and I'll show you. Thomas take the young man's mobile phone and takes a photo of him and hands it back to him. *There. That's what they look like. You know what's really the most exciting thing in the whole universe? I'll tell you. It's finding a beautiful blue planet, bristling with a vast array of interconnected lifeforms all working in harmony, all built by the same mysterious unseen force that continues to control and regulate all that fabulous complexity. All that fertility amid the arid empty black vacuum of space. Now that is fascinating. That is here and now. That is what you are part of. That is what you should be excited about. And excited about saving from all the damage we as a species are doing to it. I'll give you a new planet, son, when you leave off trashing this one.*

Oh wow. Hey I recycle, man, I don't eat meat.

I know, I know. Look, come here. Thomas hugs him until tears fill his eyes. *I will go on television, but not yet. Thanks for coming all this way. But go home and live and cherish and breathe the air of this world. Ask out that girl who works in the library that you've got a thing for. Take long walks in the countryside just after sunrise. Live your life on Earth. It's the best fucking planet on this spiral arm of the galaxy, believe me. Vote for politicians who give a shit about any of this.*

Thomas, Thomas, you are awesome. Will you autograph this photograph?

What is it?

It's you of course, from 1947. You've not aged a day.

Here's my card. Send me an email when you're ready to talk to the world. People will love you. Hey, I love you already.

Thomas waves, smiles, and shakes his head simultaneously, watching from the door, as Jeff Prentiss climbs onto his motorcycle, puts on his helmet, and roars off.

Who wiz that, Daddy? Wan o' they Jehova's or Insurance Salesmen? Mary asks from her bed, as Thomas returns to her room.

Just some UFO nut, Mary. Wanted to know how you'd travelled forward in time by 80 years. I told him you weren't giving interviews.

48

Back in London, Louise hands out magnets to her Secondary School Physics class, and tells them they are going to perform a new experiment today. She draws diagrams and equations on the blackboard in chalk, while the children split into groups of eight and construct arrays of electromagnets around a central pile of iron filings which they propose to levitate. As she finishes talking, she looks across their heads towards the view of green fields behind them being churned up by mechanical diggers, building yet more housing. A feeling comes over her briefly, of standing on the threshold of something, some new chapter whose page her hand is turning.

49

Four men of indeterminate age, in black suits, walk into a grey-painted boardroom at RAF Kinburgh Air Base. Initially they had asked for a room without windows, but being told this was impossible opted instead for one facing onto neither the sea nor any public roadway, however distant. Paranoia is the routine order of the day, a dogma they live by. Once seated, one of them opens a folder and announces an agenda. The rank and pecking-order between the men remains oddly unclear. One of them stands up from time to time to pace the room and gaze across the military playing fields in mild agitation. The wind has picked up today and leaves are falling from the mature trees around the compound, their fading colours a portent of the shabby melancholy of autumn to come.

The round of voices commences like a game, something hypnotic in their manner of speech, each similar to each other, a certain inner tiredness, tinged with fatalistic sadness, like the gods on Mount Olympus debating how to clean up the latest mess Zeus has made while disguised as an animal.

We've been here before, haven't we? We all know we have?

Sure. There have been Tellmans before and there will doubtless be others in future. It always plays out the same way.

Meaning?

Sooner or later, there's a message. Something he realises, or decides, he has to convey to the public, as large an audience as possible.

This one's biding his time, then.

You know why.

We do?

We do and he does. As ever, the only solution is to discredit the witness. Often once he raises his head, but probably better before he even does so.

How?

We use the police.

Dangerous. Always leaky as a sieve, especially out in the sticks like this.

Then we use the leaks. We announce him as a wanted man. Something private, embarrassing, no public dimension. Like a paedo.

Too strong. You want publicity, not hysteria.

Something financial then? Obscure trading crime.

Too complex to manufacture collateral collaboration in the relevant fields.

A murder, or rape?

Possibly, keeps it small and personal. A crime of passion, a few sordid details, enough to remove sympathy, you know the sketch. Stole an old lady's jewels. Buried the wife under a new concrete floor, that sort of thing.

We'll get working on it.

But we have to be confident of where he is first. If it turns into a manhunt, Raoul fucking Moat style, then we're snookered. A few days media circus only, standard tabloid vilification, then take him in, kill the story.

What about the sentence? Later interviews with fellow inmates?

Good point. It needs to be extendable. A secure institution.

Then we need some weird stuff. You know, mutilations, major psychiatric disorder. Not enough for panic, just public distaste.

Cannibalism?

Way too strong. You know better.

I was joking.

Very good. You really had us there… sighs the most silent of the four laconically, now standing still up at the window, watching the cadets running out onto the blaes pitch to begin a game of off-duty football.

Everything alright, John? Asks the agenda-reader, winking at one of the others.

It's all a game to you young lads, isn't it? But one of

*these times, our defence isn't going to work. Then we'll
need a striker.*

*That's a new one. John only invents a new euphemism
on Tuesdays...* The agenda man jokes.

And withdraws it on Thursdays? Everyone laughs, even
John as he turns around, to their relief.

*You know the drill then, right? We'll need leverage on
the Doctor and on the Detective Inspector.*

And on journalists?

*No more than usual. Quick wave of the badge should
keep them in line. Any outliers we'll deal with as special
cases. But the quack and the plod already know more
than they know they do. Time for some...*

Hedge trimming, keeping our garden in order?

Topiary... John sighs, the great metaphor mixer, back
at the window again, watching the distant young men
dodging and dribbling around each other with the elusive
white flash of a ball between their boots. *There's
something creative in that. But no prima donnas please.
No own goals...*

*

Seated cross-legged on the polished wooden attic floor of
Annie Bevan's flat, Thomas watches the entire scene of
the four men in black suits in the grey-painted room,
playing out on a glowing colour sphere he is holding in
his hand. Young Bruce comes stomping into the room
laughing, and Thomas smiles, switches the sphere back to
solid silver and bounces it across the room for the boy to
catch. Thomas stands up and crosses the room to the
hallway were he picks up the phone and dials Doctor
McCaffrey's number: *Hey Doc, it's me. Remember you
said you'd help me if the thing I feared started
happening? Well, it's starting now.*

50

At 5.00pm the following evening, as he's preparing to lock up the surgery, Doctor McCaffrey receives a telephone call from Detective Inspector Drummond. *You were right, Jimmy. We were right. British Intelligence have just been on the phone. They want to take both you and I in together.*

When?

More or less now. Their car will be at my door in five minutes apparently, then we can come over and pick you up in fifteen.

Where are they taking us?

The Air Base. Where else?

Extraordinary Rendition is it?

Not all that extraordinary. Relax. They just want information, they say, then they'll leave us alone.

*You keep saying 'we'? What do **you** know about Thomas Tellman?*

Well, you just reminded me of his name, thanks, Jimmy. Maybe I know more than you realise, or I realise. Or maybe it's about what they want me to know, or to start believing and telling everyone.

I think I get your drift. Nothing for it then.

*

Two cars arrive, one of them Drummond's with an Intelligence official inside, the other one a black Audi with two further officials, one of them driving. The convoy then heads off out of Kinburgh to the Air Base, whose gates they are waved through without questioning. The doctor takes comfort from arriving with a policeman, as antidote to the general air of threat and misdemeanor which seems to hang heavy in the air.

They are quickly led up the stairs to an unprepossessing room within a timber-plank clad annexe painted in shades of grey and blue. Coffee and tea are offered but refused.

The official sits opposite them and begins, while one other plain-clothes man stands on guard outside the door, the back of his head visible, occasionally taking calls.

So, gentlemen, thanks for coming in to help us with our enquiries. We'll try not to detain you long. We'll start with you, Inspector. What do you know about Thomas Tellman? He pushes a couple of photograph across the table to him.

Not all that much. A nurse, or local authority carer, came in to file a report with us a month or two ago, saying that someone, who I now realise was probably the man who you are interested in, had suddenly appeared at the house of an elderly lady who he claimed was his daughter. Further claiming that he has been missing for the last eighty years and hadn't aged. I dismissed the story as nonsense of course and the witness as scarcely credible, being probably motivated by some kind of personal grudge or another. It's all here in my file, such as it is, I've brought you a copy.

Thank you, Inspector. And you, Doctor?

McCaffrey clears his throat. *I too have brought along a photocopy of my file, the medical records of Thomas Tellman. The first part is historic, a document dating from 1948, since it is my considered judgement that the gentleman who I examined at my surgery is the same individual, however unlikely that may sound, as the Thomas Tellman who went missing, presumed dead while on active duty in 1948. I took the liberty of testing a sample of his DNA and having a local university compare it to DNA still detectable on items of clothing that were owned by the 'original' Tellman, as it were. They are a perfect match, right down to the degree of degradation in the older sample, concomitant with the passage of eight decades.*

Unusual steps to take, for a General Practitioner. But go on please... the official says, taking a few notes.

The patient wanted a general medical check-up, so that he would potentially be able to get a National Insurance number, a job, driving licence, bank account and insurance and so forth, so I conducted a full physical examination. His condition and fitness seemed consistent with the age of 26 years which he ascribed to himself. I did however find a couple of significant anomalies in his physiology, matters which while causing him no discomfort or ill-effects, would attract widespread medical interest in any other situation where patient confidentiality were not at stake.

Go on, please... The official asks again.

Syndactyly. In layman's terms: while his fingers were normal, all of his toes on both feet were fused. X-ray revealed that the bones inside were fairly normal, but that the skin tissue extended completely around all five falanges and metatarsals, including the hallux.

He has webbed feet in other words?

Yes, you might choose to phrase it like that, but to an extraordinary, and as far I can gather, unique degree. Human syndactyly is a generally rare birth defect, due to some failure in foetal development, and typically results in only partial fusion of one or two fingers, rarely toes, all of which can be corrected with surgery, skin grafts in extreme cases. Tellman's is the most extreme case I know of.

Anything else, Doctor?

Yes, while his genitals appeared superficially normal, he had, as far as I was able to ascertain, no testicles inside his scrotal sac.

You mean he was a eunuch, effectively?

That term is seldom used these days, and often misunderstood, although it makes a fascinating topic for historical research, in terms of the noble roles afforded to them in ancient societies. Castrations today are much more common than perhaps the average layman realises, for a variety of reasons, often related to cancer and its complications. A man can function perfectly well without one or even both testicles, can even generate testosterone from other sources within the body, certainly with occasional top-up injections.

Did someone castrate Tellman, did you think?

I don't believe so, there would be signs, marks. As with

his fused toes, I believe this condition to be simply how he was born.

But are those observations on his original medical records of 1948?

No.

That's a bit of a contradiction then. How do you account for that?

I don't. Unless my medical predecessors somehow missed those details.

That doesn't sound likely, surely. Did the subject offer any explanation of his own?

I think he muttered something about him being injured when his rescuers took him on board their ship, and them having to perform restorative surgery on him, but I didn't take him seriously at that moment.

How do you personally believe therefore, that Thomas Tellman came by his webbed feet and missing gonads?

I have no scientifically feasible explanation. But my most logical hypothesis, based only on the facts I have, is that he is the product of a more advanced stage of human evolution.

Can you be more specific, Doctor?

I mean, toes are basically vestigial, we have no uses for them. Our feet used to be another pair of hands, for swinging around in trees with, but now they're just hooves basically. He is like one of us, but as if born several thousand years into the future. His intelligence, his memory and awareness, struck me as extraordinary. Although I did not carry out any detailed psychological tests, let alone brain scans. I should also add that he had no body hair.

But we see it on his head in these photos, Doctor, do we not?

That isn't hair, strictly speaking. It's not organic, which is why it doesn't grow, and Mr Tellman will never need a haircut. I got a sample tested at the same university as looked into the DNA for me. Our nearest equivalent would be some kind of plastic, but engineered to have a fibrous form very closely resembling human hair in texture and colour.

What do you make of that, Doctor?

Again, any logical hypotheses also sounds absurd. But if anything, it's a possible clue as to the patient's origins, and to a degree of deception, either on his part or the part of others responsible for his sudden re-appearance here. He seemed unaware that his hair was inorganic, and that his 1948 counterpart had body hair, but it's hard for me know when he is, or is not, telling the truth, given that his central belief, which he does apparently believe entirely, is that he was born in 1922 and went missing in 1948 and travelled for 80 of our years without ageing. All an irresolvable impossibility, from our perspective and current scientific understanding.

Thank you, Doctor. Does that conclude the substance of your report? Can we ask that you keep all this confidential?

You can ask, but there's no real need. Why wouldn't I? Medical records are confidential, so I won't by definition, as a professional, be passing the details of this on to anyone else without the patient's consent. Can I ask that you do the same?

The offical laughs, not unkindly. *Well, maybe I'd mirror your comments and point to motivation. Why would we want to reveal any of this to a larger audience?*

True. As I understand your work and your interest, which is to say only vaguely, your concern is to prevent public panic when anomalous evidence comes to light redolent of technology far in advance of that of the Ministry of Defence department of Her Majesty's government.

The official looks at him with narrowed eyes, wondering if he detects a hint of irony or sarcasm. *Well, that concludes the first part of our meeting, and in our second I would like to present you both with what we know about the subject, Thomas Tellman, and what we would ask yourselves, Inspector Drummond particularly, to pass on to the public in terms of an official explanation of this case.*

Go on please... Drummond interjects smiling, definitely with irony this time.

The individual you know as Thomas Tellman is an alcoholic vagrant with a history of schizophrenia originally from Virginia, USA, who arrived in Scotland two years ago on a one-way ticket purchased by his estranged parents, and has been begging on the streets of Edinburgh, Dundee, and Aberdeen prior to his arrival here. While in a homeless hostel in Aberdeen he attacked and killed a fellow resident, and went on the run from the police, attempting to change his name and identity. While in Aberdeen it is believed he also acquired his interest in, and knowledge of, Ufology, as it's sometimes called, from a fellow resident who had once been a RAF pilot. Here is the abstract of our file, one copy for each of you, which we would ask you to bear in mind, and in your case, Inspector, to release as part of a press conference in the near future to see if the assistance of members of the public can be secured in order to aid in this man's apprehension.

Doctor McCaffrey casts his eye over the printed page briefly and resists the temptation to screw the piece of paper into a ball and lob it out the window.

*

After McCaffrey and Drummond leave, the interviewer goes into the next room, where 'John' has been standing, watching the meeting through a two-way mirror. *What did you think?* The agent asks.

I think it was a mistake to interview them together... John sighs, grimacing, swilling the dregs of his paper coffee cup. *You don't know what you're dealing with in places like this. They all know each other, thick as thieves. I'd say they're in cahoots already. We've probably only hardened that link, not broken it. We could lose this game unless we take it up a gear.*

*

Outside in the car park, as Drummond prepares to give McCaffrey a lift home, he produces a small hand-held metal wand from his inside pocket and scans his vehicle.

What are you up to there?

Just checking for bugs, Jimmy. All clear, right get in.

On their way out the compound gates, Drummond asks: *Well, did you believe any of that?*

No. I know an alcoholic when I meet one, even a reformed one, and a homeless man for that matter. The wear and tear, the shakes, the liver damage. It should be a simple matter to verify or disprove their story, given the very distinctive physical characteristics, abnormalities that Tellman has, that would show up in any medical history of the other man.

Drummond arrives at the main road and turns towards the town. *Yes, that's what I was thinking. I have friends in the Aberdeen City North division, I'll give them a call, make some discreet enquiries of my own, take a drive through if I need to. If their story is bullshit then I'm damned if I'm going to be used as their stooge to promulgate it. I'm too near to retirement for that. Kept my integrity, almost, this far, I'm not going to lose it now for those shite bags. They think they're above everyone and everything, think they can manipulate the public, the truth, reality. I don't like them on my patch. The RAF I can tolerate on a good day, when they keep themselves to themselves. But those cockroaches give me the creeps.*

Drummond drives around the outskirts of Kinburgh, passing the brewery and on towards the pleasant fields of wheat rolling down to the Firth. They both reminisce briefly about years gone by, the school they went to, hills they roamed freely on as kids. Drummond exclaims: *I recall we could wander around anywhere we wanted all day, hiked for miles. Our parents turfed us out in the morning and hadn't a clue where we went, unlike today's closeted collection, chauffeur driven around between sleepovers in unnecessary four-by-fours. I worry that it makes them all more timid, more entitled, less use in a crisis.*

I've had the same thought. That Tellman fellow, funnily enough, made me reflect on it. His 1940's attitudes, presuming they weren't some spectacular piece of acting or invention, reminded me of something we don't see in the young so much now. A certain integrity and sense of responsibility, an eye on the bigger picture.

The Doctor's house is in a small hamlet in the hills above Kinburgh with a view north towards the open sea. When they come to a halt, Drummond asks: *Do you ever remember us, Jimmy? That incident way back then. I know we're bug free in here, so I might as well ask now.*

The doctor flinches a little. *Jesus, Hugh. That was centuries ago, we were just kids. It was nothing, we didn't know what we were doing. What you doing talking about stuff like that for?*

I'm asking as a friend, not as a moral arbiter or town gaoler. I'm just curious. Just between you and I. You ever had any dalliances again over the years, you know... of that nature?

Give it a rest. No, of course not. It wasn't who I am. I don't understand it now. I had plenty of girlfriends after that. I've been happy with Emily.... What about you?

Same. But good to know, in case these goons try to manufacture anything on us.

Are they capable of that, d'you think?

Oh, they're capable of anything I reckon, history suggests. The only defence is to be insignificant to them. Take care now. My regards to Emily. Goodnight.

Before going to the house, Doctor McCaffrey stays standing for a moment, deep in thought, looking after Drummond's car as it vanishes down the hill, leaving behind a cloud of dust like a long twisting ghost, slowly settling back down onto the sheaves of ripe corn.

*

The Doctor takes a brief telephone call at his surgery the next day from Inspector Drummond:

Jimmy, I won't talk for long. Just to say it's as we

thought. The Aberdeen vagrant story is an invented decoy. The schizophrenic guy who killed someone in a homeless hostel was never found, suspected suicide, but he didn't look remotely like Tellman, in fact he was short, just over five feet, walked with a limp, blind in one eye and had learning difficulties. If that's the man you wrote a medical report on then I'm a monkey's uncle.

Fair enough, Hugh, thanks for calling me. We'll talk again soon... McCaffrey answers, then hangs up to return to his patient Mrs Robertson, who has been complaining of dizzy spells recently.

51

Waking up for the first time at Annie's house, Thomas decides to tell her over breakfast the decision he has made about his future. She sends Bruce out of the room to play, once she begins to realise the gravity of what he is saying.

I'm going to go down to the newspaper and television offices in Inverness today to get interviewed.

What about? Annie asks.

You know, where I went for the last 80 years. My impression of everything I've found since I've got back.

Is that wise?

It's probably inevitable. I'd hoped to keep it off for longer, but various people have been sniffing around recently, coming out to the house. Reporters, even British Intelligence. You know, spooks, nutters. I don't want them bothering Mary. If my story is going to come out, I'd rather it was my way and on my terms.

Annie sighs. *There's more to this though, more than you're telling, isn't there?*

How do you mean?

I've always sensed it. Something you're planning. Something you're holding back.

Maybe... Thomas says, and stands up with his coffee cup in his hand, to go over and gaze out the window down to the scenes of ordinary street life below. *Their tiny universe is shaken... so few drink from the fountain of truth.*

What's that a quote from?

A foolish Italian poet who lost his way, got caught up in prejudice and politics.

Dante? Looking for his Beatrice in Hades?

No, not that one. I won't lose my way. And we mustn't look back, only forward. Hades, eh? The underworld in Greek myth. The ultimate reward for the virtuous in life was to visit the Fields of Elysium and drink from the waters of the River Lethe, which granted them forgetfulness.

Well, I hope you're going to be a bit less cryptic than this on national television.

52

Janet McComish, Editor of the Kinburgh Herald is called down to reception to meet a surprise visitor, a man of indeterminate age in a black suit. He shows her an identity badge in his pocket that identifies him as a member of the Intelligence Services, asking her not to run any news stories about Thomas Tellman. *Too late...* she halts him, and switches on the large television on the wall behind him so they can both watch the live interview now underway. By the time Janet turns around, the mysterious black-suited gentleman has left the building without any further comment.

She turns back and walks towards the recording studio. She stares through the plate glass screens, her gaze gradually telescoping, zooming in past the cameramen towards the heart of the studio where Thomas is seated at the usual lunchtime discussion table with popular host Viv Denholm on her citrus-bright sofas on a desert island of stylish rugs, amid a sea of laminate flooring. A view of the Inverness riverside is always visible over the shoulders of her and her guests, one of whom today is, she announces: *Local celebrity Thomas Tellman, who claims to be an RAF pilot who went missing in 1948 while pursuing a UFO in the air over the Moray Firth. Thomas is here along with his family doctor James McCaffrey who has conducted medical examinations and DNA tests on Thomas and now believes Thomas to be who he claims to be. The catch? Thomas appears to be 26 years old, exactly the same age as when he left 80 years ago...*

Viv having thus concluded her prepared introduction to welcome viewers back after the commercial break, then smooths her skirt, checks her tie-pin microphone and retires to the sofa zone to join Thomas and James and ask them some of those hundred burning questions that the viewers are dying to ask. *Thomas, where do you believe you were for the last eighty years?*

Well... Thomas smiles, *to you it was eighty years but to me it was only about one year I'd say, although it wasn't always possible for me to judge time.*

Where were you?

Most of the time, on-board the silver hovering object that I was pursuing in my aeroplane in 1948, just before I lost consciousness.

Wooahhh. I wasn't alive in 1948 of course, Thomas, and I hope I look as good as you when I'm eighty! But this was a military plane you were flying, wasn't it?

Yeah, a Hawker Sea Fury, for RAF Kinburgh.

But that's an American accent you have there, how's that?

I grew up in Kentucky in the States, and joined the Air Force there but was transferred here at the outbreak of the war.

World War Two.

Yes, and stationed at Prestwick at first on the Scottish west coast, where I met a Scots girl, whom I married, Eleanor Anderson.

Who sadly passed away in the intervening years I believe?

Yes, in 1985.

But you had children?

Yes a boy and a girl. One of whom, Mary, is still alive I was happy to discover.

And what age is she?

Eighty seven.

Wow. Now hold on, so you left behind a seven-year-old girl, and you came back to find she was an elderly woman, eighty seven years old?

Yeah, that's correct.

What on earth was that like, finding she was still alive and finding she was so old?

Good of course to find her at all, but also painful and sad to see she had aged so much, and especially painful finding out her little brother had died in the years in between.

I'm so sorry to hear that. My sincere condolences. How is your daughter keeping?

A little infirm or else we might have brought her in today. I live with her at the moment, since we've had a lot of catching up to do, and she's really the only close family I have left now, as far as I'm aware.

Thomas, I'm going to turn to Doctor McCaffrey in a moment, because a lot of people, understandably I hope you'll agree, will be sceptical and have quite a bit of difficulty believing your story...

Sure, yeah, I get that, it's certainly understandable.

But first I want to ask you the burning question. This UFO that took you on board and took you away, you said, what was it like inside and what sort of beings – your hosts presumably – were flying this thing, and how did they treat you?

I reckon that was about three questions actually, but I'll try to just answer them quickly although I could also do so at great length. Inside this thing was very bright, filled with white light, but once my eyes adjusted I could see that most of the surfaces were silver metal, very smooth but matt, mostly not reflective, although some surfaces were also a kind of glass-like material that could change from opaque to transparent if required by the operators. They, my hosts as you put it, were not all that unlike us really, just a bit less tall and mostly much older than any of us get to be, with very pale, wrinkled skin.

Like the 'grey' aliens that have been depicted in the media and popular folklore?

Well, I've caught up with stuff like that since I've been back, with this new-fangled 'internet' gizmo that you all seem to be obsessed with. I'd say all the 'grey alien' images are similar to the way people of the past glimpsed seals and then invented mermaids, or the ancient Greeks glimpsed men on horseback and thought they were centaurs. My hosts weren't 'Greys' as such in the way you mean, but I can see a resemblance there to an extent that might explain all the rumours and myths that have arisen over the years. And they treated me very well. They know a great deal about us, maybe more than we know about ourselves. They've been studying us for many thousands of years.

Well, my word – turning to you, Doctor McCaffrey, Thomas seems pretty sane and normal, despite his remarkable claims. I know a lot of people will be dying to know now: can his story possibly by true or could there be some other explanation for what he believes?

I was very sceptical at first, as anyone would be. And being medically trained, I don't have any truck with mumbo-jumbo. Also I know how to spot key signs of someone being delusional or schizophrenic and so forth. But after my first meeting with Thomas, I was intrigued enough to organise a series of tests, whose results increasingly surprised me and other researchers. His daughter Mary still had clothes of his, and other possessions of his, even a lock of hair, from 1948 or shortly before. We were able to test Thomas's DNA and compare it to those samples, and they were a perfect match. Also his knowledge of people and events from 1948 are exceptional. We've researched a great deal of his memories, which are apparently very fresh to him, and in every case found them to be extremely accurate. I know it seems very hard to believe, impossible even, but as Arthur Conan Doyle said: 'When you have eliminated the impossible, whatever remains, however improbable, must be the truth', and I think in Thomas's case we may be close to that stage.

In part two, after the commercial break, things take a turn for the even more controversial. Viv reads out some questions telephoned in from viewers, and begins with this one: '*Do you believe in God, Thomas? Did those beings have anything to say on the subject of God?*'

Yes. They said they regarded religion as a laughable piece of primitivism on our part. They demonstrated this by asking me the simple question of whether I thought every planet out there in the cosmos with intelligent life on it would have its own Jesus, or whether I thought ours was travelling around like Santa Claus or a travelling salesman. They told me that the thing we call God, whose presence some of us think we feel, is actually Gaia, the force of life itself which is a kind of global root system, a green brain which controls all life on the planet and talks to itself through all living cells. They told me this brain is aware and able to regulate the world, even the climate, and the activities of all living creatures, and in this sense matches closely to our concept of God. They said if we wanted to worship anything, we should worship that, by paying closer attention to our stewardship of the natural environment and showing more respect and understanding for all other forms of life other than just ourselves.

That's extraordinary. But what about right and wrong?

They said that was all made up, for us to make up. Something for us to invent for each of our societies and cultures, as appropriate to each. We could rape and rob and kill each other if we liked, but any society built on that would always disintegrate. They said that what we call 'good' is only common sense, and is the only thing that works, in terms of human interaction, in the long run.

What about Jesus then?

A brilliant practical philosopher, who genuinely changed our world for the better, as did many other prophets such as Gautama Buddha, Muhammad, Mahatma Gandhi and Martin Luther King.

You do realise there's quite a lot of people who may be offended by what you just said?

The sooner the better, because we all need to grow up and wake up – rise to the occasion of protecting our environment from the harm that we ourselves are doing to it. We need to worship the earth, not men.

But what do you believe will happen if we don't? If people don't heed your warning, just as they have failed to heed many others from other people before?

Well, I have an answer to that question, which I intend to unveil next week in a very large public forum.

Really? What do you mean? A football stadium or arena somewhere?

Much more than that. A public address, not just to the media and ordinary people but to their political leaders.

What do you intend to show them?

The future.

Viv looks up and off to the right side of the cameras, to where Janet McComish is signalling to her – with a gesture seldom used except in an emergency – telling her to wind up the broadcast and go to the commercial break early. Later she will be told the reason: one of the television company's major shareholders had phoned in expressing his disquiet at the potentially blasphemous comments – especially aired at an hour he judged many of the station's older and more traditionalist viewers would be tuned in.

53

After the unfortunate confusion of 'Rookie' reporter Lesley Crawford's meeting with Mary Tellman, her next assignment turns out to be more of a scoop. What is anticipated to be a rather boring routine press briefing from the local constabulary regarding a historic unsolved case, unexpectedly turns into something else. Detective Inspector Drummond makes an extraordinary and historic announcement, with the cameras rolling, setting off political earthquakes that will create friction between British Intelligence and Scottish democracy.

I have here a public statement, a press release, that I was more or less instructed by the British Intelligence services to read aloud to camera... Drummond begins. *However, due to what I judge to be a series of major untruths contained within that statement, I am now going to make an entirely different statement, one of much greater veracity and reliability. It is my belief that, for reasons unknown, the British intelligence services are engaged in a smear campaign against one Thomas Tellman, a 26 year old male resident within this parish, a former RAF pilot who claims to have recently returned from an 80-year hiatus or possible coma state due to an encounter with an unidentified aerial phenomenon. I have no means of knowing, nor does anyone I suspect, whether Mr Tellman's claims of interaction with off-world technological vehicles can possibly be true, or just the symptom of some kind of hallucination or brain injury. I do know however, from reliable sources, that he is who he says he is and was born in 1922, meaning his apparent youth and vigour eight decades later should be a matter of scientific curiosity and enquiry, rather than persecution. Persecution being what I believe is the intention of this spurious dossier of untruths I hold in my hand, and which I have no intention of reading from today. My question to the media, to our political leaders and to the public at large is this one: what has this man really done to merit the excessive interest the intelligence services have taken in him? What has he to say, that the intelligence services wish so much to prevent him from saying?*

54

Chrissy feels like a criminal turning up for her disciplinary hearing convened by senior management at local authority Home Care. She hasn't felt so sick since she was a schoolgirl, brought before the head teacher for showing her pants, and worse, off to boys under the desks in maths class. Her anger and dread has transmuted during the past month of her suspension into something else, which today manifests itself in its ultimate expression: a kind of numb trance, in which she moves and talks mechanically.

She scarcely hears the charges against her conduct read out. When given the brief chance to speak at last, she voices her concerns over Thomas Tellman without passion, reiterates her well-meaning attempts to protect Mary Tellman from perceived harm without conviction. Fails to answer when Helen Murchison asks her if she understands and respects the rights all clients and patients have to privacy, lest their personal affairs be misconstrued and distorted by newspapers and other media. Especially, Helen emphasises, in light of the recent developments in the media which all present will have seen and heard last night. Chrissy lifts her head at this point, puzzled, unaware what everyone around the table is referring to and nodding their heads about. She and Kenny spent last night in the pub – one without television – followed by a long lie-in. She feels estranged from these people, from her surroundings, and begins to tune out instead of listening any further, taking great interest in the details of historic architecture and features behind everyone in this splendid room in a splendid building in a splendid old town. The carved oak panelling, the moulded skirtings and dado rail, the architraves around the doors, the elaborate capitals and scrolls at their head, dripping with fruit and veg and obscure little Masonic symbols... confirming of course her deepest of intuitions regarding justice: that it is all a conspiracy.

Thus when the committee's judgement is read out, one of professional misconduct resulting in her immediate dismissal and permanent ban from health care work in the public sector, she is able to hear it all out without the slightest emotion, even appearing ready to remain seated in the room after the meeting breaks up, tuned in to some higher plane and more tangible reality. She wonders vaguely what it is inside her that gave rise to this? What hidden design flaw in her being? What trigger or booby-trap that lay hidden in her attitude and outlook all these years, just waiting to snag on this peculiar chain of recent circumstances?

55

In the top floor penthouse apartment of an incongruously tall modern building above the Bassin Vergote in Brussels, a Monsieur De Smedt waits for two visitors to be ushered in; one English, one American. De Smedt is established on paper as a wealthy industrialist and respectable Belgian citizen, his assets and interests lauded, quantified, and taxed – but within a certain rarefied international circle he is tacitly known to be something more. The two guards at his front door are well-armed, but very discreetly. Everything is discreet here. Nothing too indelicate is ever too openly drawn out into the daylight to be dissected or explored; it is understood by those who visit in such circumstances that this is always the work of various unseen subordinates, the dotting of the i's and crossing of the t's. De Smedt welcomes the two men in, then offers them drinks. He strikes his guests as impossibly tall, much like the tower whose top he chooses to dominate, although neither of them are quite bold or poetic enough to crystallise the metaphor. He invites them to gaze down with him at the broad glittering canal far below, and the tracts of disused industrial land either side of it currently in the midst of transformation by mechanical diggers like rampaging dinosaurs, forging it into future green spaces for charming joggers and cyclists to whistle through in perennial flurries of fitness and joie de vivre.

De Smedt's taste in interior design is lavish but exclusively masculine, veering towards polished metals and glass wherever soft fabrics threaten to rear their head. His potted plants are predominately large and unusual cacti. His taste in ornaments and trophies betrays a certain preference for violence and the hunt. Stuffed eagles, boar's heads and antique swords, priceless dark oil paintings of claustrophobic medieval scenes. He claps his hands, to signal the transition to talking business. *Did you ever hear the one about the American, the*

Englishman and the Belgian? he asks his guests, *All of them in black suits, none of them with names – or at least not real names, the real names their parents gave them?*

The Englishman shakes his head and looks down briefly at the floor, while the American looks up and attempts an appeasing smile, lamely.

No? Funny that. Me neither. Because nothing in this room, this apartment, ever goes any further than these walls, as I trust you know. So please be relaxed, gentlemen, and tell me what's on your mind.

The Englishman produces a photograph from his pocket and hands it to De Smedt. *This man is currently in Scotland, and we believe may shortly be coming here to this city.*

A tourist? We get a great many, with so much history here.

He will be high profile by the time he gets here, we expect, not a tourist. He has become very vexatious to his home nations.

Britain?

And America, where he was born, whose accent he still speaks with. The American chips in. *Both London and Washington have agreed a substantial shared interest in this. We need there to be an incident here. Something random and almost personal in nature, no whiff of course of state involvement. Any state.*

De Smedt has been watching the American wide-eyed, with close attention, eyebrows raised. He now turns back towards the Englishman.

But he has no relatives or friends here, no connections, which is both bad and good... The Englishman adds.

I think I see, De Smedt muses, rubbing his brow, thinking deeply. *You need a motive, a low one, that leads back to nowhere other than itself, leads only to some little man in a squalid apartment, who does not read his newspapers.*

Precisely. The Englishman allows himself a smile of satisfaction. *Who has scarcely travelled, remains demonstrably ignorant of global affairs, has never been a member of any political party, at least not any mainstream or credible ones.*

Wait. De Smedt interrupts him, hand raised. *May I see that photo again? Thank you. I think I may have such a man as you seek, but of course he is by definition a trained operative of the highest calibre, with some background in the special forces. Therefore unfortunately extremely valuable as an erstwhile ongoing asset. You will need to make it clear to me whether you wish him, if it is to be he who we choose, to survive the event. Because if he does not, then the chances of him being traced back to us, the three of us in this room, would be agreeably small, very small indeed. But as I've said, extremely expensive to thus irrevocably lose him. The other thing that strikes me, strikes me as potentially fortuitous in this case, is that the man I have in mind is, how shall we say... racist. Deeply so, I believe, having some history in right-wing fringe organisations, low-level, scarcely political groups – incoherent really, but violent certainly, harassing of immigrants and so forth.*

The American nods his head vigorously. *Yes, I see your point. That's good.*

The Englishman takes a deep breath. *Would it be credible? Racial hatred, resentment of a black man in the public eye, simple racism so focused as to seek to actually make a lone wolf attack?*

De Smedt leans his head to the side in consideration, pours himself more tonic and proffers the decanter to his guests before he continues: *I believe so, although perhaps some related psychiatric issues could be thrown into the mix. What sane man after all, would risk a long jail sentence for so petty an act against a stranger merely for the colour of his skin?*

There would have to be no jail sentence, the Englishman responds.

Nor any trial. The American chips in. *Just a second man to remove him, as you alluded to. Then an apartment to be picked over, loaded with all the appropriate evidence, fanaticism, obsession and so forth. The second man must remain elusive however, unseen, unapprehended, thus remains your asset going forward. Perhaps what he undertakes looks like a suicide, even in custody if necessary.*

Well, thank you, gentlemen, for your thoughts. De Smedt puts his drink down and rubs his hands together. *I do believe, off the top of my head, that all of that sounds eminently achievable. We never talk of money here, as you know. So allow me to retire now while I consider a figure to convey to you through our intermediaries. I hope you enjoy our lovely city for the rest of your stay. I bid you good day.*

56

As Thomas opens the back door of Annie's second floor
flat on Ruthven Street, he is shocked to see a small crowd
of religious fanatics waiting for him, some carrying
placards, calling him a demon and the devils' emissary.
He is saddened to glimpse Magdalena and even the
erstwhile atheist Chrissy among them. He needs to reach
his morning appointments at the newspaper headquarters
and Grampian Broadcasting Studio unhindered. While
Annie goes out to distract and reason with the crowd, her
boy in her arms to attempt to soften their hearts, Thomas
telephones a taxi then climbs through the attic window
onto the north-facing slope, and crawls his way on all
fours along the slate roof of the terrace. Reaching the
corner house, he considers the rainwater downpipes then
curses that the old cast-iron has been replaced in flimsy
black plastic. He crosses the ridge and using the heavily-
leaved branches of an old oak tree as visual cover, leaps
towards the back garden below, landing in a parachutist's
somersault as he was trained to, without breaking any
bones. His interviewers for the day are surprised to see
him arrive in torn trousers and muddy shirt, offering him
replacements in the make-up room.

57

Tonight on Channel Six we are going to be discussing the breaking news phenomenon surrounding Thomas Tellman, a former RAF pilot who went missing in 1948 and now claims to have returned, un-aged, to the town he was stationed in. The catch? Mister Tellman claims to have been in the care of extra-terrestrial beings for the last eighty years, often travelling close to the speed of light – this being his explanation for why he has not aged relative to those he left behind, – an effect consistent with Einstein's theory of relativity. A far-fetched story, surely? Mass hysteria whipped up on social media? Or a genuine cause for scientific interest? DNA tests carried out independently by three separate universities in Britain and America, have reputedly authenticated Tellman's DNA as a match to clothing he left behind. So what as to the rest of his outlandish claims? Videos have been circulating on the internet of Tellman levitating objects, supposedly as a demonstration of the advanced technology he learned about during his interstellar travels.

In order to explore the credibility of these claims and the issues they raise, as well as the significance of figures like Tellman in social history, I am joined now by social scientist and self-described professional sceptic and debunker Professor Deanna Carvela, author of The Messiah Complex and Dogma Bites Man. Professor, what do you make of the Tellman phenomenon?

Well, for a start I'd say it distinctly reminds me of two things, one of which will still be within living memory of many viewers, and the other not. Firstly, I think of Uri Geller, who in the 1970's became an overnight media sensation by appearing to bend spoons on television. Now, history records that professional sceptic James Randi definitively exposed Geller as a fraud on the Johnny Carson show, but surprisingly and significantly I would argue, this event actually boosted Geller's fame and public belief in him rather than ruin his career. It seemed as if many people saw his failure to be able to perform his spoon-bending under pressure as a sign that he was only human like them rather than a magician. Geller was and is, in fact, a complete hoax – his bending achieved with diluted acids on his skin – but a hoax so successful that even oil companies have given him money for his supposed divining skills. The conclusion I think, is that a great many people want to believe in supernatural miracles, indeed have an in-built subconscious need to believe in such things, which shrewd tricksters now and again throughout history have latched onto and made a mint out of.

The second thing all this brings to my mind is Grey Owl, a figure who much fewer of your viewers will be familiar with. Grey Owl was an early instance of an environmental warrior, in a way, who came to prominence in 1920's America, campaigning very powerfully on behalf of native American tribes for the natural flora and fauna of the American west to be spared from the ravages of trapping and hunting by the white man. Grey Owl's cause was very noble but, as only became fully apparent after his death, he was a fraud. He was not in fact an Iroquois or Apache or mixed race as he claimed, but a plain old Englishman called Archie Belaney. I say plain, but to be fair the man did lead a very interesting life in close proximity to First Nation peoples. But my point is that although he was a fraud, his cause was noble, and his deception was put to very good use as a leading conservationist and advocate for human and animal rights. My real question therefore could be put like this: if we somehow had a time machine and could go back and expose Grey Owl as a fraud, would we choose to, given all the good he did? Despite the divided opinion that these kind of pseudo-messiahs always provoke in human history, I think almost everyone would answer the same way to the question I just posed. They'd let Grey Owl get on with it and bite their tongue. And so it is, I would suggest with Thomas Tellman. I don't believe for a moment that he's who he claims to be, or has ever been in outer space in his life, but he is saying powerful and useful things, truthful things even, that people ought to listen to. Maybe he is just a very media-savvy version of Geller or Grey Owl, who has figured out that in order to get his message across in our age of short attention spans, he needs to do it on the back of a truly outlandish story, and a visually appealing one. I wonder if he really can fly an aeroplane for instance? I would imagine and predict that something along those lines will be the next stunt he is planning.

58

Chrissy watches her television, something she anticipates having a lot more time to do for the immediate future until she finds alternative employment, probably an alternative career. She realises she has distorted her account of the disciplinary hearing to Kenny, but was unable to stop herself, feels still unable to quite face the truth now. The small hairs on the back of her neck keep standing on end and she is beset by a series of minor headaches, as if something, her very body perhaps, is at odds with her words and expressed thoughts, is seeking to signal its discomfort. Kenny will be telling all his friends how unfairly she was treated, how she did nothing whatsoever wrong, how the whole case was really about professional jealousy, personal animosities and rivalries within the department, being used to act out long-standing vendettas and grudges against her. She almost believes all this herself.

Now, incredibly, to rub salt in the wounds, Chrissy find every television channel carrying stories about Thomas Tellman, even extracts of interviews, all showing that always smiling oh-so-sincere face of his, spouting his usual nonsense about zooming around in flying saucers. How can anyone be believing this stuff? How can serious news channels be carrying it? It infuriates her more than ever. She resolves to go to the newspapers again herself and see if they are any more interested in listening to her this time. She writes out a note to Kenny saying she has gone shopping down in Inverness, to make sure he doesn't ask any awkward questions later.

*

Janet McComish recognises Chrissy, but does not dismiss her so readily this time, even brings a young colleague into the room with her, who takes notes furiously.

So you're saying you actually lost your job over this?

That you're some kind of whistle-blower? That he has webbed feet? But doesn't that potentially lend weight to the idea that he really has been consorting with aliens, or is even one in disguise?

No, because I'll bet his original medical records don't record that he had webbed feet. RAF medicals are pretty rigorous, one would imagine. Someone just has to get their hands on those. It's as if somehow he's got that GP, that family doctor hypnotised, enthralled to him, helping him back up his cock-and-bull stories.

How would he do that though? Janet exclaims. *Are you seriously suggesting he's a hypnotist? I've met him of course, I found him very charming.*

Charming? Chrissy laughs harshly. *An interesting choice of word there, don't you think?*

I mean he didn't seem manipulative. I mean, what would he want anyway? What does he stand to gain in return if all this business is made up?

Oh I don't know. Is the burden of proof really on me to conjecture that? He could want notoriety, fame, sponsorship, cover for embezzlement and tax evasion, diversion and evasion from past crimes, because if he's not Thomas Tellman then who is he? As a newspaper woman, you must know more about the multiple motives for attention-seeking than anyone, mustn't you?

Yes, perhaps I do. Maybe that's true... Janet ponders. *I do know an attention-seeker when I see one. And a racist.*

I'm sorry?

He's black. Or are you going to tell me you didn't notice?

What's that got to do with anything? Chrissy exclaims.

Your reaction against him seems to have been fanatical, almost hysterical, right from the start. I just wonder why that is.

Dear God, tell me you're not serious? I'M NOT... Chrissy checks herself, and lowers her voice. *I'm not a racist. Are you going to run my story or not now?*

59

Returning to Annie's house for dinner after another day at the newspaper offices and television studios, Thomas tries to make light of it all, grinning at the door saying, *Well, did you watch me on the telly?* But he can see by Annie's expression and her reaction that her mind is deeply troubled.

I spent twenty minutes yesterday morning trying to politely argue with a small but perfectly loopy crowd, including two friends and colleagues, who wanted to forcibly stop you from garnering any more notoriety for this town and your 'radical' views as they put it. It wasn't what I'd planned for my Tuesday morning. Bruce has been confused by it, to say the least, I've sent him to his granddad's for dinner, and as for me... well, who cares about me?

I care about you of course... Thomas sighs, trying to reach his hands out to her, which she rebuffs. *None of these consequences were intended. But what choice do I have? MI6 aren't going to leave me alone so I have to defend myself and get my message across.*

They sit and eat together in near silence for ten minutes, before Annie answers. *You spoke well, Thomas, but I'm worried about you – worried about us. Do you really understand what you're getting yourself into? The first channel ran your interview like it was a joke, a harmless bit of whimsy to lighten up the day. But then it began slowly shifting in tone, throughout the day. Clips are circulating like wildfire on the web. People are starting to take you and your story seriously. There's a tipping point after which you lose control – there are nearly eight billion people on this planet. Even your alien friends, if they exist, let alone you, wouldn't know how to safely control an audience of that size. That's a human problem and puzzle, that probably only a few creeps like Rupert Murdoch have ever figured out anything about. I want you as yourself – not as some media phenomenon.*

All this makes me scared I'm going to lose you, when I've only just found you. That would be… well, it just feels so cruel and unfair.

But I need the audience, Annie. Can't you see that?

Yes, I can as a matter of fact, and it scares me how much you're lapping it up already, how it transforms you. I thought I knew you, but I'm not sure at all that I know that man who appeared on the screen today. He struck me like some kind of demagogue in the making. Cunning, and dangerous.

Have you gone mad, Annie? It's not about me, surely you know that. I have a message to explain, about environmental destruction. All terrestrial life depends on this. We won't even have the privilege of sitting here having this conversation if the planet we're sitting on goes on fire and vanishes under meltwater.

But don't we matter then? You and I? She thumps her hands on the table, tears coming to her eyes.

Of course we do. But so does everybody else and all other life. We're all intimately interconnected. It's not a choice you ever have the luxury of making, between yourself and the world. They're always ultimately the same thing.

That's all very noble and clever, but isn't what it boils down to really is saying that you and I don't matter enough, whatever way you look at it?

*Nobody can hide from the world, Annie. What use is love between two people, a man and a woman, if one of them has no love for humanity? Compassion for **all** living things is a prerequisite for loving **one** with any degree of authority. If the man you love turns his back on the human race then he is a monster.*

Annie stands up from the table and goes to stand at the sink, gazing out over the slated roofs of Kinburgh, like so many closed eyelids, awaiting sleep. *I'm beginning to wonder if he's a monster anyway…*

60

In Brussels, Axel Verstraete sits outside his favourite cafe in Avenue Jean Volders, within sight of the Port de Hal. He sits beneath a sycamore tree whose leaves have begun to change colour as Autumn approaches, a few even free-falling down towards his table as he sips his espresso and reads the horse-racing results at the back of the newspaper. Luck has been the defining idea of his life; what saved his life when under fire in the Special Forces, what brought him to his nefarious second career afterwards with its many close scrapes with police, many chances that enabled him to take his assigned targets with clinical efficiency and earning him a formidable reputation within a very select and secretive circle. A mosquito lands on his left hand, which he allows to settle for a moment then swipes with a practised technique, combining sufficient force with economy of means. He knows they come from all the city's many canals, and that some are even rumoured to be carrying malaria again, a new invasive species coming north into Europe from Africa. They make him think of all the black faces that so irritate him in his neighbourhood, like the drug-dealers in Marseille that his mother taught him to fear and hate.

One of the few other men he knows by sight – or ever meets – within the circle of his employment now comes to join him at his table. A shuffling middle-aged figure resembling a tram-driver or bin man, but with the piercing eyes of a magistrate, the rough over-sized hands of a farm labourer. He has only ever known him as 'Tibo', avoiding even asking questions as to what quarter he might live in or what family he has, knowing this man probably lives as he does, as a soldier who has never truly been demobbed. Except there is no enemy. The enemy has no face. Their camaraderie, such as it is, does not come from heroic cooperation against some existential societal threat, but from something darker which they never discuss. Were it ever to be named, it might be the love of the hunt, the simple act of killing with precision while magically freed of the consequences, the love of weapons themselves. Perhaps there is some nostalgia in it also, some hidden yearning to be part of a team again, enlisted into a conflict with reassuringly simple objectives. Large crowds and social complication confuse him. Axel lives largely alone, making contact only occasionally with a small selection of friends, none of whom know each other. He is never more alive than at the moment he pulls the trigger and sees a man fall, as if that act somehow also plays invisibly in reverse at some level, transfers that man's spark of life back to him, merges with his own. Killing is an ancient art and trade, after all, which needs no explanation or justification for its fascination on this earth. Its timeless recurrence and attraction remain self-evident.

Tibo sits down and opens his leather haversack, from which he hands Axel a slim brown cardboard folder with information and photographs within. Axel glances briefly inside, then asks Tibo to summarise the brief in words, culminating in telling him the fee. Axel sits back, breathes in, his eyebrows lifting, at the size of the sum. *Mon Dieu. I could retire on that.*

It is a dangerous assignment, we are to be given to understand, Axel. The money takes into account the risk, the need to compensate your family members should the worst happen.

Something in Tibo's eyes, and the way he subsequently averts them, disturbs Axel, as if there is some new and concealed barrier between them, as if Tibo is keeping something back. *Of course,* Tibo continues, *to do so, the names and addresses of those relatives would have to be passed to some third party. You could trust me, I would suggest, to broker that.*

Operating amid a largely unarmed crowd, civilians, non-combatants, with only some policemen, guards to worry about? I don't see the risk consistent with the fee.

The English have a saying, Axel, regarding how one

shouldn't examine the teeth of a horse gifted to you for free.

Is that who's behind this, the English?

Tibo shrugs, inevitably, pouting, as he hails a waiter for fresh coffee. *Perhaps it's just as you say then. Not so much danger as they think, not for someone of your calibre. The ideal situation. The fee of a lifetime. It must be big, political, but the likes of you and I need never trouble ourselves with things of that nature. Men of the shadows, as we used to say.*

Axel drinks up and leaves to go home and and give the folder's contents more thought. Left alone at the table, after the waiter puts down his Americano, Tibo opens his leather haversack again and takes out a second slim brown cardboard file, as he lights a cigarette. A mosquito flies past his cheek and he raises his glowing cigarette end into its path and incinerates it without taking his eyes from the folder. The photograph inside is of Axel.

61

Father Seamus O'Hara sits with Magda in the study of the Chapel House having retrieved her from Confession, to which he judges her visits too frequent recently for so unsullied a soul. The tall Victorian windows overlook an overgrown garden for which he could easily arrange more frequent trimmings and prunings, but whose unruly appearance has always appealed to him since he first took over the parish from his elderly and disorganised predecessor. Something about it gently taunts him in a way he likes, reminds him each day of the complexity and mystery of God's plans, and the force of that great will in everything which men can neither tame nor wholly understand. Its fronds and branches reach out now and tap gently against the glass as the breeze picks up, like some aged hand ringing vainly for attention.

What troubles you, my child? he asks Magda, pouring tea into two fine china cups and saucers. *I feel almost as if you come to us too often recently. If we are a hospital for the soul, then I wonder if our cures are working for you. Is it about this man Tellman?*

How did you guess? Maybe I mentioned before my glimpse of his strange foot. But I'm worried that I shared that knowledge with someone I shouldn't have. Perhaps I am too innocent and open-hearted. One of my colleagues was about to lose her job and I felt sorry for her, so I had lunch with her and talked on too long and unguardedly. She's been obsessed with Tellman, convinced he is some kind of criminal con-man, robbing from the old lady he claims to be his daughter.

And what do you think?

About Tellman? He is a good and kind man, in whom I have never seen the slightest trace of malice, let alone evil. Although I must say I was disappointed to hear the disparaging comments he made on religion this week. You heard about them too, I take it?

Father O'Hara smiles gently. *You may be rather*

shocked I'm afraid, but I must confess I rather liked them.

Really? I'm surprised, I'll admit. Magda looks at him wide-eyed. *How come?*

The church is changing, Magdalena. It's old and needs to change with the times or soon young people such as you may turn away from it entirely, which would be a tragic failing of the duties of I and many others, would it not? I liked how he hailed Christ as a great practical philosopher. In all my days, I'd never thought to see the son of God in such a light, but I've reflected on it since and found that I consider it a helpful perspective. People today don't like being told what to do, by governments, churches, gods, or anyone else. As with adolescents, people only learn by making their own mistakes, not by being dictated to by adults, against which they will then often rebel. He said that good was common sense and that evil never worked for long, and again on reflection I find that perspective one potentially more likely to be approachable to the average man and woman of today than to tell them that evil is some kind of magical force that can be banished with incense and the right kind of prayers like magic spells.

But Father, forgive me, but you sound like you're losing faith, as if all of this around us is like… like stage scenery for some kind of performance, a play with whole centuries for acts.

Why, that's very poetic, my child, beautiful in fact. But I can assure you I am not losing faith, despite my many years on this troubled earth. In fact, I feel the opposite is true. I've felt it for some time, a new optimism growing inside me recently, a late flowering, if you will, that this man Tellman's words seemed to confirm and chime with. I understand that some people have been offended by him. But he did not say morals were unnecessary in the world. Quite the reverse in fact. He urged us to construct them as appropriate to each society, and what could be more important than that which needs building, and needs many hands working together to do so? What he was attacking was dogma, blind dogma, that causes so much regrettable division among religions and peoples, not morality and spirituality, which can be quite separate things.

But this only makes me feel worse, Father. I was persuaded by my disgruntled colleague to even take part in a protest outside the house where Tellman is staying – castigating him for his irreligious comments. Have I done wrong? Sinned?

I don't know. If you upset him and others in his household, then perhaps, but that's not irredeemable. You could apologise to them. He sounds like the sort of man who welcomes debate on moral topics. If you've spread some rumour in the world about his feet, from what I understand of how the media works, then that is only likely to add to his notoriety and publicity for his message.

I may even have helped him then?

We all make mistakes, all the time, and are sometimes inadvertently utilised by evil. But even evil sometimes does good, when the conditions are right, by the power of its negative example. It strikes me that we live in the adolescence of our world, waiting to be born into something better.

62

Mary is woken by a camera flash outside the drawn net curtains of her bedroom. Thomas comes in a moment later to check on her and peer out to see what's going on.

Whit wiz yon flash, Daddy?

Reporters I think, Mary, and their photographers. Gentlemen, and ladies, of the Press. They could become somewhat irksome, I'm starting to think. He goes to the front door and opens it, to be met with a barrage of flashes and a cacophony of requests for comment. He closes it again, then closes all the blinds and curtains in the house. He puts the kettle on and looks in the fridge. He hears the phone ring as he walks back down the hall, but Mary lifts the receiver in her bedroom.

Whit's that? Yir frae where? The union? Whit union? Whit commission? Ye mean thi Forestry Commission?

European Commission. We're running low on milk, Mary. Once I've made you your tea, I'll pop into town for some more. Thomas says, as she hands the phone to him.

*

The bicycle the wealthy art dealer loaned to Thomas turns out to be an ideal tool for a puzzle he did not anticipate having to solve. He steps outside, jumps onto it and cycles away at speed along the narrow path across the fields, too fast for anyone to follow on foot, and not wide enough to get a car down. He arrives in the centre of Kinburgh twenty minutes later to find Annie and her father and Bruce under siege at their flat by further sections of the press corps.

Ah, Tam, whit huv ye gone and done, son? Bobby greets him at the door. *We're fair scuppered here.*

The police are coming out to cordon off Mary's house… Thomas answers calmly. *I'll phone and get them to do the same here, if they're not already on their way.*

In the living room, Annie sits with her arms around

Bruce, tears staining her eye-shadow. *I'm scared, Thomas. You need to make them go away. Look what you've brought down on us all. They think you're Captain Kirk or Jesus Christ or a cross between the two. Like you're their hotline to little green men. Who knew so many people are so unhinged? Tied to reality by a slim thread. Some of them are talking about an alien invasion. Panic buying has started apparently, at supermarkets and petrol pumps.*

There goes any chance o' spare bog roll then... Bobby sighs.

I'll go to to the supermarket now for you, and any other errands. What food do you need?

Like you're gonna be able to get oot o' here any easier than us, son. In fact, hoo the hell did ye get in past that barrage?

I have my methods, they didn't even notice me.

Whit? Methods eh? Bobby grimaces, exasperated. *Talk sense, son.*

Bruce speaks up. *You can make them all go away, can't you, Thomas? You can do anything with your superpowers. You beat the Nazis. You could makes them all float away up into the air like helium balloons, couldn't you?*

Shoosh, Bruce... Annie says, holding him closer to her and running her hands through his hair, *We're all tired of all this already.*

Bobby is becoming visibly angry now, an ugly spectacle that evidently no one wants to witness. *We're tired of you, son, and all your shenanigans.*

Well, don't worry, all of you! Thomas announces loudly, creating an odd silence, even seemingly from the street outside, into which he then speaks more softly, seeking to be reconciliatory: *I'll be going soon, to leave you all in peace forever.*

63

Reporter Lesley Crawford picks up Thomas at the end of the road to Mary's house and drives him out to a local nursing home where, after weeks of investigation, she has finally located one RAF veteran still alive who claims to have served in the same squadron as Thomas Tellman. She's brought a cameraman in the backseat, who begins fidgeting excitedly with his lenses, as they pull up outside a bland modern building of home-counties-England-style brick and white render already stained by efflorescence and algae.

Benny Faulds is 103 years old and extremely frail, confined to a wheelchair, with an oxygen nasal tube permanently connected.

With the camera rolling, Benny greets Thomas, shakes his hand and they commence to reminisce together about night flights over Europe, daringly close scrapes with the Luftwaffe. Benny's hand lifts and shakes, describing deadly arcs and terminal explosions. His rasping whisper of a voice, dispensed of necessity in only small installments, speaks of brave colleagues they appear to both remember, of aeroplanes returning so riddled with bullet-holes as to be scarcely air-worthy.

64

Using a borrowed car to avoid media attention, Annie and Thomas drop Bruce and her father at his house then drive out as close as they can get to the quiet stretch of shoreline near Mary's home, to go for a walk along the beach towards evening. Thomas kneels down above the high-tide line to examine the flotsam and jetsam. *Just look at all this, even this little beach where nobody comes, Annie. When I left in 1948 this was clean, unspoilt. Nature still had the upper hand. But now look at the plastic... ring-pulls and bottle-tops intertwined among the seaweed. Fragments of white polystyrene crate, orange-brown blobs of insulation. The bottles, cartons, plastic bags, fragments of wires and circuit-boards. And those are just the things here and the things we can see. The whole ocean – not just here but all around the world – is contaminated. Detergents, fertilisers, pesticides and micro-particles accumulating in animal's guts, discarded nets entangling and choking them, fuel waste, industrial waste, human waste, all making the saltwater more acidic and less-oxygen rich, preventing sea life from constructing their hard shells. The sea bed and reefs and all kinds of underwater habitats are being destroyed by over-fishing, nets trailing along the ocean floor. The seas can absorb a quarter of human emissions of carbon dioxide, but with that ability depleted and more CO_2 in the upper atmosphere, global temperatures are rising, sea temperatures rising, producing more habitat depletion, more species loss. The warmer water and atmosphere is making the ice caps melt, raising water levels. More species destruction, including ourselves. When will all this madness stop? And why hasn't it, with so many respected voices raised against it? Something is profoundly wrong in human democracies if elected leaders, supposedly the best people among us, choose to forestall doing anything about this because it might lower their vote ratings. How* *do we end this plague of selfishness and truth-denial, short of global revolution by the unempowered?*

But although he knows Annie understands and agrees with all that he is saying, he looks up into her eyes and realises the whole world is dwarfed at that moment by the enormity of the personal pain he is causing her. But with what? But with what? With his love. Even good does harm. An inescapable paradox.

But why does it have to all be down to you to sort? Annie asks, despondent. *Just one man. Surely all this media circus is temporary, Thomas, and will let up soon. Don't you know how fickle the world's attention span is? – how quickly people move on to the next story? I don't want you to leave, despite what I said today – I don't understand why you need to.* She starts to become agitated. *Everyone always leaves me. I thought we had something, were something.*

Thomas takes her hand and they walk along the beach at the water's edge, the tide lapping over their feet, erasing their footprints. *There is no luck or fate, nobody punishing you or anyone else for anything, Annie. Bruce's father and some other men let you down, but it's all random unless you choose to focus on the negative.*

She looks at him furiously, eyes burning. *That's so easy for you to say, as if you know anything more than a summary of my life. Don't you realise how patronising you sound sometimes? Or how that enrages some people? What do you know about Frank taking smack? Trying to keep him off it, taking him to clinics, rehab centres, listening to all his lies, the heroin talking, all the promises broken, meetings not met, people let down – the fear of infection, hepatitis, the fear he'd infect or harm Bruce? Watching him fade away, that pale sweaty corpse, thinner every day, hiding him from people, throwing him out the house? The terror of his spent needles. Or my father? Oh, he seems such a great old guy now, you and him were getting on like a house on fire. But he was a hopeless drunk when I was a teenager, when my mother left him, left us – just when I was finishing Secondary*

School trying to work out who I was and my place in the world. How can you know? How can you dismiss all that with one patronising sentence? Nobody can know anyone else's pain, the horrors they've lived through, the demons that still haunt them, can they? Do you think you're above all this because some bug-eyed monsters whisked you away one day in a silver tic-tac?

Noticing they have reached the remains of a timber boat, bleached beams poking out of the sand like the skeleton of a whale, they stop and sit down together facing each other, resting on its spars. Thomas sighs and answers: *I'm sorry. I'm above nothing on this earth. I didn't mean to seem to diminish anything you've lived through. I was just trying to help with some broader perspective. Some way to guard against believing in bad luck. It's such a corrosive concept, as if God or whoever has got it in for you. Why are we arguing anyway? I'm just going away for a week. I've told you I intend to come back.*

Yes, but something in your tone of voice makes me disbelieve you. You seem nervous and worried, and you won't tell me where you going. Isn't that a bit weird? Even a friend would expect to be told something like that about you, wouldn't they? Let alone a... well whatever we are. What are we?

Lovers, I suppose.

You suppose?

I mean I suppose that's the right word. The English language is pretty hopeless on this subject. In Greek there are four words for different kinds of love. In English we're forced to confuse lust with romance, regard with duty, sin with joy, every time we open our mouths.

Greek? How many languages can you speak?

What have you got?

You know, I think I've grown tired of all your enigmatic smart-arse answers to everything all the time, like you've always got more cards up your sleeve. I watch you on television and I wonder if my boyfriend – my lover – is really real, or some kind of slick plastic fake, you know, like some 70's Sci Fi thing, a simulant or replicant or cyborg or something.

I cry real tears, I bleed real blood, Annie.

But do you feel real pain? Are you in any pain at all over the idea of leaving me right now like this? Leaving me in the dark about what and where and why and whether I'll ever see you back here again? If I'd thought you were just passing through like some kind of tourist then I wouldn't have got involved with you. I thought you were starting a new life here and needed me or someone like me to help you with that.

And you have, you've helped me find my feet. You know I didn't seek any of this publicity and notoriety out, don't you? You've been there most, a lot, of the time, so you must know. I tried to lie low, to blend in, but in the end the world came looking for me. What do you want me to do instead now? Change my name and run away with you? You're bound to this town anyway, by so many things.

Well you certainly sound like you're running away now.

In the pause between their voices the sound of the waves somehow becomes harsher, more hopeless to their ears, before Thomas continues: *I'm not. I'm going to sort something out. This fame, for want of a better word, is an opportunity that I have to use for good, to help everyone – not just you but everyone and everything alive on this planet.*

But you're going to do something dangerous aren't you? I can feel it. And you think there's a pretty good chance you'll get killed at it, whatever it is, and never come back. Why don't you just… level with me?

Thomas sighs and hangs his head, looking down at the sand for a long time before he finally answers. *All right, I admit it. You're right in some respects. I applaud your intuition. I am not entirely what I seem – but I am entirely human. You'll understand what I mean by that soon, as will everyone, in a day or two. I am about to place myself in danger. I may live and come back or I may die, but not in a way that you will know anything about. Either way there will be no pain for you to feel. Everything has been carefully calculated up to now, by myself and by the monitors, but not this, not what is about to play out next. This is the moment of maximum risk. The outcome is uncertain, and cannot yet be known. But the world will be changed either way.*

What a load of riddles! Annie stand up in exasperation and walks out of the boat wreck to pace down towards the shore. He follows her and when he reaches her at the water's edge, she turns around, saying: *I don't understand, Thomas. I don't understand you, and I wonder if I ever have. But I don't want to part like this, in sadness and anger and disillusionment. Hold me... Pilot.*

Looking over her shoulder as they embrace, his eyes alight on a thin pathway of sand linking the beach to a small tidal island. When they draw apart, he points to it, saying: *Look, a shoal – a sandbar that's called. Do you know the poem by Tennyson?*

She shakes her head sadly. *I want you, not another poem.*

Trust me, it's a good one. About crossing the sandbar between the river of life and the ocean of death. He speaks into the wind, looking both at Annie and the sea breaking on the sand behind her, but their eyes fill with so many tears that they turn away from each other in shame at the end of it :

Sunset and evening star,
and one clear call for me,
and may there be no moaning of the bar,
when I put out to sea,

But such a tide as moving seems asleep,
too full for sound and foam,
when that which drew from out the boundless deep
turns again home.

Twilight and evening bell,
and after that the dark,
and may there be no sadness of farewell,
when I embark.

For though from out our bourne of time and place
the flood may bear me far,
I hope to see my pilot face to face,
when I have crossed the bar.

*

Shame... Thomas says to Annie quietly, on the way back in the car to drop him at Mary's house, driving through dense forests of pine trees, throwing bands of shadow and light across their eyes. *Why do I feel shame? When we started out without it, proud even, of our attraction, our love.*

Isn't shame where it always ends up with Adam and Eve? Annie remarks bitterly, changing down the gears as they reach the main road. *And what is love anyway? Got any alien answers for that one? Mating glue? Gene exchange?*

Adam and Eve are still going, still going forth and multiplying, as far as I can see. He answers. *Love is everything, Annie, here and on every other star.*

Their final kiss outside Mary's door is like a plea, a severance, the pain travelling slowly inwards to begin its hidden work in both of them, the ancient wounds that only amnesia, not even time, can heal.

65

Alan Lyons, Director of the Scottish International Airshow lives in a beautiful house overlooking Prestwick beach. He has just returned from his morning round of golf when he gets a phonecall from his Events Organiser asking him to turn his TV on and watch an ongoing interview with Thomas Tellman. *Could this be the guy that was in touch last month saying he wanted to bring a Hawker Sea Fury to the show, but couldn't produce any paperwork?*

Alan looks at the captions rolling across below the screen. *Captain Thomas F Tellman. Yes, it very well might be. Did we take him seriously?*

Maybe not seriously enough... I think we told him it was too short notice but there might be a few free slots towards the end of the day.

Damn... Alan frowns. *I like the way you're thinking. Can you get back in touch with him urgently and offer to give him big billing? And how many tickets do we still have for sale? Could we release more, upgrade the crowd capacity? Good. Let me know how it goes. This could be very good for us. Very good indeed.*

66

Around ten at night, Inspector Drummond's wife alerts him to the sight of a strange man in a black suit in their driveway examining his tyres. Drummond checks his discreet infra-red cameras, then tells her to quietly lock the doors and stay put after he goes out. Going via the garden shed, he approaches the agent silently and rapidly from behind and whacks a bicycle chain across the back of his head, punches him twice in the face then drags him across the concrete paviours to the metal railings where he handcuffs his right wrist to the bars. As the intruder moans in pain, he slides the transparent plastic cover back over the chain then uses it to beat the man further, mostly on his legs and sides, concealed areas, enough to leave him able to still walk, but in debilitating pain. Drummond knows the man is dangerous, knows he is probably achieving nothing by this except ending his own career when various invisible strings will later be pulled to relieve him of duty. But it's still worth it. He'll probably get to keep his pension, to avoid any fuss or inquiry. He'll go quietly, he thinks, but damn, this is good, just to get this payback for once.

Once he's sure the man is incapable of any imminent movements, let alone combative ones, he reaches into his pockets to retrieve his I.D, kneels down at a safe distance just beyond his shoes and addresses him:

What was the plan then, sunshine? Let the tyres down? Tracking device, car bomb? I never thought I'd meet someone like you, like this, you know, on my own patch. It's not what I signed up for. Bet you don't even have a real name do you? Just a little shite of the state sent to lie and cheat and mess the fucking world up with your nefarious little schemes. The British Empire's over, didn't anyone tell you? You go fuck off back to Surrey or Milton Keynes or wherever spawned you and never come here again. Go get an honest job, why don't you? I've spent my life maintaining law and order in this town, in

Douglas Thompson

this community, because that's what this is, a community. People know each other here and look out for each other. You're beneath contempt, not above the law. I'm the fucking law around here, and you're not above me, or above a good kicking for that matter. Just count yourself lucky I didn't break both your legs. Because next time I will, and that goes not just for you but all of your slimey little cronies. Got it? I'll phone a taxi for you. They can patch you up at the air base and fly you home to your mummy.

67

Channel 7 interview Thomas for his views on the climate emergency and on the intentions of possible alien civilisations studying the Earth; International Affairs editor, Dominic Fullerton, seems more interested in one topic than the other, however. *It's well understood, Mister Tellman, that action by world governments is urgently required in order to slow down and reverse the effects of global warming, but I must press you again; will you give us more detail on the exact nature of the alien civilisation that you claim gave you sanctuary for the last eighty years? What star system? What planet around that star system? Are you scared that astronomers will disprove the feasibility of whatever location you cite? Why not tell us tonight on this programme?*

As I've said already... Thomas answers very affably, *for various reasons that will become obvious this week, as soon as tomorrow in fact, in a detailed statement I'm going to make in a major public forum, the answer to that question will change everything – so I want to reveal it at the time of my own choosing in order to have maximum impact relative to the other parts of my message.*

You do realise you sound like a politician already? So much for a fresh voice, fresh angle and perspective. The News From Nowhere as some people are calling you. What are your connections with the various campaigns that are now running in your name, asking people for donations and subscriptions? Campaigns such as 'Tellman Tells It', 'Saint Thomas Global' and 'Tellman Extraterrestrial Incorporated'?

No connection whatsoever, obviously, as I've stated many times already. They've only just appeared.

May we see your naked feet by the way?

Excuse me?

There's a story in the Guardian this morning, suggesting that you have webbed feet, and are thus some kind of alien impostor. Ridiculous, I know, but easy to disprove. Will you slip a shoe and sock off to let us see, just to be sure?

Thomas laughs good-naturedly. *Will you take yours off at the same time?*

What? Why would I? What's the point?

Why would I?

To disprove the allegation?

Anyone can make any absurd allegation. I could accuse you of having seven toes right now, and ask you to disprove that.

Okay... Dominic chuckles sourly, *nothing to lose I suppose.* He slips his shoe off and freezes, then begins stammering: *Wh-wh-what the... hey, oh no, no, that's not right, no, no...!*

Thomas sits eerily relaxed in his chair as Dominic becomes more and more hysterical.

My toes! Oh my god, what's happened to my toes? This isn't... it's not... can I get some help out here?! Help!

On live television Dominic rolls his trouser leg up and and yells hysterically while clutching his naked foot – which the camera and the world behind it can clearly see consists of five perfectly normal and fully functional and independently operable toes, which he nonetheless repeatedly bemoans as de-formed and fused together into a weird amphibian mass.

Thomas and the cameramen and studio-hands calm Dominic down and encourage him to put his shoes back on so he can resume the interview.

They sit back down and Thomas continues: *I think your toes were lovely, Dominic, webbed or not, thanks for sharing them.* Thomas smiles at the cameras, judging that they are still running. *There's no point debating a thing which people are bound to have widely divided points of view on, depending on their upbringing and social milieu. If global warming continues unchecked and water levels continue to rise then webbing between your toes could well be a very useful adaptation. Nothing at all to be ashamed of. I hope you've given a big empowering boost tonight with your bravery, to young people the world over who have been the victims of body-shaming. What a boring world it would be if we were all identical. One man or woman's private minor deformity is another one's secret fetish in this day and age. I also hope you put up a helpline at the end of this programme with a link to a webpage of facts and resources, so that impressionable people out there don't start asking plastic surgeons to make their feet look like yours.*

Dominic wipes his pale forehead with his handkerchief, and reaches for his glass of water, as he consults his notes, resolved to get back onto the subject.

68

Thomas walks in to Mary's room as she finishes her supper, knowing it may perhaps be the last time, since he intends not to wake her in the morning.

That wiz guid, Daddy. Ah'm ready fur a wee sleep noo. Aw, but whit's oan yer mind? Ah kin see there's something vexin' ye. Spit it oot.

He sits down on the edge of her bed. *I have to leave tomorrow, Mary, at first light. In fact I'll be out the door before dawn, so you won't see me.*

Whaur ye aft tae?

The truth is, I didn't just come back to see you, Mary. I came back with a message from the beings who rescued me back in the forties. It's a good message, a noble mission. Maybe the most noble any man has ever undertaken.

Braver than Wirld War Twaw, Faither? Ye saved fowk already, did ye no?

They always need saving, Mary. Maybe we all do. Saved from each other. Saved from ourselves. Maybe the only way to save ourselves in fact, ultimately, is by saving others. The minister and the priest would certainly say so.

Mary's eyes fill with tears. *Aw naw, Daddy, dinnae tell me yir no cummin' back.*

Thomas takes her in his arms and they embrace for a time so long that it seems out of time. An aeon of regret and longing in which all the stars and nebulae wheel through space, implode backwards towards the dark heart at their centre, their missing source. *I'll try, sweetheart. I'll do my best. But I can't guarantee I'll make it this time.*

They pull apart and gaze at each other, as he runs his fingers through her hair. *My daughter, my beloved daughter...* he whispers. Her eyes and his each sparkle with light and tears, overflowing. *At least we had this precious time together again. Think of it all as a dream, if that helps. The same goes for life. Because maybe it is, ultimately.*

Her old gnarled hand reaches out and her fingers intertwine with his, age and youth, the ruined living and the beautiful dead, decay and immortality.

69

Seven o' clock in the morning. Bright sunlight, moderate cloud cover, light winds. Thomas Tellman walks out across the most isolated section of moor bordering on the RAF Kinburgh munitions testing range. The only sound is a desolate sea breeze blowing through the long swaying grasses. He reaches the base of the ten-foot high fencing, pauses and looks around himself to check he is not being observed. He throws his back-pack clean over the fence in one high arc. He then takes his jacket off and hurls it up so as to land on top of the barbed-wire, takes several paces back then runs at top speed and leaps up briefly onto his balanced coat then rolls right over on his arms in order to land standing up on the other side, facing inwards. He looks down at the minor wounds sustained on his skin, and kneels down to take disinfectant and bandage from his rucksack. He gets up a few moments later and continues walking straight into the heart of the abandoned area of sandy scrubland.

After walking for fifteen minutes he reaches a particularly complicated area of sand dunes over which a small silver sphere has been hovering for the last three months. He raises his arm towards it to shape his fingers into an obscure hand signal and a blue pulse of light briefly emerges from it in response. Thomas sits down and waits, watching for the next five minutes as a vortex of localised winds blows the sand away from a large concealed object. Gradually the gleam of metal emerges, the brightly painted colours of RAF markings and camouflage stripes. Although ultimately an instrument of war and destruction, the machine is also exquisitely beautiful – honed to its function with great economy of means, and perfectly preserved.

Thomas stands up, dons his leather flight helmet and goggles from his rucksack and reaches out for the propeller, starting it on his second attempt, the rotors speeding up. He kicks the last of the sand away from the wheels then climbs onto the wing, slides back the glass canopy and clambers down into the cockpit. He checks his instruments then releases the throttle; begins taxiing and turning towards the open section of ground nearby, then bumps up onto the disused runway – blowing with sand, and somewhat pot-holed, but still serviceable. He turns away from the sun, lowers his goggles and accelerates as rapidly as possible as his Hawker Sea Fury shakes and trembles under his expert control until he feels it become almost weightless, a sublime feeling he remembers and loves. Then with the grace of an angel the aeroplane lifts off into the glorious light of an autumn morning, fraught with possibility, everything waiting to be won.

70

Thomas feels delighted beyond measure to be back in the air. As if this is his true home, rather than Earth below him or the planets he visited, rather than any future or the past he came from. Here, only here, is where he belongs, in the pure moment. The burn of fuel, the fierce blast of air rushing and rattling endlessly against him and his extended body: this suit of metal armour, exquisite design expressing the timeless longing of humankind to emulate the birds. He knows it's small and puny – laughably so, even – compared to the technology of those who saved him and took him out of his own time. But, even so, he sees now with clear vision and renewed perspective how beautiful the creations of human beings are. The modesty and honesty with which they express our spirits, our bargaining with the world we find ourselves in, cast out from Eden.

Thomas turns onto a south-west course and takes a long journey of nostalgia down across the spectacular peaks and glens and lochs of the Highlands back towards where his life in Scotland first began: the Ayrshire coast. He keeps the Cairngorms on his left and the Great Glen on his right; that ancient geological fissure that cuts Scotland in half like a scarring of the mind, the split in national character, the itch scratched by Stevenson, Hogg, Scott, explained by Lyle, crossed by Telford, exploited by the science of Kelvin and so many others. So much genius generated by the need to overcome landscape and the past, loving and hating alternately, soaring though enslaved. Country of two languages and cultures combined in one. Doppelgängers, changelings, selkies; people of two worlds, every one.

The colours below are stunning: the purple of heather, the citrus green of grassland, the vivid orange of moors, the cool white of peaks that never thaw, sailing above all human reason. Lochs in shades of blue from cobalt through cerulean to almost green where sandy beaches hide below. At times flying lower, he sees herds of deer fleeing down slopes from him, cows and sheep turning in confusion. And then there are the roads, much more of them than he remembers from eighty years ago, and each one strung like the beads of necklaces with little beetles crawling, the glinting metal of cars going to and fro like daisy chains of ants, antennae touching as they pass, enacting their human infestation on the pockmarked corpse they are so busy making of the Earth.

Nearing the Atlantic ocean, and keeping the long distinctive profile of the Cowal peninsula and the isle of Arran below and to his right, Thomas slowly descends towards Ayr. Delighted to see Prestwick, the long sandy beach between there and Troon, it stirs memories of his first arrival in Scotland when he met Eleanor. His heart weeps, remembering her – their first happy days of courtship, his mind reeling like bleeding through old faded photos, innocent and yet cast in heightened chiaroscuro by the drama of ongoing war in Europe. His reverie is broken by noticing the frenetic activity around the new international airport to his left, sleek white airliners coming and going. He lives and moves in a different world now, the rash of civilisation festering, poison reaching out from engines and factories, fertilisers and pesticides. Streams and rivers race to the sea as if in distress, no longer carrying purity and meltwater snow, but recirculating their own demise, unable to cleanse the technological toxin descending on them, of plastics, hydrocarbons, sulphides, acid rain.

The crowds on the ground at the International Airshow outside Ayr have been told over tannoy to expect the possible arrival of a very rare and special period aeroplane with a celebrity pilot. The organisers remain uncertain up to the last minute however as to whether the whole thing might be a hoax or a stunt, have contingency excuses ready to trail out, alternative distractions to assuage possible crowd disappointment. But none turn out to be necessary. Thomas Tellman does indeed land his Hawker Sea Fury onto the runway with little difficulty, a mild crosswind from the sea shaking the fuselage. Opening the cockpit and standing up, he takes off his goggles and waves to a growing crowd. Some of them are wearing green baseball caps with a 'TT' logo on them created by his recently inaugurated internet fan clubs, each masterminded by god-knows-who. An organising official clutching clipboard and mobile phone sprints across the tarmac and shouts and gestures up to Thomas, inviting him to taxi round towards a lane off the main runway, where he can step down and converse with his hosts.

Arriving there a few minutes later, Thomas is surprised and slightly alarmed to see how many 'green caps' there really are, and that they already have banners with his face on them and captions like 'Let Tellman Save The World', 'Tell It To The World, Tellman', 'Doubting Thomas Puts The World's Governments To Shame', and even 'Tellman For First Minister'. He wants to talk to humanity, but are these its best representatives? People so eager for a saviour and a leader? So ready and willing and even desperate to project onto any such leader all the hopes and dreams of their entire lives, something by definition nebulous and unanswerable, an equation in which no one, no human hero, can do other than ultimately disappoint. And if not these people then whom? Unless…

He thinks about it. From Abraham Lincoln to Martin Luther King, from Jesus of Nazareth to William Wallace; what is the essential ingredient to grant them the perfection they sought, the statue that may never be tarnished in their eyes thereafter? Death, oblivion. Thomas understands this, and already knows therefore that this must be the ultimate course that his aeroplane has plotted out. He knows this fate and is at peace with it. Indeed, it is not a fear, but his goal.

But on this subject and many others, Thomas remains reticent as he addresses the crowd. *Next comes the fun bit!* he laughs. *Watch the progress of this little aeroplane on social media! I'm taking the message next to the heart of democracy, to all of our leaders, where they sit complacent in their gilded palaces of power! The climate crisis necessitates a revolution! Democracies must be run by an informed majority, not corrupt privilege.*

'Anoraks' mill around, marvelling at the pristine condition of the Hawker Sea Fury. Event technicians ask him if he needs refuelling, to which he shakes his head and taps his nose, citing invisible technological advantages about which he intends to give an explanatory lecture at one of his next venues. The crowd overflows with excitement, laughter and tears, autographs are given, photos taken posed standing with the great man of the media moment, babies handed up to be held and kissed as history is made. History seems almost visible and tangible for a rare moment, revelling in its own self-construction.

And yet somehow, secretly, Thomas is relieved when he gets to taxi back to the runway and feels one of the world's last propeller-driven fighter aircraft lifting him off into the fresh air again, and the hands and hopes of human expectation all falling away from his shoulders like flimsy cobwebs, leaving him supremely alone, one man in the blue sky under the sun, laughing and alive.

71

Thomas turns north-west and sets course for the first city within reach, to begin his plan to raise awareness further for his mission. He has had time now to study the internet, the worldwide web, and has come to understand its enormous capacity for both good and harm, connection and loneliness, truth and disinformation. He understands that sight is after all the primary sense in humans, and therefore that everything depends on visual images expressing compact statements of ideas, concise metaphors. He contrives to create a series of arresting photographs, a succession of livestream movies that people will pick up and begin to disseminate exponentially. He knows he is a herald of vital information flying in the face of a tornado of complacency. If only as a matter of short-term expediency, he must make himself and his message into the same thing.

Reaching Greater Glasgow, rising up over the Glennifer Braes, Thomas is amazed to see how vast and sprawling the city has become. Aiming for the city centre like the bull's eye of a dartboard, he approaches and comes down low over the weird new shapes of Finnieston Quay, the Armadillo and Hydro, flies between new and old, a gleaming white bridge like a futuristic trapeze act, and the rusting Stobcross Crane, icon of past industrialism. Sightseers reach for their phones and the police and security services begin panicking, sirens and alarms going off. Crossing the enormous wound of the M8 motorway, cut down into the city's street-grid like the veins of heart bypass surgery, he aims west and finds his intended jugular: Saint Vincent Street. He glides down carefully between towerblocks and steeples, down into a long canyon of glass towerblocks and beautiful stone Victorian buildings dripping with elaborately carved decoration. If this was New York then the echoes of the eleventh of September 2001 would be unbearable. But at this moment of space and time, office workers run to their windows in awe, some even at a level high enough to look down from above onto the passing spectacle of Tellman's Sea Fury with its RAF markings speeding by, its gloriously brash propeller noise reverberating between the gridiron architecture. The street leads, as he knows, to George Square itself – front of the City Chambers, seat of local government – where crowds of citizens are congregating and look up to see his aeroplane slicing daringly above their heads and the proud domes, spires and campaniles of their familiar buildings.

From there, Thomas rises up towards the ancient cathedral and its necropolis; city of the dead, of graves and tombs winding around a green hill reminding him of the probable ultimate destination of this, his final flight and last adventure.

72

Thomas follows the M8 east across the country, like a vast snake, a twisted spine or carotid artery, leading all the way to Edinburgh. The quantity and speed of cars and buses and lorries passing underneath amaze him, the intensity of traffic risen across the decades to the level of hysteria. Glimpsing the wonderful old castle up ahead on its ancient outcrop, he lowers down at Haymarket in order to fly down Shandwick Place – then round onto Princes Street and its Gardens to pass low over the heads of crowds of shoppers; startling everyone, amazing some, terrifying others. Then veering over the sea of glass tents that make up the roof of Waverley Train Station, he finds the Scottish Parliament at the foot of the Royal Mile. He flies close and low enough to make a pointed statement over the boat-like roofs of the complex, and the curiously shaped ponds outside. Thomas drops a payload of leaflets and seed bombs onto those waiting below before rising rapidly in order to shadow the progress of the long footpath winding up the base of the Salisbury Crags, bidding farewell to Arthur's Seat and climbing further into the sky to gain greater speed then heading due south again.

73

Thomas would have welcomed the opportunity to visit Newcastle, Manchester and Birmingham, but finds he has unwelcome company by the time he crosses the border: two RAF aeroplanes, of a much more modern variety than his own. F-35 Lightnings; he admires their sleek lines and maneuverability at close quarters. They buzz him, attempt to hail him and harass him, force him down. He climbs higher towards a drifting formation of clouds, and his pursuers are puzzled to intermittently lose visual contact, even radar contact from the ground, off and on for the next hour. At times they almost call off the pursuit, believing Thomas to have somehow simply disappeared, before establishing visual contact again and resuming their chase and intended intercept.

Approaching London itself, the Ministry of Defence go into meltdown. With the Prime Minister on the phone, they finally obtain authorisation to ask their pilots to open fire on Tellman's aeroplane rather than risk a potential terrorist attack as he enters metropolitan airspace. Thomas begins rapidly dropping altitude above Walthamstow, levels off above Hackney Downs, by which time the pilots have already twice tried and failed to use their weaponry, their fingers inexplicably freezing over the triggers – beset they will later conjecture, by some kind of brain fog or muscular seizure of unknown cause.

London Fields, Haggerston, Shoreditch, Spitalfields flash by at exhilarating speed, the ever-intensifying mass of traffic and architectural complexity tingling Thomas's cerebral cortex into pleasurable overload. Unlike everyone else, he knows he isn't going to die just yet. Thomas likes a challenge. Enjoying himself, he adopts the most provocative and daring trajectory imaginable: straight through the financial city at under five hundred feet in altitude, steering between the dense tangle of towerblocks around the Gherkin and the Walkie-Talkie.

Office workers, those not yet evacuated, press themselves against the glass facades in awe, cameras and phones clicking and flashing. Shoppers and workers down below are stunned by the plane's shadow passing over them and the unfamiliar sound of its propellers churning through the congested urban air. The tall buildings seem to spit Thomas out across the Thames where he crosses London Bridge above cheering crowds then rises up for a victory loop around the soaring civic church spire of The Shard. Then south again, climbing in height and increasing in speed, drifting in and out of cloud and visibility, Thomas exits Britain high above the white cliffs of Dover.

74

From Dover to Thomas's next destination is a remarkably short hop in an aeroplane, freed of all the vagaries of maritime and logistical boundaries. He remembers the way all too well – Calais and Dunkirk particularly – and knows that compared to the last time he flew the route, under constant fire from German air defences, this can only be easier. Although the roads and traffic, the extent of conurbations, have all proliferated since, he knows certain landmarks remain constant. The Terneuzen and Albert canals that wind down to Ghent and Antwerp from the Scheldt Delta; the triangular relationship that Brussels forms with those two cities. He drops down over Bruges and Ghent close enough to glimpse their glittering waterways and cacophony of medieval spires and towers, red roofs and grey stone Gothic lacework, recalling some smaller Europe of history books – of horses and carriages, of barges and galleons, when Man was still small upon the Earth, counterbalanced by Nature. The industrial hinterlands around these and every other city strike him like the smoke-black exhaust trails fanning out behind something in distress, back-firing engines.

More sleek silver jets – F-16 Fighting Falcons – join him upon leaving Ghent, but as escorts this time rather than as harassment, the president of the European Commission having agreed to meet him, albeit somewhat incredulously with regard to his preferred method of arrival. Brussels begins to take shape beneath him, a vast and bewildering sprawl; but he knows to look for the long axis of the Bouldevard of Leopold whose orientation coincides almost exactly with his own route, as if reaching out to welcome him. He drops altitude to below a thousand feet over the boulevard, approaching the cross it makes as it intersects with the wide stately waters of the Canal de Bruxelles. Once past, he knows he must curve south over the historic quarters centred around the Baroque stage set of *The Grand Place*, always swarming with sightseers. Now at below three hundred feet, his shadow ripples over the cobbles below like that of a sparrow hawk. Cameras capture him flying in front of the white lacework steeple of the Hotel De Ville, in livestreams beamed around the world.

Steering south-west he descends over the intense network of densely wooded parks of the Koningswijk quarter and the Parc de Bruxelles. He uses the roof of the Royal Palace itself as the final landmark to guide him down into his most audacious manoeuvre of all: using the long straight down the Rue De Luxembourg as a runway on which to land. Fortunately the police have largely cleared the streets in reluctant compliance, anticipating that the plan Thomas has emailed in advance to the Commission will indeed be followed to the letter. Faced with the choice of acceptance of this extraordinary international visitor, or attempting to shoot him down, the Air Force have opted for damage limitation and containment. One overhead wire just after the junction with the Rue du Commere comes dangerously close to his undercarriage as the Hawker Sea Fury's wheels begin to fold down. The sight of the antiquated little plane gliding down to head-height between the long parallel lines of genteel facades is breathtaking. The overleaning branches of trees are as much of a hazard as high street signs, the ability to roll the plane still allowing for minor last minute tilts. His wingspan is clear of lamposts but perilously close to any parked cars, forcing him into various gliding slaloms even as he bumpily touches down.With apparently only inches to spare, Thomas pulls the landing off, skidding and rattling along the cobbles of the Place de Luxembourg and taxiing around a cenotaph for dead industrialists, the green copper statues of the John Cockerill monument. He comes to a rest at last in front of a comically diminutive white doll's house of a building: all that is left above ground of an erstwhile train station and the annihilated Leopold quarter, behind which now rises the vast bulk of its usurper and replacement: the numerous modern buildings of the European

Parliament, stepping up in receding cascades of intimidating power. He cuts the fuel, opens the cockpit, and breathes a long sigh of relief.

The crowds are held back behind cordons, as Thomas is greeted by EU officials and armed guards and escorted across the Espace Leopold and under the elliptical forms and soaring arches towards the entrance to Parliament.

75

In Kinburgh, as all across the world, people crowd and hunch around their televisions, monitors and myriad device screens to watch Thomas approach the podium.

Louise, who has come to stay with Mary again over the weekend, has wheeled a television into Mary's room for them both to watch. On her mobile phone she has been showing Mary film of her science pupils attempting Thomas's anti-gravity experiments.

Annie Bevans sits on the sofa with her dad and Bruce, clutching their hands with white knuckles of tension.

Helen Murchison watches the screen in her kitchen while she and her girlfriend prepare an evening meal together.

Chrissy watches in cold rage subsumed into silence, shouting inside herself as to how people can stomach this spectacle, wondering how many others out there might be of a like mind to her, and how to make contact with them.

Magdalena watches with her mother, comforting each other quietly in Polish, eyes flicking from time to time from the screen to her statue of the Virgin Mary and baby Jesus on her mantelpiece.

Doctor James McCaffrey watches on his secretary's computer terminal in his surgery reception, having just sent his receptionist Sarah home. He's not sure why he wants to be alone, unless it's some vague impulse to distance his wife from involvement in the whole Tellman business and the continuing fear that his office will be attacked by protesters – or shady governmental agencies.

Detective Inspector Hugh Drummond watches in the living room of his suburban home, pouring himself a gin and tonic, and shouting to his wife to come and join him. He puts one arm around her, and with the other surreptitiously checks that his handgun remains concealed where he left it, under the right hand arm rest.

Major Leslie J Kelsington switches the television in his office off, and goes out to take a stiff walk around the parade ground, then strolls further out, absentmindedly checking the perimeter fencing for any breaches.

Janet McComish is working to oversee production of tomorrow's issue of the Kinburgh Herald, with her star reporter Lesley Crawford who has secured her reputation with the excellent nursing home lead and the consequent film they've been able to sell to numerous major channels. Taking a break, Janet and Lesley sit down together to watch the television reports on Thomas. Janet's pug, Griselda, leaps up onto Lesley's lap, causing Janet's right eyebrow to lift in a twinge of incipient jealousy.

Professor Radim Hromádka, working late in his lab at Aberdeen university, is too absorbed in his work to stop, intending to watch the news later. The levitating metal donut in front of him begins to wobble, then slips its tether and moves about the room as he rotates the voltage dial on his electromagnetic field spectrometer.

The Reverend Desmond Baliol watches the small television in his vestry, as he changes out of his ecclesiastical gown in preparation for driving home. But feeling suddenly overwhelmed by what he is hearing, he reaches for his bible and kneels on the floor to pray, facing the small stained-glass window on the west wall, whose patterns of red and green light fall dramatically across him. Eyelids closed, his lips move while the commentary continues to play in the background.

Father Seamus O'Hara doesn't have a television, preferring the delights of a good library. His recent meeting with the Reverend Baliol has re-kindled his interest in some of the more esoteric tomes in his own collection. He takes down his copy of Robert Kirk's 'The Secret Commonwealth' recalling there was something in there about time and invisibility which he wishes to find again, and returns to his evening armchair to read it by the fireside. He glances up occasionally at the pleasant glimpses of sky and greenery that his overgrown garden affords, fronds and branches waving in the evening breeze.

'John' the secret service head of section watches on his

mobile phone, while sitting on board a jet to London. Most of his fellow operatives aren't watching at all, at their various homes scattered around greater London, seeking to divert themselves and their loved ones on other pursuits, to block out their sense of professional failure that they allowed the situation to slip through their fingers and get this far.

Jeff Prentiss, editor of UFO Watch Magazine, digs into a team bag of popcorn at the watch-party he and his fellow extraterrestrial enthusiasts have arranged for the Thomas Tellman weekend.

Doctor Yasin Khatib has no time for television, working beyond his shift at Raigmore Hospital to save the life of a father of four with open-heart surgery.

RAF veteran Benny Faulds sitting in his nursing home, is jocularly quizzed by the nurse bringing him his dinner, as to whether he enjoyed his hour in the limelight talking to his old pilot friend, to which to her surprise he replies: *Ah dinnae ken who he wiz. Ah nice lad right enough, but ah'll' tell ye wan thing fur sure: he wiznae Tommy Tellman.*

Annie returns from the toilet pale and shaking, having just seen her pregnancy test turn blue. To conceal her feelings as she calms down, she goes over to the window then slides the casement up for some fresh air. Her son and her father behind her remain engrossed in the television. Leaning out the window, placing her hands on the sill, she notices a white butterfly, perhaps the last of summer, flitting through the air towards her. Too weary to flinch, she closes her eyes and feels it nudge against her nose, then looks down to see it has come to rest on the back of her right hand.

The wild animals outside Mary Tellman's house slowly emerge to begin their sunset rituals. The field mouse darts across between the bin store and the house, gathering up his usual rain of crumbs. The snails begin their agonisingly slow pilgrimage across the dry patio slabs towards the heaven of slow drips from the external standpipe. The brood of swifts, now fledged and grown to maturity in the garage roof, complete their final group-formation training flight around the house then set off together on their impossibly long journey south for winter, from which they will nonetheless return unharmed next spring. The pine marten, believing himself to be stalking a vole, fails to notice the fox watching from the woods who is in turn stalking him. The bees return to the hive, preparing to wind down flight operations and keep alive by shivering against each other all winter like so many Emperor Penguins at the South Pole.

The waves down at the beach continue to wash against the pebble shore with their ancient rhythm. The sun continues to lower towards the horizon, slowly turning orange to red. The leaves of deciduous trees change colour and prepare to fall. The enigma of life and death goes on, adjusting itself across aeons by mysterious increments. Only the creature called Man, the most nervous of Gaia's children, frets over grand meanings, labouring under the delusion that he might be in charge.

76

Thomas takes to the podium at the centre of the hemicycle, the famous auditorium within the Paul Henri Spaak building of the Espace Léopold complex, and addresses the parliament:

Ladies and gentlemen, representatives of the twenty-seven states of the European Union, Madame Speaker, I want to begin by thanking you for kindly allowing me to address this parliament today and thereby to address all of the citizens of Europe and of the wider world. My message is an urgent one. I have achieved notoriety recently as an ex-RAF pilot who went missing in 1948 and thereafter travelled aboard what is commonly referred to as a UFO; an unidentified flying object or flying saucer. I was treated well by my hosts, with whom it appears to you that I travelled for the equivalent of 80 years of time here on Earth. But such was the speed at which we travelled that, true to the principles set out by Albert Einstein, only one year went by in terms of my own biological ageing.

Now I would draw your attention to two things in the opening statement I have just made. Firstly that I did not, and never have since my return to Earth, refer to the beings that acted as my hosts as 'aliens'. The second significant fact is that I said that it "appears to you" that I travelled for 80 years. Well, here comes the crunch. Such was the speed at which the craft which carried me travelled in its voyage beyond our solar system that upon returning here not 80 but 8000 years had actually gone by on Earth. I found myself therefore returning to a future Earth that scarcely resembled this one. Much of life as we know it, fertility and species diversity, had all but perished due to the global warming which went unchecked in the 21st century. I returned to a ruined and depleted, desert world. Allow me please to now show you film I have with me of that world and of my hosts, whose physical appearance I have often been asked about since my return and that I know many of you here today are keen to learn more about. This will be a shock, I warn you, after which I will leave you all a few minutes to digest the information and recompose yourselves.

The film, generated by a silver sphere that Thomas unleashes from his pocket like a white dove to hover above his head, shows the Earth seen from space with its familiar recognisable continents but with unfamiliar colouring, gradually revealed to be due to the preponderance of desert over vegetation, as the camera re-enters the atmosphere and begins a rapid descent over Asia and Europe, coming down to land in an almost unrecognisable South America. *This used to be the Amazon Rainforest...* says a voice off camera, of the desert in front. The camera slowly pans to reveal Thomas attired in a space suit of unfamiliar design, with his helmet under his arm, then standing next to him two apparently alien beings. Breaths are drawn within the parliament, some delegates beginning to weep, some even fainting as the camera zooms in more and more closely on the beings' faces as they begin to speak in an only partially intelligible language with subtitles on screen underneath. Their dark eyes sparkle like the blackness of space fraught with stars, pinpoints of light and hope amid the velvet night of bleak despair.

So now you all see at last. How very old and wrinkled and wizened they look, how tired, how anaemic. The so-called aliens, the so-called 'greys' are in fact our future selves, a product of the degraded Earth that they will inherit from us. Stunted and shrivelled due to a depleted gene pool, they are physically our inferiors but by way of compensation, mentally far more advanced. They had to become so in order to survive at all, in order to overcome the enormous environmental challenges that we will leave them with. But how and why, you may ask therefore, do I come to be here again, 8000 years into the past in order to arrive again at this moment with you, your present? I believe that most of Earth's scientists, though not all, currently believe travel backwards in time to be theoretically impossible. I can tell you however, that although it is rare and carries many dangers, it is for the people of the future, far from impossible. Only a great danger or tragedy, and critical mission to attempt to avert the disaster that brings that tragedy about, would merit them attempting such a journey. I am in fact that journey, that mission, delivering this message now.

Climate change and environmental damage and species depletion has now gone beyond the point of any possible natural recovery. Global warming due to the accumulation of greenhouse gases within the upper atmosphere cannot now be undone by any action of humanity with its present level of technology. The oceans are contaminated with plastics and the extinction of species on land and sea cannot be halted. This has been widely predicted it seems for the last forty years, known to everyone within this chamber and the majority of their constituents and yet, even still, galvanising human societies into taking remedial action has proven impossible. This is, it seems, the tragic flaw and irony in the human character. Only when things have gone beyond the point of no return does the point of return dawn on us.

But I come bearing good news, not only bad. I have therefore brought twelve gifts from the future: advanced technological solutions that once mastered and deployed will correct human damage to the world and restore the eco-system to its desirable equilibrium over the next five to ten years. I have already emailed the formulae for these to numerous key universities across the globe under open-source patents, anticipating that many different businesses and industries will be generated from them rather any single wealthy individual seeking to profiteer through market monopolies. The patents are as follows:

One. An anti-gravity drive that utilises electromagnetic field radiation to produce reactionless thrust, thus transforming transport systems and eliminating the need to burn fossils fuels any longer.

Two. Meta-metal alloys to form self-repairing

materials essential in order to perfect vehicles driven by anti-gravity drive.

Three. A thin-film photovoltaic paint, also a meta-material, that can be applied over any surface, including existing transport vehicles in order to generate substantial energy from daylight. The aeroplane I flew here in, for instance, was coated in this material to a thickness of 500 microns.

Four. A version of this same paint which can be made invisible and visible again instantly by passing a specific electric signature through it, thus rendering whatever object it covers invisible also. The paint on the aeroplane I arrived in was also of this specification.

Five. Micro wind turbine technology at the molecular level. The leading edge surfaces of the nose-tip, wings, and fins of the aeroplane I arrived in were also of this specification.

Six. Using the same principles that enable trees to digest the carbon dioxide we produce, and exhale oxygen in its place: a biologically engineered novel plant form, called moss-ivy, that can grow across almost any urban surface. I have dropped spores of this over each city I have flown over today and so it will already be growing quickly. It's appearance is pleasant, creating an effect akin to romantic ruins overgrown, but is harmless to building fabric and all terrestrial life forms.

Seven. A synthetically-engineered organism which can thrive at high altitude in Earth's atmosphere and consume greenhouse gases, expelling oxygen it its place. Once the ozone is repaired to healthy levels, and the organism is no longer required: it will naturally die off in the oxygen-rich environment it has itself created.

Eight. A similar synthetic organism engineered to repair human damage to Earth's oceans by re-oxygenating and de-acidifying.

Nine. A self-repairing bio-synthetic micro-robot that will replicate itself within Earth's oceans then act in groups of several thousand at a time to gather and harvest all forms of plastic pollution and coalesce these into islands, which it will then digest back to harmless organic versions of their constituent elements. As with those repairing the ozone, these organisms will die off once they have completed their task by virtue of exhausting their own food supply.

Ten. A further bio-synthetic technology, effectively an artifical extremophile, that can thrive on, digest, and therefore safely eliminate over a period of several decades, all forms of harmful radiation from nuclear fission reactors and weaponry.

Eleven. A new technology for energy storage, lighter and more efficient than any current battery on Earth: an allotrope of Silicon whose complex three-dimensional structure at the atomic level effectively creates a molecular battery of infinite life.

Twelve. A bio-synthetically engineered protein that can be easily adapted to taste identical to all forms of natural organic meat protein, thus enabling the consumption of animals by humans to be made illegal.

...And now that I have delivered this message, time is running out, for reasons that I must explain in a moment. I know that you will have many questions, but I anticipate that by far the most significant one will be how to pay for all this. Fortunately the answer to that is extremely simple, particularly in the midst of a climate emergency. The billionaires and millionaires on this planet, those who have amassed vast personal wealth, did not do so by printing their own dollar bills, or synthesising gold out of the air like latter-day alchemists. They gained their wealth, obviously and unarguably, from other citizens or from governments and organisations who again in turn ultimately gained their wealth dollar by dollar, Euro by Euro and so forth, in this century or in a previous one through inheritance, from ordinary human citizens. Therefore all wealth on Earth belongs to all its citizens, not to any one individual. That wealth incidentally, is ultimately only a token of course, of the underlying wealth of the planet itself, meaning its natural resources.

This even means our very selves, our bodies, the sweat of our labour, our great ideas, the inventiveness of our minds: all these are also natural resources, not possible without the air and water and bountiful food by which every healthy human body and mind achieves adulthood and wisdom in the first place. Therefore everything, our very selves, belong not to ourselves, but to the planet and every other living thing upon it. All of us are designed by Gaia, the Earth's integrated biological system, to be servants with a role to play, not consumers – not idle princes sitting around speculating on what and who to exploit for personal gain. Here endeth the moral portion of my lecture, which is after all only pure logic and common sense.

Finally then, before I depart the podium, I feel obliged to leave you with the most mind-bending part of my message, which not all of you may be able to grasp, and even those of you who do grasp it may, paradoxically, be forced to forget it shortly afterwards. I am not of course, for obvious reasons, going to impart to the Earth's scientists today or any other day the secret of how to build technology capable of sending people backwards in time. If the human race can't be trusted with even its own planet yet, then what sort of mess would it make of time? All you need to know for the moment is the following, and some of your theoretical physicists have I believe, nearly figured this much out already. Travel to the past can either be by a novel intervention or a causal loop. A novel intervention is highly dangerous because of the risk of altering history, but once made, it will always instantly collapse to become a causal loop, meaning that history books will thereafter record at some level or another, in small print or large, as a major event or mysterious minor incident, the fact that someone from the future suddenly appeared there and made an impact. What I am telling you in short, is that this is not the first time I have been here like this, addressing you all and saying similar things. The history books of the future that I saw recorded that I did appear here, but also of course, that I failed to make a difference, hence why the devastated desert world I was sent back from still came to, or comes to, exist.

A causal loop in time, once established, becomes a safe means by which to travel to the past. Although I can know I have been here before saying this, I cannot know how many times before I have been here, for reasons that the extremely intelligent among you will be able to work out after a reasonable period of thought. It could be twice, three times, it could be an infinity of times. The only thing that is certain is that I will keep being sent back by myself and my hosts until the outcome is satisfactory – which is to say at the point when humanity does indeed finally heed my pleas and correct its behaviour and adopt remedial measures sufficient to rescue the terrestrial ecosystem and avert future disaster. But here's the best bit, the very hardest bit to grasp or believe: if I am successful this time then I will shortly thereafter cease to exist, vanish spontaneously from this reality, since the future that sent me back will have ceased to exist. Is anybody out there still following this? Hands up! Good. I have no means of knowing what form this joyous annihilation of myself is going to take, if as increasingly looks likely to me, I have been successful this time. Now you can see why I have taken such extraordinary steps to publicise my journey here and to make much more of a mark on history than I know the future history books currently record. Now you know how I was able to take such ridiculous risks, the wings of my low-flying aeroplane missing lamp posts by a matter of millimetres and so on. Now you know why jet pilots were unable to change my trajectory or fire missiles at me. Because I was and am, protected by the force of history – a very strange, mysterious and intangible force, whose power is nonetheless very formidable indeed. Any theologically-inclined among you might like think of it as the hand of God, although the hand of time or fate might be a safer label. Even the physicists and theoreticians of the future have yet to devise formulae and identify particles and waves to explain that force, so perhaps those romantic primitivisms shall forever remain as close an approximation as any possible to unmasking the ineffable.

And now, ladies and gentlemen, Madame Speaker, if you will excuse me, it has been a very long day and I am very tired. I would now like to step down from the podium and step outside to return to my modest little aeroplane in order to set off again in search of my life's mysterious negation and annulment that I hope history will shortly dispense to me in return for having saved the ecological future of this planet from ruin, and thereby altered the future of the human race to be a brighter one.

Thomas receives a standing ovation and rapturous applause. The sound of cheering makes his ears and those of everybody else ring. He slowly pushes his way outside through the crowds of MEPs asking him questions, then likewise through the assembled press representatives bristling with cameras and microphones and shouted questions. Then further out, into the fading daylight outside, into the yet larger crowds of the general public, some shouting and crying, some screaming and pleading, some loving, some hating, some protesting, some cheering on. To many in the crowd, Thomas is their perceived messiah come at last, to others he is some sort of demon as foretold in ancient scripture, come to inflict the very hell that he claims to wish to avert. To most sane people, mostly sitting at home, he is either a flamboyant conman or a stray pilot who lost his way in space and time.

77

The professional assassin Axel Verstraete moves his way quietly through the crowds of bystanders, one hand in his pocket, caressing his loaded pistol. History is full of men like him. He has no pretensions to any grand philosophical perspectives, no sophistry to justify his existence and his acts. He knows he is just a cog in a vast set of dirty wheels, a cockroach whom other more powerful, unseen men, manipulate like a chess piece. He is Gavrilo Princip, who could not believe his luck when Archduke Franz Ferdinand's motorcade took the wrong turning in the streets of Sarajevo and came to a halt in front of him with the gun ready in his pocket, thus starting World War One. He is James Files, who shot John F Kennedy from the Grassy Knoll, Jack Ruby who shot the innocent idiot Oswald. He is John Wilkes Booth who crept up behind Abraham Lincoln in his balcony booth at Ford's Theatre. He is James Earl Ray, who shot Martin Luther King from the second floor balcony of the Lorraine Motel in Memphis. He is Nathuram Vinayak Godse, who fired three bullets into the chest of Mahatma Gandhi. The list is undoubtedly endless, reaching far back into the dismal reaches of human history. How telling that so few of their names trip off the tongue, while that of their victims do.

Nonetheless somehow the eyes of Thomas Tellman and Axel Verstraete find each other over the heads of the frenetic crowd and lock for a moment in a strange kind of recognition, a kind of convulsive opposite of love. The notion that time is constant and always passing at a uniform rate is more delusion than fact. Perceptually: time slows down for both men, and all sound fades out into a background murmur until all that each can hear is their own heartbeats. Thomas smiles in joy and relief as Axel raises his pistol, squeezes the trigger and the bullet leaves the barrel of the gun and crosses the air between them. This is the future arriving and departing, the hand of the universe's unknown and unknowable Creator at last reaching out to touch Thomas and answer his question. He feels the bullet tear into his chest, puncturing flesh, sinew, vein and bone, and the fire of pain and dissolution beginning within him. The planet is being saved.

In the confusion that follows, few people fully comprehend what has occurred and that Thomas has actually been hit. By the time he has re-crossed the cordoned plaza and reached his parked aeroplane in the Place de Luxembourg, a trail of blood is trickling out of his left trouser leg. Grimacing as he pulls himself back up onto the wing, the bullet itself falls out onto the cobbles below, like some fatal arrow from antiquity, its work of the gods duly done. He shall of course, now die. Thomas re-starts the engine and wheels the plane around to taxi north-west in order to gather speed and finally take off among the trees of the Square de Meeûs. From there to climb rapidly and erratically above the city. Sunset is coming on in the sky over Brussels, a full moon rising up over Flanders. Various witnesses believe they observe a very bright white light in the sky, akin to the moon, that Thomas's aeroplane appears to climb towards, almost vertically for a while until, after the light briefly intensifies to the extent to which it is almost painful to look at, both light and aeroplane disappear altogether.

78

A white flash makes televisions and computers all around the world briefly blank and re-boot. People find they have stopped in mid-sentence and that they are unable to remember exactly what it was they were thinking and speaking about only a moment earlier. The images and broadcasts which come up on the re-started devices are not of the European Parliament in emergency session, but of whatever routine humdrum piece of scheduling was previously supposed to have occurred that day. A football or tennis match, a day at the horse races. Human beings forget because it is something they are very good at. Just as they forgot the last Ice Age, what Stone Henge was for, the Viking invasions, two world wars, the Black Death, Spanish Influenza, and the assassination of peace-making leaders by villainous usurpers bent on war. They forget. Indeed, it is a vital function of consciousness without which none of us would ever have the strength to go on. How else do we cope with grief and loss, loath though we'd be to admit it? How else did Jackie Kennedy cope with the vision of her husband's head fragmenting across her lap? We forget. Sometimes only for a few moments at first, but bit by bit, in order to go on living at all: sooner or later, we forget. It is essential. Maybe words, books, are our only safety net.

79

January 1948. Pilot Captain Thomas F Tellman takes off in his Hawker Sea Fury aircraft from the military airstrip at RAF Kinburgh, on the orders of base commander Colonel Henry Deacon in response to civilian and traffic police reports of an unusual aerial object near Bonar Bridge. Accounts of an eastbound circular object, between 250 and 300 feet in diameter are received from Spinningdale and Dornoch. At about 1:45pm, Sergeant Charles Blain sees an object from his position in the control tower at RAF Lossiemouth. Two other witnesses in the tower also report a white object in the distance. The base commander reports an object he describes as *very white* and *about one fourth the size of the full moon... Through binoculars it appeared to have a red border at the bottom... it remained stationary, seemingly, for one and a half hours.*

Witnesses at Milltown Airfield describe the object as having the appearance of a flaming red cone trailing a gaseous green mist and observe the object for around 35 minutes. Another observer at Easter Airfield notes: *The UFO was a strange, grey object, which looked like a rotating inverted ice cream cone. Just before leaving it came to very near the ground, staying down for about ten seconds, then climbed at a very fast rate back to its original altitude, 10,000 feet, levelling off and disappearing into the overcast sky heading 120 degrees. Its speed was greater than 500 mph in level flight.*

Throughout the event, Sergeant Blain remains in radio communication with Tellman, who begins a steep pursuit of the object. Despite warnings regarding his dwindling oxygen supply, Tellman ignores suggestions that he should level his altitude and try to see the object more clearly from a safe distance. There will later be some disagreement among air traffic controllers as to Tellman's last words as he communicates with the tower: some sources reporting that the pilot described an object

Directly ahead of and above me now, moving at about half my speed... It appears to be a metallic object or possibly reflection of sun from a metallic object, and it is of tremendous size... I'm still climbing... I'm trying to close in for a better look. Then finally, incredibly: *My God, I see people in this thing.*

Tellman continues to climb. According to later RAF reports, once he passes 25,000 feet he blacks out from lack of oxygen and his plane begins spiralling back towards the ground. Witness reports identify Tellman's Hawker Sea Fury in a circling descent. His plane crashes into the Moray Firth at 3.16pm. By 3:50pm the giant craft can no longer be seen from RAF Kinburgh, but reports continue as the UFO travels southward towards the Cairngorms.

A major sea search is conducted to recover Tellman's aircraft. The official story becomes that the UFO was just a silver weather balloon catching the light. Maybe. Except that there weren't any in the sky that week. Probably. Maybe. Except.

When the aeroplane is finally winched up off the seabed of the Moray Firth, no body is found in the cockpit.

80

A late summer evening in August. Mrs Mary Tellman is being given her medication by Doctor McCaffrey, seated at her bedside. Horizontal bars of yellow-orange light and shade from the lowered blinds fall across their hands and faces. Nearby the trees of the pine wood sigh in a soothing sound that fuses with the waves of the sea in the distance somewhere far behind them. *Why did you never move away from here?* he suddenly finds he has asked her quietly, then feels surprised at himself. Sighing, the old lady seems to ignore his question, although perhaps what she says answers it in some other more roundabout way than McCaffrey could expect:

I had a dream, last night, Doactor, a gey queer one. Ma faither came back. Walked right out o' they woods ower there… still wearing his pilot's uniform. He hadnae aged a day. An we were sae happy to see each ither again, glaikit wi' it, an we had a good greet thigither, at whit time had done tae us both. Both wheeched awa' oot o' thi time we kent sae well, and plopped doon in this unco future that we cannae mak heed nor tail oot o'. We were parallel, he said, that wiz the wurd he used, like. Parallel in oor fates. But then he became upset agin tae see how auld and withered ah had become, his luvly wee perfect daughter. So in thi dream like, he started tryin' stuff, weird balms and surgeries, replacing bits o' me, trying tae stop me dee'in, tae mak me young agin…

Mary pauses, and sees that Doctor McCaffrey has become uncharacteristically wide-eyed, rapt by her narration, waiting for her to go on, as if their roles have reversed for a moment and she is in charge, revered elder of the tribe. *Ah had tae tell him in thi end, tae give it a rest. Dinnae bother, faither, it's nae use. It wiznae natural whit he was tryin'. Just let me dee in peace. Mibbe immortality will be a thing fur people o' the future, but ah dinnae fancy it much, it's nae fur me.*

McCaffrey nods, then Mrs Tellman changes the

subject. *Did you see Annie Bevans came by thi ither day? One o' the nurses, the carer girls. Ah hudnae seem her in a wee while, turns oot she'd been pregnant, been awa' for a couple o' years... ah must hae lost track o' time. She brought her wee girl aroond to see me. Were you no here? Ah lose coont o' who comes an goes frae this hoose these daes, right enough. Well, she gae me a wee fricht, a reet start. The wean was the double o' myself at that age, thi double, I swear it, a dead ringer as they say, a bright wee floo'er bloomin'. Like whit dae ye call it? Reincarnation. But ah had tae stop mysel' Doactar. I winted tae ask whae thi faither wiz, but ah couldnae and ah didnae. See these modern lassies, single mums an' a' that. Ye daren't ask, dae ye? Then it came to me in a way, that it didnae matter. Didnae matter at a'. Whaur's ma ain faither been these last eighty odd years? My mither brought us up withoot a man, coped because she hud tae. Aye. It's a sair ficht. We're a' orphans at thi end o' thi day.*

After giving Mary her latest course of pills and making sure she is comfortable, Doctor McCaffrey closes his case, slotting the old brass nibs shut with a click as a million times before in his long professional life. Before he leaves the house, he pauses to look again at the old black-and-white photograph of Mary Tellman as a child with her father, where it rests on the mantelpiece. Looking up, he sees the dark green pine trees outside stirring and swaying on a breeze picking up from the sea, and has the odd momentary impression that there is something anthropomorphic about them, as if they are watching him on behalf of something; nature perhaps, or time or fate, whatever those invisible things might conceivably mean to a man of science.

Later that evening he writes his entry in his diary at the desk in his study before going to bed as follows:

As a doctor perhaps I have to discipline myself to remember sometimes, that in the grand scheme of things my failures may be as important as my successes. I mean knowing when to let go. Life would have no flavour somehow, no savour, no preciousness, no poignancy, if we thought it was of infinite length. Maybe the apparently linear nature of time, time itself, is only an illusion, that might be by-passed and overcome. That would mean that we never really die anyway. Take time out of the equation, and what is left is just a sea of characters, each one like stars in the night sky. Or like jewels, shining diamonds set in black velvet, existing forever each within their own allotted slot of time and space. Whatever and whoever happens even once, happens eternally. Death is, and can only ever be, what never was.

*

Next day, emerging from the Chemist's on Main Street, Doctor McCaffrey catches sight of Annie Bevans holding her daughter by the hand, and waves to her. Bright sunlight dances on the green canopies of trees swaying in the manicured planters of the pedestrian precinct, a gentle breeze whispering again of an autumn soon to come. He goes over to chat, uncharacteristic of a man in his habitual haste, bends down to say hello to the little girl and looks into her shyly sparkling eyes, gasps at her astounding resemblance to the photograph he looked at the night before.

What is it, he will reflect and wonder upon later, that waits there in the eyes of a child, timid and biding its time, impatient for its release into adulthood? A wave of life breaking upon the shore of the world, confident, self-contained, somehow knowing-without-knowing, that it has strength to draw upon from invisible dimensions, that it is one with the others before, and with the many to come after.

~ ~ ~

Douglas Thompson

Acknowledgements

Thanks to all the encouragers & inspirers, including but not limited to: Peter and Alison at Elsewhen, my late mother and all her local authority carers for love and stoicism, to my late brother Ally for an education in Ufology, to Rona for sheltering the alien, and to her mother Margaret for time travel and the milk of amnesia.

Elsewhen Press

delivering outstanding new talents in speculative fiction

Visit the Elsewhen Press website at elsewhen.press for the latest information on all of our titles, authors and events; to read our blog; find out where to buy our books and ebooks; or to place an order.

Sign up for the Elsewhen Press InFlight Newsletter at elsewhen.press/newsletter

ENTANGLEMENT
DOUGLAS THOMPSON

FINALLY, TRAVEL TO THE STARS IS HERE

In 2180, travel to neighbouring star systems has been mastered thanks to quantum teleportation using the 'entanglement' of sub-atomic matter; astronauts on earth can be duplicated on a remote world once the dupliport chamber has arrived there. In this way a variety of worlds can be explored, but what humanity discovers is both surprising and disturbing, enlightening and shocking. Each alternative to mankind that the astronauts find, sheds light on human shortcomings and potential while offering fresh perspectives of life on Earth. Meanwhile, at home, the lives of the astronauts and those in charge of the missions will never be the same again.

Best described as philosophical science fiction, *Entanglement* explores our assumptions about such constants as death, birth, sex and conflict, as the characters in the story explore distant worlds and the intelligent life that lives there. It is simultaneously a novel and a series of short stories: multiple worlds, each explored in a separate chapter, a separate story; every one another step on mankind's journey outwards to the stars and inwards to our own psyche. Yet the whole is much greater than the sum of the parts; the synergy of the episodes results in an overarching story arc that ultimately tells us more about ourselves than about the rest of the universe.

Douglas Thompson's short stories have appeared in a wide range of magazines and anthologies. He won the Grolsch/Herald Question of Style Award in 1989 and second prize in the Neil Gunn Writing Competition in 2007. His first book, *Ultrameta*, published in 2009, was nominated for the Edge Hill Prize, and shortlisted for the BFS Best Newcomer Award. *Entanglement* is his fifth novel.

ISBN: 9781908168153 (epub, kindle) / 9781908168054 (336pp paperback)

Visit bit.ly/EntanglementBook

THE RHYMER
an Heredyssey
DOUGLAS THOMPSON

The Rhymer, an Heredyssey defies classification in any one literary genre. A satire on contemporary society, particularly the art world, it is also a comic-poetic meditation on the nature of life, death and morality.

A mysterious tramp wanders from town to town, taking a new name and identity from whoever he encounters first. Apparently amnesiac or even brain-damaged, Nadith Learmot nonetheless has other means to access the past and perhaps even the future: upon his chest a dial, down his sleeves wires that he can connect to the walls of old buildings from which he believes he can read their ghosts like imprints on tape. Haunting him constantly is the resemblance he apparently bears to his supposed brother, a successful artist called Zenir. Setting out to pursue Zenir and denounce or blackmail him out of spite, in his travels around the satellite towns and suburbs surrounding a city called Urbis, Nadith finds he is always two steps behind a figure as enigmatic and polyfaceted as himself. But through second hand snippets of news he increasingly learns of how his brother's fortunes are waning, while his own, to his surprise, are on the rise. Along the way, he encounters unexpected clues to his own true identity, how he came to lose his memory and acquire his strange 'contraption'. When Nadith finally catches up with Zenir, what will they make of each other?

Told entirely in the first person in a rhythmic stream of lyricism, Nadith's story reads like Shakespeare on acid, leaving the reader to guess at the truth that lies behind his madness. Is Nadith a mental health patient or a conman? … Or as he himself comes to believe, the reincarnation of the thirteenth century Scottish seer True Thomas The Rhymer, a man who never lied nor died but disappeared one day to return to the realm of the faeries who had first given him his clairvoyant gifts?

Douglas Thompson's short stories have appeared in a wide range of magazines and anthologies. He won the Grolsch/Herald Question of Style Award in 1989 and second prize in the Neil Gunn Writing Competition in 2007. His first book, *Ultrameta*, published in 2009, was nominated for the Edge Hill Prize, and shortlisted for the BFS Best Newcomer Award. Since then he has published more novels, including *Entanglement* published by Elsewhen Press. *The Rhymer* is his eighth novel.

ISBN: 9781908168511 (epub, kindle) / 9781908168412 (192pp paperback)

Visit bit.ly/TheRhymer-Heredyssey

Existence is
Elsewhen
Twenty stories from twenty great authors
including
John Gribbin
Rhys Hughes
Douglas Thompson

The title *Existence is Elsewhen* paraphrases the last sentence of André Breton's 1924 *Manifesto of Surrealism*, perfectly summing up the intent behind this anthology of stories from a wonderful collection of authors. Different worlds… different times. It's what Elsewhen Press has been about since we launched our first title in 2011.

Here, we present twenty science fiction stories for you to enjoy. We are delighted that headlining this collection is the fantastic **John Gribbin,** with a worrying vision of medical research in the near future. Future global healthcare is the theme of **J A Christy's** story; while the ultimate in spare part surgery is where **Dave Weaver** takes us. **Edwin Hayward's** search for a renewable protein source turns out to be digital; and **Tanya Reimer's** story with characters we think we know gives us pause for thought about another food we take for granted. Evolution is examined too, with **Andy McKell's** chilling tale of what states could become if genetics are used to drive policy. Similarly, **Robin Moran's** story explores the societal impact of an undesirable evolutionary trend; while **Douglas Thompson** provides a truly surreal warning of an impending disaster that will reverse evolution, with dire consequences.

On a lighter note, we have satire from **Steve Harrison** discovering who really owns the Earth (and why); and **Ira Nayman,** who uses the surreal alternative realities of his *Transdimensional Authority* series as the setting for a detective story mash-up of Agatha Christie and Dashiel Hammett. Pursuing the crime-solving theme, **Peter Wolfe** explores life, and death, on a space station; while **Stefan Jackson** follows a police investigation into some bizarre cold-blooded murders in a cyberpunk future. Going into the past, albeit an 1831 set in the alternate Britain of his *Royal Sorceress* series, **Christopher Nuttall** reports on an investigation into a girl with strange powers.

Strange powers in the present-day is the theme for **Tej Turner,** who tells a poignant tale of how extra-sensory perception makes it easier for a husband to bear his dying wife's last few days. Difficult decisions are the theme of **Chloe Skye's** heart-rending story exploring personal sacrifice. Relationships aren't always so close, as **Susan Oke's** tale demonstrates, when sibling rivalry is taken to the limit. Relationships are the backdrop to **Peter R. Ellis's** story where a spectacular mid-winter event on a newly-colonised distant planet involves a Madonna and Child. Coming right back to Earth and in what feels like an almost imminent future, **Siobhan McVeigh** tells a cautionary tale for anyone thinking of using technology to deflect the blame for their actions. Building on the remarkable setting of Pera from her *LiGa* series, and developing Pera's legendary *Book of Shadow*, **Sanem Ozdural** spins the creation myth of the first light tree in a lyrical and poetic song. Also exploring language, the master of fantastika and absurdism, **Rhys Hughes,** extrapolates the way in which language changes over time, with an entertaining result.

ISBN: 9781908168955 (epub, kindle) / 9781908168856 (320pp paperback)
Visit bit.ly/ExistenceIsElsewhen

STUDENTS ℃F MYSELF

RHYS HUGHES

There are few students in my class. When one considers what the subject is, this isn't surprising. I teach myself.

In other words, I impart to my students facts and fancies based on my life and ideas. It's the least popular class in the university and I doubt it will be funded for another term. But none of that is my fault. I wanted to teach a proper discipline such as ecology, but the authorities wouldn't let me. They insisted that I teach myself; and as a result, I do so.

The students are given an assignment. They each have to write a short piece about how I spend my free time. But this is information I've always kept secret. I can't imagine how they're expected to know anything about my private life, certainly not in detail.

Clearly I'm being spied on. Unless it's guesswork?

I read the essays anxiously.

Yes, only some of them have got it right…

"If I said he was a Welsh writer who writes as though he has gone to school with the best writing from all over the world, I wonder if my compliment would just sound provincial. Hughes' style — with all that means — is among the most beautiful I've encountered in several years." SAMUEL R. DELANY

ISBN: 9781911409793 (epub, kindle) / 9781911409694 (112pp paperback)

Visit bit.ly/StudentsOfMyself

INTERFERENCE

Terry Grimwood

The grubby dance of politics didn't end when we left the solar system, it followed us to the stars

The god-like Iaens are infinitely more advanced than humankind, so why have they requested military assistance in a conflict they can surely win unaided?

Torstein Danielson, Secretary for Interplanetary Affairs, is on a fact-finding mission to their home planet and headed straight into the heart of a war-zone. With him, onboard the Starship *Kissinger*, is a detachment of marines for protection, an embedded pack of sycophantic journalists who are not expected to cause trouble, and reporter Katherina Molale, who most certainly will and is never afraid to dig for the truth.

Torstein wants this mission over as quickly as possible. His daughter is terminally ill, his marriage in tatters. But then the Iaens offer a gift in return for military intervention and suddenly the stakes, both for humanity as a race and for Torstein personally, are very high indeed.

Suffolk born and proud of it, Terry Grimwood is the author of a handful of novels and novellas, including *Deadside Revolution*, the science fiction-flavoured political thriller *Bloody War* and *Joe* which was inspired by true events. His short stories have appeared in numerous magazines and anthologies and have been gathered into three collections, *The Exaggerated Man*, *There Is A Way To Live Forever* and *Affairs of a Cardio-Vascular Nature*. Terry has also written and Directed three plays as well as co-written engineering textbooks for Pearson Educational Press. He plays the harmonica and with a little persuasion (not much persuasion, actually) will growl a song into a microphone. By day he teaches electrical installation at a further education college. He is married to Debra, the love of his life.

ISBN: 9781911409960 (epub, kindle) / 9781911409861 (96pp paperback)

Visit bit.ly/Interference-Grimwood

HOWUL
A LIFE'S JOURNEY
DAVID SHANNON

"Un-put-down-able! A classic hero's journey, deftly handled. I was surprised by every twist and turn, the plotting was superb, and the engagement of all the senses – I could smell those flowers and herbs. A tour de force"
– LINDSAY NICHOLSON MBE

Books are dangerous

People in Blanow think that books are dangerous: they fill your head with drivel, make poor firewood and cannot be eaten (even in an emergency).

This book is about Howul. He sees things differently: fires are dangerous; people are dangerous; books are just books.

Howul secretly writes down what goes on around him in Blanow. How its people treat foreigners, treat his daughter, treat him. None of it is pretty. Worse still, everything here keeps trying to kill him: rats, snakes, diseases, roof slates, the weather, the sea. That he survives must mean something. He wants to find out what. By trying to do this, he gets himself thrown out of Blanow… and so his journey begins.

Like all gripping stories, *HOWUL* is about the bad things people do to each other and what to do if they happen to you. Some people use sticks to stay safe. Some use guns. Words are the weapons that Howul uses most. He makes them sharp. He makes them hurt.

Of course books are dangerous.

ISBN: 9781911409908 (epub, kindle) / 9781911409809 (200pp paperback)
Visit bit.ly/HOWUL

About Douglas Thompson

Glasgow writer Douglas Thompson won the Herald/Grolsch Question Of Style Award 1989, 2nd prize in the Neil Gunn Writing Competition 2007, and the Faith/Unbelief Poetry Prize 2016. His short stories and poems have appeared in a wide range of magazines and anthologies, including *Ambit*, *Albedo One*, *Chapman* and *New Writing Scotland*. Variously classed as a Weird, Horror, Sci Fi, Literary, or Historical novelist, he has published more than 17 novels and collections of short stories and poetry since 2009, from various publishers in Britain, Europe and America.

https://douglasthompson.wordpress.com/